Nixie Drake's past has caught up with her...

Nixie's thoughts were a jumble as she floated in one of *The Celestial Ghost's* outrigger holds. The shattered remains of *The Raccoon's* forward compartments were strapped down in the cavernous chamber. While the nose of the ship appeared undamaged, the hull just aft of the multi-cabin was splayed like the exploded barrel of an old cartoon musket. Long rectangular sections of titanium plating were bent outward at odd angles. The interior bulkhead that once separated the hold from the multi-cabin was dished in from overpressure.

Nixie curled herself into a fetal ball as she floated next to the lifeless hulk. A horrible emptiness filled her, and she closed her eyes tightly in an attempt to shut out the painful reality encompassing her. She relived the moment when the shock wave had shaken Captain Grit's cabin. She could still feel the sharp g-forces that slammed her body back and forth as *The Raccoon* was torn apart beneath her. The emotional battering was even worse. Nixie's life had exploded with the ship, and her energy had vented out of her as surely as *The Raccoon's* propellants had flooded into space.

...and her life hangs in the balance.

MERIDIAN'S SHADOW II:
NIXIE'S RISE

For Jackie,

Thank you for your kindness.

Dan

MERIDIAN'S SHADOW II: NIXIE'S RISE
Copyright ©2012 Daniel T. Moore

Published by
Dan Moore Productions
Liverpool, NY
www.danmoore.com

Cover art by Jason D. Moore

ISBN 978-0-9834283-9-8

March 2012
Printed in the United States of America

Visit www.meridiansshadow.com

This novel is dedicated to my goddaughter,
Sarah Ingerson Townsend.
You are an amazing woman, whose courage
and loveliness light up the lives of those around you.

.

FOREWORD

Meridian's Shadow became a series because of characters that appeared in my imagination. When I thought of these amazing people, I knew I had to tell their stories. The first book is about Sprite Logan and her parents, Hunter and Adrianna. This is Nixie's tale. She is a young smuggler, whose life comes crashing down around her. Old memories haunt her, and she must face her brutal beginnings in order to claim her future.

The opening sentence of this book reveals Nixie's peculiar dialect. She is a brilliant, but uneducated woman. If you stumble over her words, you might want to read them out loud. Her meaning will shine through.

I am indebted to my wife Diana, for her constant encouragement and unfailing grace. Without her support, none of these stories would be possible. I also wish to thank Jackie Jones for helping me with my battle with the English language.

Now, fasten your seatbelt and make sure your tray is in an upright and stowed position. Nixie's day has gotten off to a rough start, and things are definitely going to get worse before they get better!

Dan Moore

March 2012

CHAPTER ONE

"We needs the money, Spiffy! It's 'spensive to keep this dippy ship from droppin' parts all over the system! Wheeze takes what worky-derk we can gets." The girl's gravelly voice resonated from her chest cavity like a perverted wind instrument. She glared at her copilot, who was floating next to her on the flight deck of *The Raccoon*, an aging transfer ship.

Nixie Drake wore a purple jumpsuit that zipped up the front. Her head was freshly shaved, revealing a small birthmark high over her left ear. Her fingers were stubby, with nails chewed to the quick. The short, seventeen-year-old woman had girlish features: a doe-like face dotted with freckles, small breasts, and slender, pencil-thin arms and legs. Strangers often mistook her for a girl five years her junior, and Nixie depended on it. She could play the part with ease, concealing the truth that lay beneath her innocent exterior.

"I got a shiverin' feeling 'bout this run, Nix." Spif was a handsome man, the kind of guy who looked good in anything. He was frightened and angry, but still looked like a vid-star. He gave Nixie a concerned look. She could tell he was struggling to control himself. His eyes were filled with dread. "We never shoulda done this."

Nixie gave him an exasperated sigh, and then she hurled a torrent of words at him like a crazed dictionary with all its pages pulled apart. "Cap'n Grit calls the shotty shots 'round here, Spiffy. He okeedokeed this jobber right tight, he did. We's gonna foller hors d'oeuvres like beer follers brandy on this shipper dipper." She slammed her fist against the instrument panel, which set her body tumbling about her center of gravity. Nixie was a hardened smuggler with a razor-sharp mind, but no formal education. She had been on her own for almost as long as she could remember, spending her childhood years on the Moon in the corridors of Copernicus Base. She had never spent a moment in school. Rather, she taught herself Standard English from old vid-casts and movies. Her odd dialect often confounded the people around her.

Spif's eyes narrowed. He pushed away from his seat and rendezvoused with a small piece of paper floating over Nixie's shoulder. "Damn that Ice," he muttered, venting his anger. He returned, hovering in front of Nixie. "Tell her to stop littering on the flight deck!" Spif held up a gum wrapper. "It's Fruity-Juice. Her brand." He balled it up and flicked it toward Nixie, the tiny projectile hitting her in the chest before she could snatch it out of the air. "You should get your Captain Grit to issue a command about chewing gum on the flight deck." He spat the words at her.

Nixie snatched the wad of paper. "Tells Icy yourself, Spiff-ball. Grits don't have no grouse with it. Me neither, as I sees it." She launched the crumpled wrapper back at him.

Spif snatched it out of the air, making a sour face. "I've been thinking about things, Nixie. When Captain Grit recruited me for this crew, he sent you. You spoke for him back then. You sweet-talked me into joining up." Nixie listened intently, but offered no rebuttal. "When I first saw *The Raccoon*, I couldn't believe my eyes. It hardly held an atmosphere, much less flew. I wondered what I was getting into. Grit was obviously putting together a new crew on an old ship." Nixie nodded. "I've talked to Ice and Slake about it. The same thing happened to them. None of us have ever seen Captain Grit."

"Whats yer pointy point, Spiffy?" Nixie was perturbed.

"I want to see him." Spif motioned toward a hatch on the rear bulkhead of the flight deck.

"Gritty won't sees you, Spiffy." She gave him a stern look.

Spif clenched his fists in defiance. "I have a right to speak with my captain."

"He don't sees nobody but meezy wheezy. You nose-hairs that."

Spif catapulted out of his seat, crossing the compact flight deck in the blink of an eye. He grabbed a handhold next to the hatch, bringing his body to a stop in the zero-g. There was a small plaque screwed to the portal. It read, "Josiah Grit, Captain." Spif raised his hand to knock on the hatch.

Nixie pushed away from her seat and bumped Spif as she came to rest next to him. "You's donut wants to dooze that, Spiffy. Grit's got a baddy-ass temper-tantrum, and he mighty likely send your butthole outside for a suckin' swim. How's your breasty stroke in vacuum?" Nixie gave him a sly smile. Spif was always thinking about sex. She hoped the innuendo would distract him. It didn't.

Spif balled his fists and planted them on his hips. "There are too many secrets around here, Nix. Grit's got us carrying sealed cargo. We never do that. We don't know if it's a load of crackers or some virulent disease. We've never dealt with this client before, either. I've heard he's a real hard-ass. Why are we smugging unknown materials? It's not safe, no matter how much he pays us." Spif's tone was pleading.

Nixie could tell he hated groveling with her. It was an affront to his masculinity. She remembered the first day she had invited him to join the crew. She would never forget his initial hesitation, how he had bristled at negotiating terms with a young girl. Spif still looked good, though; maybe even better. She thought men were more handsome when they were subservient. "You gots to trusty trust Grit. He's gots more 'sperience than you does." She could tell she was losing the argument.

"It's not too much to ask, Nixie. I want to face the man and hear it from his own lips. Why are we taking these risks?" Spif was boring a hole through her with his eyes.

"Things been squeezy 'round 'bout, Spif. Wheeze had lots o' teeny tiny smugs, but nothin' coverin' over our bills. Case yer not notifyin' much, *The 'Coon's* jiggered by bale wire and ducky tape."

"I want to see Grit."

"He won't see ya, Spiffer-doodle."

"Why?"

"You nose-hair wise. Got his face all blundered up fightin' Meridian scurity."

"I know!" Spif nodded his head, having heard the story too many times.

"Got his-self pop popped through the forward viewport. Spent three minutes in sucky space-nothin'. Bubbled his smacker up bad. Doesn't like company." Nixie gave Spif a matter-of-fact look, suggesting the story explained everything.

"So what?" Spif shot back. Nixie masked her surprise. Spif had always been awed by the story. Now he was dismissing it as fiction. "I am tired of hearing you tell his damned legend. I don't like taking orders from a..." Spif sized her up, looking for the right word. "I have never liked taking orders from a girl!" He said it like a curse. "It's time for the captain to face me, man to man." Spif punched the hatch control. Nothing happened.

"Heezy keeps it locky docked, Spif." Nixie gave him her best glare.

Spif swore under his breath and started banging on the hatch. "Captain Grit! It's Spif! I want to talk to you!"

Silence. Not a sound escaped from the captain's cabin. Spif was rattled by it, his courage shaken by the lack of response. Nixie put her hand on his arm, urging him to refrain from another round of knocking. "Besty you nots dooze that," she warned. "The vacuum poppy popped his ear drummers, too. Gritty's kinda deaf. You're lucky ducky he didn't notice you hump dumping his hatch like that."

Spif took a breath, glancing at the hatch and then at Nixie. "You know what I think, Nixie?" The small woman stood her ground, her hand still on Spif's arm. "I think Captain Grit is dead, and you're keeping it from us."

Horror marched like an alien army across Nixie's face. Her eyes went wild for a second, and she pulled away from Spif. Her cheeks turned red, and she sucked in a long breath. Then, with a power unexpected from such a small body, Nixie shrieked at Spif. "Hell's bells to you, goddamn Spiffer!" The two moved apart for different reasons. Spif gripped the handhold by the captain's hatch and pulled himself backward, fearing Nixie's wrath. The tremendous force of air from Nixie's mouth was like a vernier thruster, pushing her head back and threatening to put her spinning head to toe. Nixie kicked at the bulkhead and twisted away from Spif, propelling herself toward the flight deck hatch. Then she disappeared into the bowels of the ship.

* * *

The first inhabitants of the Moon came to Cabeus Settlement at the Lunar South Pole in the late twenty-first century. Meridian Earth sent them there to mine ice deposits and perfect the technologies necessary for a sustained presence on the Moon. The modest outpost was very successful as men and women demonstrated humanity's keen ability to adapt to new environments. Meridian Off-World was established, and Copernicus Base, or the Cuss, became the first major habitat, tapping water ice like its predecessor and then developing a formidable ore mining and processing operation.

Over the one hundred fifty years since its inception, The Cuss had grown into a bustling city, sheltered under a vast complex of concrete domes and tunnels. It had served as the headquarters for Meridian Off-World, until disagreements with Meridian Earth over the establishment of a presence on Mars caused a veil of distrust to descend between them. A large base had already been established at Jackson Crater on the far side of the Moon, and Meridian Off-World relocated their center of operations there, to avoid the prying eyes of their Terran counterpart.

Copernicus Base remained an important industrial center, its spaceport serving as a major waypoint for lunar commerce. Her vast stores of oxygen and hydrogen, drawn from the lunar ice deposits deep beneath the surface, provided for her own needs as well as thousands of other small settlements and mining operations. The Cuss was a popular and necessary regional supply depot. Her corridors were filled with a human stew of every sort of person imaginable.

The Copernican spaceport and mining operations were located on the south side of the base. This was the realm of the hardworking men and women who wrestled the native elements from the grip of their lunar mother and poured out their health and longevity to produce the raw materials used to build Meridian's off-world empire.

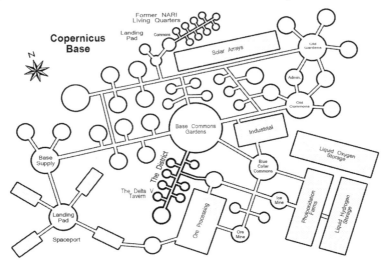

A small complex of domes, threaded together with a central corridor, was nestled conveniently between the spaceport and the ore processing plant. This was "The District," the underbelly of the Cuss, where all manners of liquid and physical pleasures were available. Those who labored hard went there to lose themselves, their minds occupied with lust for a cold drink and hot sex.

A lone figure walked southward from the large garden in the Base Commons toward The District. He had a weathered face and hard eyes. His hair was heavily oiled and slicked back. There was a tattoo of a woman on his forearm, and he walked with a determined step. His body was lean, and there was a sizable bulge between his legs. The protuberance swung back and forth beneath his pants as he moved.

There was an unspoken threat in Pierre Antoine, an aura of melancholy mixed with a sociopathic disregard. A naked woman stood at the threshold of one of the brothels that lined the central corridor of The District. Pierre looked at her, first gazing deeply into her eyes and then at her body. They both knew she was eye candy for potential customers. She had no pride, no shame. She appeared to be a bag of used skin. What little color remained in her pale complexion drained away as his eyes lingered on her. Pierre knew he had screwed her. He knew because of her reaction to him, rather than any memory he might have had of their encounter. He gave her a menacing smile, and she withdrew into the brothel. Pierre laughed to himself, amused by the absurdity of a naked whore trying to hide her body.

He walked toward the end of the corridor and paused in front of the last dome on the right. It was the Delta V tavern, a popular watering hole. He checked his wrist comp and then looked back the way he had come, scanning the passage for any possible threat. A man in his position had to be careful. Then, he pushed his way through the massive doors that covered the entrance to the tavern.

A woman of older middle age stood silently behind the bar. She was a portly woman, powerfully built. She glanced in his direction, and their eyes met. Pierre knew Kate Sloan. She had been the owner of the Delta V for as long as he had been in the Cuss. Unlike the whore in the corridor, Kate didn't flinch at the sight of him. She held his gaze with a steady confidence. She was the only woman he knew who wasn't threatened by him. He didn't care. She was too old and fat to be of any use to him.

There was a modest late-afternoon crowd in the public area of the tavern. Perhaps half of the tables were occupied, some with lone drinkers, others with men and women with sex on their minds. A bank of large viewports filled the outer rim of the dome, offering a panoramic view of the stark lunar landscape and the spaceport. Several transfer ships stood on the pad.

Pierre Antoine turned away from the scene and studied the far corner of the room. A man was sitting alone at a small table, tucked into a half-alcove in the wall. The concavity offered a modicum of privacy. The man looked up and gestured toward Pierre. He nodded in return, threading his way through the tables toward him.

"Pull up a seat," the man said.

Pierre sat down across from him. He had known Remson Burke for many years. Remson ran a large shipping business, and the two men had worked together more than once. While most of Remson's work was legitimate, the projects he pursued with Pierre were not.

"Been a while, Rem." Pierre caught the eye of a barmaid and summoned her with a quick twist of his wrist.

"Like a planetary alignment, Pierre," Remson muttered. "My needs and your services come together, and we make a deal."

A young woman stepped up to their table, her scalp bald, her jumpsuit worn but clean. Pierre looked her over like a rancher examining a cow. "What'll you have?" she asked.

He swung his arm smoothly off the table and reached for her. As his hand grew close to her buttocks, the woman shifted her weight, moving her body away from him. Pierre let his hand drop to his side. "A Forty-Two, if you please, mademoiselle." He spoke French only to his female conquests.

"Coming right up," she replied evenly, turning away from the table.

"Nice piece of meat," Pierre commented. "I could find a use for her."

"I wouldn't, if I were you," Remson countered. "That's Kate Sloan's daughter. You touch her, and your corpse will likely be found with your head bashed in."

Pierre rolled his eyes, unimpressed. "The old woman doesn't threaten me."

"She should. Kate's like a mother to everybody in The District."

Pierre studied the cost-benefit ratio of adding the nubile barmaid to his collection, then decided that he had better things to think about. He turned back to Burke. "Why am I here?"

"I have a certain friend at Rinker's Knot. He needs some supplies."

Pierre raised an eyebrow. "Rinker's is way the hell out on Vesta. It's a four-month trip to the Asteroid Belt."

"That's right. My guy is used to paying shipping charges. It will be worth your while."

"How much product does he require?" Pierre felt excitement rising within him. He loved closing on large orders.

"I'd say thirty."

"Three zero?"

"That's right. All female, under the age of fifteen. No fat ones. Any skin color will do."

Pierre glanced across the tavern; the barmaid was returning with his drink. He smiled at her as she approached the table. "There's your Forty-Two, Mr. Antoine."

Pierre was surprised. "You know my name."

"I do," she replied confidently.

"Then you know I can have you, if I want." His mouth smiled, but his eyes were cold.

"I have refused much more powerful men than you, Mr. Antoine." The woman turned away dismissively and went on about her work.

"God, I want that," Pierre muttered.

"I think you'd find her too much to handle," Remson remarked.

"I doubt that." Pierre took a long pull on his drink.

"She's just like her mother. If you're going to mess with her, wait until this job is done. I don't want your death messing things up."

The Frenchman laughed. "Okay, okay."

"How long will it take you to get the shipment ready?"

"Three weeks, maybe more. That's a lot of units. It will require considerable discretion."

"I'll want to inspect the cargo and sign off on it before you depart for the Belt."

"No problem." Pierre gave Remson Burke a toothy grin. "Now, let's talk about payment."

* * *

Meridian Corporation was the largest commercial enterprise in the solar system. Meridian Earth had been established in the late 21st century to develop technology for sustainable lunar prospecting and habitation. As the company grew and established a footing on the Moon, the Meridian Off-World Division was created. Then, as humans began to colonize Mars, Meridian Mars was formed. Conflicts arose between Meridian Earth and her off-world divisions, and the company fractured. Meridian Corporation established its headquarters at Jackson Base on the far side of the Moon and thrived. Meridian Earth could not compete economically with her off-world counterpart because of the immense cost of placing goods into Earth orbit.

Space Elevator Four hung majestically in geosynchronous orbit above the South China Sea. Tethered by six slender nanotube ribbons anchored on the Island of Sumatra, approximately one hundred sixty kilometers south-southwest of Singapore, the platform was the orbital gateway to Southeast Asia. The elevator had been in service for a year and was one of five such nanolifts girdling the equator. Each of these revolutionary orbital systems provided low-cost transit to and from the Earth's surface. The elevators were causing a seismic shift in the economic balance between Earth-based manufacturers and the gigantic Meridian Corporation that had ruled off-world commerce for over two hundred years.

Sprite Logan stood quietly before one of the immense viewports on the observation deck. She wore a dark-blue jumpsuit with a scarf wrapped around her neck. A woolen watch cap was pulled over her head, covering her ears. She was a slender young woman, six months into her twentieth year. Her eyes were bright, revealing her keen intellect. Her body was lean and muscular, her breasts firm, her hands small yet powerful. Her skin was deeply tanned, unusual for someone who had spent the last three years on the Ice Line, the boundary between the outer gas giants and the inner rocky planets. She could feel her heart racing in her chest, partly from excitement and partly from fear. She had spent four months on a transfer ship from Rinker's Knot, a supply base on the asteroid Vesta, and was now at the threshold of her college career. She was on her way to Cornell University's orbital campus, located at the Earth-Moon L1 point. In a couple of hours, she would board a jumpship that would take her to her new life.

Sprite watched the scene spread before her. Scores of spacecraft were clustered around the waist of the platform with even more cued nearby, waiting for their turn to approach the docks. The ships moved in slow motion, their AI guidance systems chattering back and forth, choreographing a graceful mating dance. The tranquil scene belied the well-orchestrated chaos a few decks below her. Men and women, partnered with intricate machines and AIs, directed the loading and offloading of passengers and cargo into the central core of the platform. The observation deck was perched at the top, or starward, end of the elevator. A hundred meters below, on the earthward end of the platform, a long tubular passageway jutted out, paralleling the orbital plane. Six nanotube ribbons hung down at intervals along the structure, disappearing into the atmosphere below. Half a dozen nanolift pods, each embracing its own ribbon, moved up and down the slender cords in an endless cycle, carrying their loads from orbit to the Earth's surface and back again.

Sprite felt the synthetic gravity pressing the soles of her feet against the decking. It was new technology, touted by Meridian Corporation as one of the company's great scientific advancements. The boast was one of Meridian's many lies. Sprite knew full well who had developed the new innovation.

Sprite's uncle was Prescott Logan, a comp specialist and encryption expert. His wife Maria was an accomplished physicist. They had become entangled with Meridian Corporation almost twenty-five years earlier and had fled to the Asteroid Belt. Maria's goal had been to make their secret home more comfortable, and it was she who had developed the synthetic gravity system. A couple of years ago, she and Prescott licensed the technology to Meridian through a dummy corporation. The deal made them financially independent. That wealth was making Sprite's college education possible.

Sprite gazed through the large viewport, feeling a wave of gratitude fill her. The pull of the synthetic gravity and the amazing generosity of her aunt and uncle mingled within her, creating a profound moment she could not share. She was proud of her family, but she knew firsthand how important it was to keep a low profile.

Three years earlier, Sprite's parents, Hunter and Adrianna Logan, had been working on a project to create nanoscale machines that could be taught to destroy harmful pathogens. When a saboteur's bomb unleashed the un-programmed nanobots, the tiny machines killed many of their friends. Amos Cross, the leader of Meridian Corporation, wanted to use the bots as a weapon. He forced her parents to work at Meridian 6, a research settlement in the Asteroid Belt. When they refused to cooperate, Amos had one of his agents kidnap Sprite. Her parents rescued her, but now they were enemies of Amos Cross, his hatred for them burning like an eternal flame. Since that time, they had been hiding in her aunt and uncle's home.

Sprite looked down at her carry-on bag, making sure it was wedged between her leg and the aluminum silicate glass of the viewport. She glanced around, taking inventory of the people around her. She took note of an unshaven man sitting a few meters away. He was staring intently at one of the overhead screens, which protruded from the ceiling. He wasn't interested in her. Sprite's eyes shifted to a woman dressed in a gray jumpsuit. She was standing across the observation deck, looking directly at her. Sprite turned away and stiffened. Her father had warned her. "Don't react," he had said. "Stay calm. Blend in. Never run." Sprite peeked at her again out of the corner of her eye. The mysterious woman was looking in her direction. Sprite turned away slowly, gripping the rail that ran along the viewport and willing her body to be still. There was a sudden movement in her peripheral vision. She glanced up, expecting the woman to be at her side. Instead, a young man who had been sitting between them rose from his seat. The strange woman's face burst into a radiant smile. She mouthed something, perhaps the man's name, and stepped toward him. They embraced warmly. Sprite let out her breath.

She tried to shake off her anxiety. As much as she was excited about going to college, she had dreaded the long trip. Although she had used three different names since leaving her parents, she still felt exposed. At any moment, one of Amos Cross's security officers might detain her. Many times over the last four months, she had wanted to turn around and return to the safety of her uncle's home, but Sprite wasn't going to succumb to her fear. To do so would mean that Amos Cross had won.

Sprite reached down and felt the card comp in her pocket. The tiny device was the size of an old-fashioned credit card and contained Wiley/Athena, Sprite's artificial intelligence and his mate. In reality, her card comp hosted a compressed copy of the digital beings. Wiley/Athena had taken up residence in the Deep Core Retention Well beneath Meridian Corporation's headquarters at Jackson Base. The card comp periodically synced with the real AIs, permitting Sprite to stay in touch with her friends. Sprite wanted to talk to Wiley/Athena, but she knew it would not be wise to do so in public. She patted the slender rectangle and smiled.

In a few days, she would be studying advanced digital intelligence on Cornell's orbital campus. Her father's best friend, Tyson Edwards, taught there. The educational habitat offered top-flight instructors and a secure environment. Sprite couldn't wait to see a familiar face. Uncle Tyson and his son Kell had been with the Logans when they were under Meridian's thumb. Sprite felt a warm tingle through her body at the thought of seeing Kell again.

A young girl brushed by her. Sprite jumped, chastising herself for letting down her guard. She watched the girl walk away from her. The child was alone, sliding her fingers along the handrail; her eyes were glued to the sweeping panorama beyond the viewport. She was oblivious to everyone and everything around her. The girl couldn't have been more than ten years old. Her body still sported a layer of baby fat. The elastic of her pants was pulled way up above her waistline. She wore a multicolored top, which was tucked into her slacks; the image of a popular children's ANI character was emblazoned on the back. She had a beaded purse slung over her shoulder. It flopped back and forth as she bounced along. Her blond hair was shoulder length; an Earther, Sprite reasoned. Off-world women kept their hair short. It was more convenient in zero-g. The girl was the personification of innocence. Sprite couldn't remember the last time she felt that way.

Sprite turned away, refocusing her gaze on the ships cued up at the docks. There was a sudden motion to her left. She looked back toward the young girl. She was gone. There was no place for her to go, Sprite thought. She pivoted away from the viewport and glanced down the aisle that curved around the circular observation deck. In the distance, she saw a flash of color, then the image of the ANI character bobbing up and down. The child's mother, a woman with copper-colored hair, gripped the young girl by the shoulder and dragged her quickly through the press of humanity loitering on the deck. As the pair disappeared around the curvature of the observation area, Sprite could tell the youngster was upset with her mother. Sprite understood. She had felt that way about her mother, too.

There was a commotion behind her. A woman shrieked. Sprite whirled around to see a man and woman pushing their way through the crowd. "Molly! Molly Winters! Where are you?" The woman's eyes were constantly moving, darting back and forth. The man with her was beside himself. He was panting, obviously exhausted from the frantic search. He planted his feet and tipped up his head. Then, with a loud voice, he spoke. "Any of you see a girl, ten years old, blond hair, about this tall?" He gestured with his hand. "She's wearing a 'Wiry Willie' sweatshirt."

"Where is my daughter?" the woman wailed. "She's gone!"

CHAPTER TWO

N ixie Drake barreled through the Raccoon's multi-cabin like a slug hurled from the muzzle of a shotgun. The air currents from her passage sent dust particles skimming across the compartment. She slammed feet-first into the aft hatch, which led to the cargo hold. Bouncing back, Nixie grabbed a handhold, her body swinging around by her wrist. She applied a counteractive force to steady herself and then pushed off more carefully toward the hatch.

Nixie punched the actuator button, and the hatch opened ten centimeters before closing again. "Damn doofy hatch!" she snarled, punching the button a second time. This time, the hatch issued a pathetic squeak like a dying bird and opened. Nixie threw herself through the opening as the portal closed again. The hatch hadn't been working right for three months. It was supposed to open properly and remain open. Instead, it was like a slow motion guillotine, threatening those who traversed the threshold with dismemberment.

The Raccoon was nearing the end of her journey. The transfer ship had left Mars two months earlier and would return to lunar orbit within a few weeks. None of her crew was happy about wasting half a year on a single run. They much preferred shuttling cargo between the Earth and the Moon, or better yet, jump-shipping high-value products between lunar bases. Nixie had announced this run, and the crew had immediately pushed back, complaining about the long duration of the job and the marginal payback. Nixie defended Grit's decision to make the trip, spending a lot of her good will in the process. The rest of the crew couldn't show their anger to the captain; it just wasn't done. However, they could complain to Nixie. No one was happy.

The Raccoon's cargo hold was almost bare. A few pallets were laden with crates and flight cases, each representing a small shipment. Some were legitimate, others were not. They were smugglers, providing discrete transport services for paying customers. The crew scavenged the occasional derelict ship, and when funds allowed, they bought contraband to sell to distributors on the Ice Line. The tens of thousands of miners and prospectors in the Asteroid Belt were always looking for exotic and often illegal materials.

Grit's business had dried up unexpectedly. There was no money. Nixie and the crew had been dipping into their personal reserves to survive. One special pallet of goods was paying for this trip. It was strapped to the deck in the middle of the hold, housed in a large blue flight case with biometric seals.

Almost six months ago, Remson Burke had approached Nixie at Copernicus Base. He was well known around the Cuss as a major shipping contractor for Meridian Corporation. In addition to his legitimate business interests, there were rumors that he was involved in rather shadowy activities. Nixie knew this was not uncommon. Burke wanted to hire them to pick up a large item on Mars and bring it back to Copernicus Base. They were to meet a Mr. Jedro Skye at Inca City near the Martian South Pole. He demanded the utmost discretion. No questions. Furthermore, he told Nixie the cargo was sealed and could not be inspected. This was highly unusual. Even smugglers liked knowing what they were carrying.

Nixie agreed to Remson Burke's outrageous terms against her better judgment. He offered an acceptable but not extravagant fee and would not budge when she countered with a higher number. Her crew needed the work, so she accepted Burke's modest terms, and the wheels were set in motion for the run. Now they were carrying the mysterious blue case across the void. Nixie couldn't wait to get the thing out of her hold.

Slake was pumping away on a stationary zero-g bike near the hold's forward bulkhead. His hair was pulled back; the fine brown strands were braided into a single dreadlock, which hung from the center of his occipital bone and descended like a hemp rope between his shoulder blades. Slake had wound the dread about his waist, tying it off like a belt. The man wasn't tall or short, fat or thin. He was average. He had droopy eyes and a mouth that found its rest in a frown.

Nixie somersaulted to the nearest exercise machine and grabbed its handlebars. Her body swung up until she was inverted. Slake always looked better upside-down. "Gonna killy willy that Spiffer!" she snapped. Slake kept pumping at his pedals. "He's a male show-ver! Don't 'spect women, kids, or dults!"

"Dults?" Slake wasn't the sharpest tool in *The Raccoon's* tool chest.

"You know, Slakee. Old peeps."

"You mean adults."

"That's whats I says, dumby!"

"Spif might have a point." Slake wasn't paying attention.

"A point?" Nixie shouted. "I'll pound his point!"

Slake jumped at Nixie's outburst. He slowed his pace, now reviewing their short conversation and wondering what he had missed. "Then again, maybe he doesn't," he offered.

"Betsy yer butt he don't have no point! He's a spineless jelly-rope turd. Goin' hind my backside tryin' to see Cap'n Grit and the like. He don't bleeve me 'bout this run!"

Slake stopped pedaling. He looked at Nixie. "The run *is* a bit out of the ordinary." He gestured across the hold toward the large blue flight case.

"Out-of-the-ord-nary!" she shouted, scrunching the words together. "We smug. That's what's we dooze. Remson Burke pays on the pickle barrel, and we jump like a rope-a-dope!"

Slake wiped his forehead, then shrugged noncommittally. "Then again, maybe the run is pretty normal."

Nixie picked up a towel that was clipped to the unoccupied exercise machine and flung it at Slake, hitting him in the face. "Right-a-roony, slow-wit! Mighty not beezee the tightest job, but there's moola in it.

'Member that, tofu!" Slake clutched the towel to his face. He seemed to be hiding behind it, waiting for Nixie to forget he was there.

Nixie shot away into the center of the hold. Her aim was perfect, snagging a strap on the large pallet that held their mysterious cargo. The outspoken young smuggler hovered before the case, running her hand across the non-skid surface. She wondered what it held. Was it a fortune that could set her crew up for life? Was it a deadly toxin that could kill them? Perhaps it was evidence for a murder trial or embarrassing possessions of a sexual nature. Nixie was naturally curious and quite paranoid. To be honest, she agreed with Spif. It wasn't safe to carry sealed items. The "not knowing" alone could cause discomfort among crew members. It already had.

She pushed away from the troubling container and floated sternward toward the propulsion deck. The steady throbbing of the engines became louder; low harmonics were resonating her chest like a base speaker cabinet at a rock concert. This time, when she punched the hatch actuator button, the titanium portal slid open. A wave of heat flowed through the opening, pressing against her face.

Ice hovered naked in front of the tangle of pipes and conduits protruding from the Raccoon's engine. She was as slender as a reed, except for her breasts, which punctuated her chest like a pair of small mountain peaks. She was hairless, and her skin was pale, smudges of grease and dirty sweat marking her like a living abstract painting. She pivoted at the sound of the hatch and floated with her feet and arms spread apart, gazing at Nixie without expression. Even naked, Ice was formidable: a powerful female warrior, undaunted.

"You's a messy two-shoes, Icy!" Nixie was still angry, and the tone of her voice showed it. Ice didn't respond. "That damned Spiffy plucky ducked a gummy wrap on the flighty deck. Your brand." Still, no response. "Polly-jize next time you sees 'im, okeedokee?" Ice was motionless, beads of sweat dripping off her body. "Got that, Icy?" The stoic woman wrapped her fingers around a pipe and rotated away from her. "Got that, door nail?" Nixie shrieked.

Ice was a mystery. She was quiet, always observing the people around her. She had no "tells," no gestures or facial expressions that revealed what she was thinking. Even her body hid its surprising strength in a slender frame with long, but hardened muscles. As *The Raccoon's* engineer, Ice knew everything there was to know about the ship's systems. She had been the first to join Nixie and Grit and had single-handedly resurrected the ship's dilapidated power plant. Over the years, she had watched Ice perform miracles with broken components, nursing *The 'Coon* back to life on more than one occasion.

Nixie stared at Ice's back. She could see every vertebra marching down the woman's spine. She pulled at the zipper on the front of her jumpsuit, inching it up a few teeth. "Cover yer butt, noody! Shouldn't be skinny dippy on the 'pulshun deck." Nixie saw a red mark on Ice's leg where a hot pipe had burned her skin. "Might toast somethin' 'portant."

Ice pirouetted in the zero-g until she faced Nixie. "Too hot," she announced. Ice reached for a rag that was jammed into a notch formed by a pair of closely-spaced cables and wiped the sweat from her forehead. The beads of perspiration were replaced by a streak of brownish grease. Nixie was always amazed at Ice's indifference toward clothing and modesty. Her dispassionate crewmate never wore more than a thin application of liquid clothing, claiming actual clothing was too bothersome. Nixie found Ice's attitude amusing, even fascinating, but behind her bluster, Nixie was much too modest to take off her clothes in public.

"Tis warmer than snotty-snot in here, Icy," Nixie agreed. "I can sees yer points." Nixie twisted her face. Somehow, her last comment didn't come out right. Ice didn't seem to notice. The naked warrior stuffed the rag back where she found it and turned toward the complex propulsion system. She slid herself gracefully toward the tangle of pipes and came to rest in front of them. She turned sideways and squeezed behind a manifold. Ice glanced at Nixie and raised her hand, summoning Nixie with a flexed index finger.

Nixie lanced across the propulsion deck and stopped her forward motion by grabbing a stout pipe. She looked for a way to join her crewmate in the maze of waveguides and plasma channels. She flipped over and pressed herself between two pipes. She could feel the hard metal against her pelvis. Nixie wiggled into the space under Ice and twisted so she could see the device in front of her friend. "Wassup?"

she muttered peevishly. Nixie wasn't happy about tight spaces. She wasn't sure how she'd get out of the tangle of engine components.

Ice pointed toward a portable engine monitor that was floating nearby. One of the engine sensors was out of tolerance, its readout blinking red on the small screen. Nixie's eyes narrowed. Before long, the anomaly would trip the Master Alarm, dumping the reactant mass and creating a massive radiation leak. It was a life-ending problem. Nixie stiffened in alarm. She looked quickly at Ice, who was motionless and reticent. The younger woman studied her eyes. Ice had no fear. "*'Coony's* gonna smitereen us?" Nixie wiped a bead of sweat off her nose.

"Nope." Ice's voice was deep for such a slender woman.

"Gonna trippy-dip the Master Alarm..." Even saying the words gave Nixie a shutter. The alarm was ear-shattering, a sound dreaded by every professional space traveler.

"Yup."

Nixie shook her head. "*'Coon's* got oldy bonies, Icer. She gonna have a strokee-dokee? Just what Cap'n Grit needs: a busted shipper with a Cadillac arrest."

Ice snorted, but said nothing further. She reached behind a squat canister that adjoined several pipes. Nixie could see a small knob that was almost hidden from view. Ice braced her body by straddling an insulated pipe and gently turned the control. Nixie heard a change in the droning pitch of the Raccoon's engines. She glanced again at the portable monitor. The readout turned yellow, then green.

"Design flaw." Ice's tone was crisp, matter of fact. "Not dangerous. Just hot." She disconnected the sensor monitor and slithered expertly out of the conduit jungle, leaving Nixie to free herself.

Nixie slithered out from between the conduits and waveguides. Ice was covered with even more grease smudges, her body bent as she focused her attention on another piece of apparatus. "You gonna 'poligize to Spiffer for the wrapper dapper?" Ice didn't respond. Nixie wasn't sure if Ice ignored her or didn't hear her over the rumble of the engines. She didn't care about the wrapper. It wasn't her issue. She glanced once more at the stoic woman and left the propulsion deck.

* * *

Rene Winters sat next to her husband Stephen in the small security office on Space Elevator Four. Her eyes were red, and she clutched a rumpled tissue in her hand. She wore a satin jumpsuit with gold buttons. She was a woman of status: her nails freshly manicured, her golden hair cut in the latest style, a large diamond ring on her finger. Stephen's arm was snaked around her shoulders. He was a small man with a chiseled face. His hair was flecked with gray. A well-worn corduroy sport coat hung loosely on his narrow frame. His silk shirt was open at the collar, and an expensive wrist comp with inlaid silver was strapped above his left hand. The Winters were familiar with the finer things, but at that moment, their world had disintegrated around them. Their daughter Molly was missing.

Officer Greenleaf sat across from the couple, a pad comp in his hand. He was sympathetic, but unimpressed by their grief. He had seen too many couples like this to get involved in their pain. He would walk them through the process and send them on their way. The odds were never good when a child went missing, especially a young girl.

"Let's make sure we have all the facts," he intoned in a deep mellifluous voice. "You say your daughter was about ten years old and one hundred forty centimeters tall?"

"She *is* ten years old," Stephen corrected him.

"Yeah," breathed Greenleaf impatiently. "Got that. And she had blond hair, dressed in dark slacks with an elastic waistband and a multicolored top?"

"She *has* blond hair! Stop using the past tense. Molly is still alive, damn it!"

"I understand your concern, sir." Greenleaf was working his way down his checklist. "And you say there was a picture of Wiry Willie on the back of her blouse?"

"It's a sweatshirt," Rene whispered. "Her favorite. We gave it to her last month."

"Where was she the last time you saw her?"

"We ate lunch in the VIP lounge next to the observation deck," Stephen repeated for what seemed to be the tenth time. "She was excited and ran out ahead of us onto the observation deck." Rene began to sob again. Stephen pulled her close, his eyes moist with his own tears. His voice began to crack. "She wanted to see all the spacecraft lining up at the docks." He paused as a wave of guilt surged over him. "I told her we'd catch up..."

"Don't, Stephen." Rene turned her head and grasped her husband's hand. "It's not your fault..."

Stephen ignored his wife. "I let her go ahead of us. I paid the bill. By the time Rene and I left the lounge, she was gone." He pulled his hand away from Rene and buried his face in his palms. "I should never have let her go," he whispered.

Officer Greenleaf scanned his pad comp. "That was about thirteen hundred hours, local time?"

"I don't know," Stephen mumbled. "I can't remember."

Greenleaf set the pad down on the seat next to him. He wanted to get the parents out of his security office. Family usually got in the way of investigations, especially hopeless cases like this one where kids disappeared with little or no trace. Experience told him there would be no more clues. He hadn't had lunch yet, and hunger was a higher priority than needlessly frustrating himself with frantic parents and a dead-end kidnapping case.

"We can pay ransom," Rene pleaded.

Greenleaf cleared his throat. "That's not how it works off-world, ma'am. The odds of being caught skyrocket when a kidnapper makes contact with the family. Nowadays, they don't do that. They take children for other reasons."

Rene gasped. Stephen looked up at the officer, a look of abject horror on his face. "What reasons?" he asked.

"They sell 'em," Greenleaf answered bluntly. "Sex trade on the Ice Line, most likely."

Rene slumped over into Stephen's arms, sobbing uncontrollably. Stephen gave the officer a withering glare. "You didn't have to say that!"

Greenleaf was dispassionate. "Best you know the truth, Mr. Winters." The security officer shifted in his seat and picked up the pad comp. "Now. I think we have everything we need," he said mechanically. "Why don't the two of you catch your flight and leave the detective work to the professionals?" Stephen's face clouded; he was unable to fathom what Greenleaf was saying. "We took a few statements from some of the other passengers on the observation deck. Our surv-cams show your daughter leaving the deck with a woman with copper-colored hair. We didn't get a look at her face, but we've put out an Amber alert."

"We can't leave." Rene had pulled herself back up, her eyes now blazing with a mother's determination. "We aren't going anywhere without Molly!" Stephen nodded in agreement.

"Suit yourselves, folks." Greenleaf knew better than to try to dissuade them. "There's nothing else you can do, but if it makes you feel better, knock yourselves out. I guarantee that..." He glanced back at his pad comp to refresh his memory. "...that Molly is long gone by now. The people who took her know what they're doing." He reached into his jacket and removed a thin plastic card. "You can reach my office with this. The squad AI will let you know if we catch a break in the case."

Greenleaf rose and opened the door of the small room. He held it open, sending a clear message that he was done with them. Stephen got to his feet and tugged at his wife's arm.

* * *

Nixie Drake's memories of her childhood home were like indistinct shadows cast upon wispy fingers of fog. Sometimes she dreamed of her sisters, bleating and whimpering babies who cried out to her through their helplessness. She felt them reaching for her, smothering her. Then she would wake, grateful it was a dream. Nixie couldn't remember her mother. Perhaps she had died before her memories began. She wished she could forget her father. She couldn't remember his face, but she knew he was bad. He touched her in ways that scared her. That's why she ran away.

Nixie had learned quickly how to take care of herself. At first, she hid in the lush green area of Copernicus Base Commons. She would watch people walk by. She was tempted to ask them for help, but realized they would only take her back to her father. Hunger had gripped her, and Nixie learned to steal food. She found a loose grating and moved into the massive service tunnels and corridors that crisscrossed the base. She became a nocturnal huntress, scouring the garbage bins for food and clothing. She found a discarded vid-screen and took it into her hideaway. With it, she expanded her vocabulary, making up English grammar on her own.

During one of her expeditions, Nixie had foraged through the trash bins outside the Delta V, a popular tavern in the District, the seedy section of the Cuss. The discarded food was good there. She was confronted by a pedophile who tried to rape her. Kate Sloan, the owner of the Delta V, intervened and took Nixie into her home. Nixie joined a group of smugglers when she was nine years old. She was born for the work. By the time she was twelve, she had become Captain Grit's recruiter, helping him assemble her present crew.

Nixie took a deep breath before pushing through the open hatch that led to the flight deck. She avoided Spif, who was still at the controls. Out of the corner of her eye, she saw him glance at her. Nixie translated to the stern bulkhead and came to a stop in front of Captain Grit's cabin.

"You going in there?" Spif's voice was strident.

"Yup." Nixie didn't want a repeat of their earlier conversation.

"I want to see him." Nixie could tell by the sound of his voice that Spif had left the command console and was moving in her direction.

"I'll askee 'im," she said without turning around. Nixie punched a code into the actuator and squeezed herself through the hatch before it was fully open. By the time Spif arrived at the portal, it was sliding shut.

"Ask him!" Spif shouted as the hatch hissed shut against its seal.

* * *

Sprite Logan settled into the large jumpship at Dock D-12 on Space Elevator Four. She would have liked to ride one of the six nanolifts down to the Earth's surface, but the elevator was just a waypoint on this trip. Within a few hours, she would arrive at Cornell's orbiting campus at the Earth-Moon L1 point. She would make new friends and begin her training in advanced artificial intelligence.

Sprite was tucked in next to a small viewport, perhaps thirty centimeters in diameter, in the starboard bulkhead near the stern of the jumpship. All she could see was the dull silver fuselage of the jumpship in the neighboring dock. She glanced across the aisle, taking note of the other people in her row. An elderly man was seated by the port bulkhead. Perhaps he was a professor. Two of the passengers were students. She was certain. There was a young mother with a small child in the seats next to her. Sprite relaxed. She was safe for the time being.

Sprite straightened her right leg and pulled the slender card comp out of her pocket. She pressed her thumb to its surface. A sensor recognized her. The inner workings of the tiny device came alive, linking with the earset in Sprite's right ear.

"Audio only," she commanded quietly.

A familiar voice whispered to her. "Hi, Sprite! We see that you are on the jumpship at Space Elevator Four, Dock D-12. Are you enjoying your trip?"

Sprite grinned. "Hey, Wiley. I'm good."

A second voice whispered through her earset, more feminine, with a silky timbre. "Hello, Sprite."

"Athena! I hope Wiley is treating you well." There was a pause, and Sprite grinned, knowing that her comment required a huge bump in Athena's processing bandwidth.

"There are eight-point-seven million references to the phrase, 'treating you well.' I am not aware of Wiley 'treating me,' but our processes complement each other in an efficient manner. I am satisfied with Wiley's presence in my neural network."

Sprite snorted, and the little girl sitting next to her gave her a curious glance. Wiley had been Sprite's best friend for many years. He was an artificial intelligence, or AI, which used to reside solely on her card comp. Originally created to be a digital assistant, Sprite had encouraged her synthetic friend to think for himself. When Sprite was kidnapped by Amos Cross, Wiley and Athena joined forces on a Martian server. They transferred themselves to the Deep Core Data Retention Center at Jackson Base. Ever since that time, Wiley had ceased referring to himself alone. It was always "we." Sprite thought of the pair as husband and wife, and in many ways, they were.

"The new synthetic gravity system is installed on the space elevator," Sprite offered. "It feels good."

"We are glad you think so." Sprite thought she could sense a bit of pride in Wiley's voice, but she wasn't sure. "It has been interesting brokering the synthetic gravity system for your aunt Maria. Meridian Corporation has been trying to track down the source of the technology but has been unable to do so."

Sprite smiled to herself. Wiley and Athena were the perfect ones to shield her family from Amos Cross. He would look for human beings, never knowing that AIs embedded in his own network were the ones brokering the deal. "I want to send a message to my mom and dad," Sprite said quietly.

"Ready." It was Wiley's voice this time. The AI had set up an undetectable data path. Meridian Corporation's formidable resources would not be able to locate the source or destination of the message.

Sprite greeted her parents warmly. "I'm on the last leg of the trip. If you hear about a girl being kidnapped on Space Elevator Four, it wasn't me. I saw her, though. I'm okay." Sprite's voice began to shake as she remembered her own kidnapping. "I'm fine. I can't wait to get to school. Tell Uncle Prescott and Aunt Marie that I miss them. I love you." Sprite paused, and Wiley closed out the message file.

"We'll let you know when they answer you, Sprite."

Sprite thanked the AI and then settled back into her seat, trying to shut out the memories of Amos Cross and her horrible ordeal.

* * *

Stephen and Rene Winters sat dejectedly in two of the hard plastic seats that lined the observation deck on Space Elevator Four. Stephen's corduroy jacket was draped around Rene's shoulders. Her golden hair was mussed, her hands covering her mouth, her eyes glistening with hopeless tears. All thoughts of making their connecting flight were wiped from their minds. They didn't know what to do, but they couldn't bring themselves to leave the place where Molly had disappeared. Stephen's face was ashen. He gripped his valise in his left hand and massaged Rene's shoulder with the other.

Scores of other passengers surrounded them, passing back and forth in front of them, families chattering excitedly to one another. However, Stephen and Rene were all alone. They were the helpless and unwilling participants in a horrific scenario where nothing was clear. They sat on the cold plastic chairs, balanced on a razor's edge between hope and grief.

* * *

"I'm Nixin' a fit, Gritty!" Nixie hovered in Captain Grit's cabin. Her face was flush with frustration and rage. "That damn Spiffer! No 'spect from him! Never! If I had a pair," she grabbed at her crotch, "or hair-skin legs, then the mighty-tighty Spifferoon would pay his dues to whats I says." She paused to take a deep breath. Nixie could feel her heart pounding, her blood charging through her arteries. "Spiffy wants in here!" She spat out the words. "'magine that, Gritty? He's wantin' to put his peepers on you!"

Nixie's voice was piercing. A piece of strapping resonated somewhere above her, among the pipes and conduit which crisscrossed the ceiling. She grabbed a handhold and slammed her body to the other side of the compartment, coming to rest in the folds of Grit's sleeping harness. She looked across the cabin, her eyes blazing, a tear forming and then floating away from her face, a perfect sphere.

"They don't 'spect me, Gritty." Her voice trembled now, low and hollow. "After alls I done, pullin' this and scrappin' after that." She glanced down at one of the hook-and-loop straps of the harness. "Yous 'n meezy puts this crew-cut together, didn't we? Put our butts waysy-daisy out on that limbo. Weezy-deezy a team."

Nixie sniffed, then wiped her face on the sleeve of her jumpsuit. "What's I do, Gritty?" Calmer now, she untangled herself from the sleeping harness and translated across the cabin. She put a hand on Grit's shoulder, but the Captain didn't say a word.

CHAPTER THREE

Molly Winters was terrified. Everything had happened so quickly. One moment she was gazing out of the immense viewports on the observation deck, and the next she was being whisked away by a stern-looking woman with copper-colored hair. At first, she thought it was her father, but he had never been that violent. By the time she realized she was in the hands of a stranger, the powerful woman had one arm wrapped tightly around her shoulders and the other firmly over her mouth. They trotted quickly away from the viewport, putting distance between themselves and the crowd of people on the observation deck. They passed through a hatchway, and a second person met them: a man with cold eyes. Molly felt an unwelcome prick in her arm, and she felt herself falling down a long, billowy tunnel. Then, everything went dark.

When Molly awoke, she could tell she was weightless. Something heavy and thick was over her head. It was dark. Her mouth was full of cloth. She was unable to make a sound. A tight cord of some kind was wrapped around her wrists. Her fingers were numb. Her legs were held together. She had to pee.

What had happened? Molly had no idea, but she knew it was bad. She felt tears in her eyes, a gut-wrenching spasm in her stomach. She pulled her knees up and hyperventilated through her nose. She could not utter a sound, but she focused her will, summoning a mental image of her mother.

* * *

Amos Cross was a small man with almost limitless power. He was the chief executive officer of Meridian Corporation and had a reputation for his ruthless leadership. The product of a horrifically abusive home, Cross shunned close relationships and terrorized his subordinates. He had an uncanny ability to identify the psychological cracks in the people around him and use that knowledge to intimidate and control them.

Cross's office occupied the uppermost level of the sprawling Meridian Corporation Headquarters at Jackson Base. It was an empty room, an immense holochamber that he could manipulate at will. Cross was in a foul mood, born of a night filled with troubling dreams. He stood in the middle of his office, which resembled a patch of low-cut grass stretching as far as the eye could see. There were storm clouds overhead and the low rumble of distant thunder.

The great man stood before a small rectangular table. Leaves of virtual paper were neatly stacked upon its surface. Cross paced back and forth, barking orders to a nameless underling who was having the worst day of his life. "I don't want excuses! Do your job, or I will destroy you!" With a cock of his head, Cross terminated the connection. He thought of his new executive assistant, and the neural implant in his skull summoned her automatically. Within a few seconds, a soft chime announced her arrival. A section of distant prairie changed shape as a rectangular slot appeared in the image. In the opening, Cross could see the muted lighting of the corridor outside his office door. A woman stood at the threshold, waiting hesitantly for his invitation to enter.

"Come!" There was exasperation in his voice, as though the woman was late. This was the first time she had reported to his office since being hired, and Amos Cross already seemed disappointed.

"Is there something wrong, sir?" Meredith Frank inquired meekly. She wore a one-piece chocolate-brown jumpsuit under a hunter-green blazer. Her hair was pulled back into a bun at the back of her head. A turquoise scarf was tied loosely around her neck.

Cross ignored the question. He stared at her for a solid minute without speaking. Then he turned his back to her. Cross waved a hand,

and a virtual screen appeared in front of him. "Get me the human resources director!" he barked. Cross could have set up the link with his implant, but he wanted his new assistant to see this.

A woman dressed in an impeccable ruby-colored business suit appeared on the screen in front of Cross. She frowned briefly, then recovered with a formal smile. "Yes, sir?"

"Who oriented my new assistant?"

"I did, sir."

"You should have told her how to dress appropriately. She's a disaster! I'm going to send her back to your office when I'm done with her, and I expect you to personally brief her on proper grooming and personal hygiene." Cross could hear his new assistant gasp quietly behind him. He smiled to himself.

"She has a hygiene problem? I didn't pick up on that when I met with her."

"She stinks of cheap soap. Her wardrobe is all wrong. Her hair is terrible. I expect you to fix her!" Cross cut the connection abruptly, then paused before turning back to his new assistant.

"What is your name?" His eyes were menacing.

"Frank, sir. Meredith Frank. I did my best..."

"I don't care about your best, Ms. Frank. It is a testament to the miserable state of human kind that you rose to the top of the prospect list for this position. I don't see how this is going to work."

"I really want this job, sir. I'll do anything..."

"Don't bother me with empty promises. It's pathetic. I am sick and tired of being disappointed by my executive assistants. Did you lie on your resume?" Cross had already screened up the document.

"No, sir."

"It says here that you actually went to school and studied business administration."

"That's right, sir. I graduated at the top of my class."

"That's a joke!" The woman winced. "Your employment with me is temporarily suspended until you address some personal issues. You are to go directly to the office of human resources and meet with my director. She will brief you on what to wear and what fragrances are acceptable in this office." Meredith Frank's face was flush with shame. "Do you understand me?"

"Yes, sir."

"Then go! Get out of my sight and don't come back until you're clean and proper." The woman turned, suppressing the urge to sprint out of the office. "And Ms. Frank."

She stopped dead in her tracks and faced Amos Cross once again. "Yes, sir?"

"I think you might look good in carmine."

"Purplish-red, sir?"

"If you want to work for me, you better not question my suggestions, girl." His voice cut her with surgical precision.

"Yes, sir."

Cross turned away without another word and began berating another employee on his comlink.

* * *

Slake hovered by the food dispensers in *The Raccoon's* multi-cabin. The odor of garlic hung in the air. The other members of the crew had gathered for the evening meal. There was no day or night on the ship, of course. Evening was the time leading up to the sleep period. It was customary for the crew to share morning coffee and the final meal of the day. Years of association had molded them into a family: a mildly toxic and dysfunctional collection of people who regularly flip-flopped between affection and irritation.

Spif and Nixie were definitely in an irritation phase at this point. They hung on opposite sides of the cabin, their backs turned to one another. Ice floated across from Slake, watching him prepare the meal. Her eyes followed the tip of his long dreadlock. It had become unfurled from his waist and was slowly rising on a current of air. Slake was completely unaware of it. Ice pursed her lips and blew toward the dread. The mischievous shaft of air struck the rope-like appendage. The soft bristles at the end of the dreadlock brushed Slake's ear.

Slake was startled by the sensation. He had just filled a squeeze bag full of hot coffee and was preparing to screw the cap on the flexible container. Without thinking, he brought his hand up to his ear and compressed the bag of coffee against the side of his head. A brown column of coffee squirted across the multi-cabin. Ice pushed away from a handhold, her mouth wide open. She approached the long horizontal column of coffee and caught most of it with one gulp. Slake, now realizing what he had done, turned in time to see Ice's face just centimeters from his own. Startled again, he released the squeeze bag and contorted his body awkwardly to avoid a collision. Ice, as graceful as a swan, brought up her hand and caught the bag. She put her thumb over the open nozzle. Gripping a handhold, she flipped over and pushed herself back to the other side of the cabin.

"What did you do that for?" Slake whined. "You scared me half to death!" Ice hovered without expression, sucking noisily on the container of coffee. He glared at her, but she acted like nothing had happened. Nixie snickered, and Slake gave her a stern look before turning back toward the beverage dispenser.

"Let's eat," Slake announced a few moments later. Nixie and Spif turned around, but avoided eye contact. Slake gave each of them a bag of coffee and a container holding a warm Italian sandwich. Ice glanced at her two warring crewmates, then looked at Slake. He shrugged. An uncomfortable mood settled over them as they ate their meals in silence, each biting carefully into the food to avoid spreading crumbs in zero-g. Slake was the messiest eater and was constantly policing shreds of food from the cabin.

"What did you tell Grit about me, Nix?" Everyone looked up as Spif's voice broke the uneasy silence. "You tell him to dump my ass at the next port?" He was deathly serious, his face set like a piece of granite. Nixie met his gaze, then returned to her meal. Spif glanced at Ice and Slake, then nodded to himself. Once again, he turned to Nixie. "Why is it that you are the only one who can visit the Captain?"

Slake's eyes shifted from Nix to Spif, then he began to nod. "It's a fair question, Nix," he offered.

Ice remained frozen in place.

"Answer me, damn it!" Spif slammed the cover down on his sandwich container, cracking the unbreakable plastic.

"Don't nosey knows," Nix replied. Her voice was quiet but there was an edge to it.

"Maybe Grit's your lover," Spif wisecracked. "Maybe he likes pokin' his probe up your butt." Nixie stopped chewing, looking up at him with a look that was a mix of astonishment and pain. Spif continued. "Maybe you like the feel of him, huh?"

Slake started to laugh. Nixie flung her dinner toward the deck and lunged at Spif. She crossed the cabin in a flash, her hands outstretched. She grabbed him by the neck and slammed her forehead into his face. There was a sickening crack as Spif's nose was shattered. Slake moved in behind Nixie and grabbed her around the waist. He looped the fingers of his free hand through a handhold and pulled her away from her victim. Nixie had no interest in killing Spif, although her hatred for him burned hot enough. She just wanted to hurt him, and she did. Spif clutched his nose. Bright-red spheres of blood were bubbling out of his nostrils and floating around his head.

Ice put the last piece of her sandwich into her mouth without a word. The skirmish did not impress her, one way or the other. She chewed and swallowed, taking one last sip from her coffee bag. Then, Ice opened a nearby locker and withdrew a slender piece of paper about the size of an old-fashioned microscope slide. The words "Fruity Juice" were printed boldly in stylized lettering on flat paper panels. She removed the wrapper, exposing a stick of chewing gum. Ice popped it into her mouth and, crumpling the wrapper, flicked the wad of paper to the far end of the multi-cabin.

Slake fumbled in the first-aid locker and pulled a couple of cotton balls from a zip-lock container. Spif pushed them into his tortured nostrils, stemming the flow of blood. The multi-cabin was a mess. Bubbles of coffee and blood, along with fragments of food, hung everywhere. Spif was bouncing around the space in slow motion, too intent upon his injuries to bother holding himself in place. Nixie had withdrawn to the aft bulkhead and was rubbing the large bump that was forming on her forehead.

"That's it!" Spif gurgled, spitting a viscous mass of bloody mucous across the cabin. "I've had enough!" He gripped a handhold violently and pushed toward the aft hatch. Nixie, thinking he was readying a counter attack, moved away. Spif slammed the actuator button. The hatch refused to open. "Shit!" he screamed, hitting the button again. The portal screeched open, and Spif flung himself through it, barely clearing the threshold before the hatch slid shut.

"You shouldn't have done that, Nixie," Slake muttered. "I've never seen him that mad before."

Nixie had her arms wrapped around her chest; her face was sprinkled with Spif's blood. She glared silently at Slake, her eyes boring a hole through him. Her heart was beating loudly. It filled her ears with a cadence resembling that of a war drum. The fragile peace among *The Raccoon's* crew was shattered.

The aft hatch slid open, breaking the uneasy silence in the multi-cabin. Spif glided through the opening, a portable plasma torch in his hand. The aft hatch clanked shut behind him. "I'm going to see the captain," he snarled, pushing his way across the cabin toward the flight deck.

They all tumbled through the open hatch. Spif was first, followed closely by Nixie, who had been jolted out of her funk by the sight of the torch. Ice was the last one to enter the flight deck, and she sealed the hatch behind her. Regulations were clear about using a torch on a spacecraft. All hatches to a compartment had to be closed when there was an open flame.

"Pleasy wheezy, Spiffer!" Nixie cried. "Gritty only walkie-talkies to me."

"Open the hatch, Nixie." Spif was like a bull scuffing his hooves in front of a toreador. He was a living, breathing bomb. His fuse was lit, and it was only a matter of time before he exploded. Nixie tried to pull him away from Captain Grit's hatch, but she couldn't budge him. Spif was operating on pure adrenaline. His muscles were like iron, far too strong for the girl.

"Open it!" Spif raised the plasma torch, his finger on the ignition trigger. A look of horror marched across Nixie's face. She swore at

Spif. Then, in a rare display of resignation, she entered the code into the hatch actuator.

Nixie stood aside and let her crewmates float into Captain Grit's cabin. She felt the flush of shame and embarrassment on her cheeks as she followed them in.

"Where is he?" Spif demanded.

"It's empty." Slake had a keen grasp of the obvious.

Nixie sucked in a deep breath. Ice hovered at the far end of the cabin and pulled the chewing gum out of her mouth. She unceremoniously stuck it to the underside of a rectangular box that protruded from the bulkhead. Then she cleared her throat, drawing everyone's attention. A small figure was sitting on top of the enclosure like Humpty Dumpty. A miniature seatbelt made from hook and loop strapping held it in place.

It was the figure of a pirate, a child's toy. It was about thirty centimeters tall, from the peak of its Davy Jones hat to the bottoms of its black boots. An obligatory patch covered one eye, and the remnant of a plastic sword was fitted into the left hand. The silver tip had been broken off a long time ago, leaving a dull gray stub with a brass-colored hilt just above a hand with cloth fingers. The figure wore a captain's jacket with brightly-colored pantaloons. Its face was unreadable, the mouth sewn into the cloth in an expressionless straight line.

"What in hell is that?" Slake scratched his head, a look of befuddlement on his face.

"It's a doll, you idiot!" Spif gave Nixie a withering look. Her chin dropped, her cheeks turning red.

"What's it doing in Captain Grit's cabin?" Slake's eyes were scanning the compartment. "And where is the old man, anyway? Is he in the head?"

Ice hung motionless near Nixie.

Spif curled his lips; his voice dripped with sarcasm. "Don't you get it, Slake?" He ripped free the hook and loop strap and snatched the pirate doll from its perch. "This is Captain Grit!" Slake looked puzzled. He glanced at Ice, then at Nixie who was trembling. Spif waved the doll in the air. "This is our great leader! There is no Captain Grit!"

Slake finally understood, but then looked puzzled again. "Then who's been issuin' the orders?"

"You are so stupid!" Spif had the doll in his fist, its broken sword pointing at Nixie. He was like an irritated school teacher waving a chalkboard pointer at a cheating student. "We've been workin' for her all along!" He threw the doll at Nixie. "We've been taking orders from a kid!"

Slake pivoted toward Nixie. "Is that so, Nix?" Nixie's eyes were moist and red. She offered Slake a tiny nod.

Everyone heard a deep rumble that shook *The Raccoon's* space frame. There was a single shake that rattled the pipes and conduit in the cabin's overhead spaces. The bulkheads flexed like a wobble board, and Nixie felt her ears pop from the overpressure. Then there was an ear-splitting explosion from somewhere aft, and the cabin went topsy-turvy.

At first, the cabin rotated around them. The sudden change in orientation was startling. Then the cabin moved sharply to the side, and Nixie collided with Slake as everyone smashed into the starboard bulkhead in a tangle of arms and legs. Fortunately, the wall was cushioned and absorbed most of the force of their impact. The lights went out, and a chorus of warbling alarms sounded from the flight deck.

Nixie bounced off the padded bulkhead and flew back across the compartment. She hit something hard with her leg, and then she felt a handhold. She curled her fingers around it and held on. Everything that wasn't fastened down slammed around in the cabin, like a handful of bolts in an empty coffee can. She heard grunts and moans in the darkness. A flash of reddish-orange light like a rotating beacon spilled through the flight deck hatchway, then disappeared. Nixie concentrated on the dark opening. The strange light appeared again. Nixie watched it swing past the forward viewport. Several fountains of fire were spurting from a crumpled mass of metal. Nixie's eyes clouded, and she felt consciousness slipping away. It occurred to her that the flaming debris resembled the Raccoon's tail section. Then everything evaporated into a cottony-dark mist.

CHAPTER FOUR

Molly Winters listened to the muted sounds around her. She heard a faint rushing of air. It was similar to the sound she had heard on the jumpship earlier that day, when she and her parents had arrived at Space Elevator Four. In the distance, perhaps on the other side of a bulkhead, there was a muted purring. It was familiar, too. She was on another jumpship, and the propulsion system was engaged.

There was a solid clanking sound, and Molly could hear the pitch of the engine change slightly. Then her body bumped against something hard and flat. She jerked. The ship had undocked. Molly was floating, and the jumpship's velocity had changed. The cabin had moved under her, and she had collided with a bulkhead. She felt the slight g-force pressing her against the aft wall.

Molly couldn't see. She couldn't move. She grunted through her gag and strained at her bindings. Molly wanted to cry out but couldn't. She screamed in her mind, hoping to reach her parents through the sheer power of her thoughts. "Momma! I'm on a jumpship! It has just undocked from the Space Elevator! Look here! Please!" She felt the cold fingers of panic marching up her spine. Molly began to shake uncontrollably. She was in the hands of strangers, alone, in trouble. With every passing second, her parents were farther and farther away. She wondered where she was being taken. There was no answer, just the subtle hiss of air and the muffled whine of the jumpship's engines.

* * *

The *Celestial Ghost* was like a phantom. Her hull was pitch black, making her a shadow moving slowly through the dark void of space. Optical instruments could not detect her. The stars would wink out as she passed by, her darkened mass obstructing their light. Then she was gone.

The Ghost was a full-sized transfer ship. She was a flattened cylinder with an oval cross section which flared at the stern, where three ion-emitters, which resembled old-fashioned radar antennae, protruded from her hull. Her flight deck was positioned in the forward section of the hull, which broadened into a saucer shape. Four large nacelles girdled her amidships. They were outrigger holds, each attached to her waist by a stubby, wing-like strut. A fifth nacelle, much smaller than the other four, hung at the end of a telescoping appendage, which protruded from her belly just astern of the flight deck.

A man hovered before a bank of instruments on *The Celestial Ghost's* flight deck. "We've got something, Sarah."

Captain Sarah "Raven" Miles pushed away from her console and skimmed across the cabin. Her body ricocheted off a padded support column and lined up perfectly with the sensor station. She flipped through a single somersault and then gripped the handhold over the man's head. Raven swung to a stop and moved next to him, positioning her head in order to read the display.

"What have we got, Eagle?" She spoke with a smile, exuding a kindness and warmth with every word and gesture.

Ed "Eagle" Mortenson grinned at his lover. He reached up and touched her shoulder, pulling her head next to his own. "There's a contact about fifty thousand klicks off the starboard bow. There was an explosion."

"A ship?" Raven's face drew taut with concern.

"Had to be," Eagle replied. He pulled his hand back from Sarah's shoulder and punched a few keys on his workstation. "Sensors indicate it was a transfer ship. There are multiple targets, suggesting she broke up. There are two large pieces with a ton of smaller ones. One is really hot. I think it's the stern section. It's moving away from what appears to be the forward compartments at about half a klick per second. Doppler shows both major pieces spinning on multiple axes."

"Is it propagating?" Raven rubbed Eagle's shoulders, her eyes intent on the instruments in front of them.

"There was an impulse that coincided with the explosion, but nothing after that. Whatever she was, she's offline now."

Raven looked across the flight deck. "Falcon?"

A slender, one-armed woman hovered at the ship's helm. Halcyon Michaels, known to her crewmates as "Falcon," peeked her head over a large console that squatted next to her station. "Yes, Ma'am?"

Raven smiled to herself. Falcon was the most formal member of the crew. She was their pilot: a steady unflappable presence at the controls of *The Celestial Ghost.* "Eagle is sending you coordinates. Lay in a course. Looks like we've got another salvage site."

Falcon's bone-thin face split into a wide smile. "Yes, Ma'am! Shall I expedite?"

Raven glanced back at the sensor readings in front of Eagle. She nodded her head. "Yup. I don't want anybody else scooping this up before we get there."

The Celestial Ghost's vernier thrusters flared briefly as Falcon adjusted their course. The dark craft yawed to starboard as the ship's artificial intelligence locked on to the new heading. Then, the powerful ion-emitters glowed with bluish fire as balls of plasma erupted from the generators, pushing the great ship forward on an intercept course with the shattered remains of *The Raccoon.*

* * *

The air in Captain Grit's cabin was filled with the acrid smell of burning insulation. An emergency light flickered through the hatch from the flight deck. Nixie coughed, then grimaced from a shooting pain in her leg. There was a large bump on her shin, but no blood. Slake hung motionless in the middle of the cabin. An ugly bruise covered his forehead. Spif and Ice were gone.

Nixie swam across the cabin and checked Slake's pulse. He was alive. She grabbed his sleeve and pulled him, one handhold at a time, through the hatchway and onto the flight deck. Several large cabinets had tipped over, spewing their delicate contents across the decking. Wires hung everywhere. Spif was hovering at the controls. Nixie could see Ice's legs sticking out from under the console. All the screens were dark. Nixie gave the emergency light a whack, and the light stopped flickering. Spif looked up at her without a word. The cotton balls in his damaged nose were stained dark with blood, one of them hanging from a nostril by a single fiber. His disgust was written across his face.

"We's still breathin'," Nixie offered.

"Not for long," Spif shot back. "Life support is offline. Hell, everything is dead!"

"Wha' what happened?" It was Slake. He had his hands to his head. "I must 'a hit something." He opened his eyes. "Everything is kind of blurry. Hey, it's cold in here. Turn up the heat, will you?"

"No can do, Slake." Spif's voice had a hint of fear in it. "There was an explosion. *The 'Coon* is dead."

There was a sputter of light on the main console. Ice slid out from under the control surface. Norman, the ship's artificial intelligence, was booting up. Everyone held their breaths.

"Standby power is at sixty percent," Norman said. "I am ready for your commands."

Spif gave Ice an appreciative nod. "Ship status, Normo."

The AI was silent about ten seconds. "I am confused, Spif," he announced at last.

"Why is that?"

"I cannot find the ship." Everyone hovered in stunned silence. "Where is the ship?" the AI asked.

Spif scratched his scalp. "Backtrack, Norman. When was the last time you sensed *The Raccoon?*"

There was another delay. "My last contact with the ship was twenty-six minutes ago. The ship disappeared in one-point-four seconds."

"Was there an explosion on the propulsion deck?"

"No, Spif. Memory analysis suggests the first anomaly occurred in the hold," Norman reported. "There was a sudden overpressure and temperature increase before telemetry was lost. This was followed by an extreme drop in cabin pressure, suggesting a hull breach. I pulsed a distress packet automatically. Voltage was then disrupted in the main power busses. I experienced a total data loss at that point."

"Did something hit us?" Spif was shaking his head.

"No, Spif. The anomaly occurred inside the hull."

"What is the condition of the emergency life-support system on the flight deck?"

"I don't know, Spif."

"Why, Norman?"

"I cannot find the flight deck. I have no real time data."

Spif pivoted around until his was facing Nixie. "There was an explosion in the hold," he said, as a matter of fact. "All of our cargo was non-lethal, except for that mysterious box." Spif jabbed a finger at Nixie. "Shall we blame Captain Grit for bringing it on board?" He gave her a withering glare. "Oh, I forgot! There is no Captain Grit. We can thank you for killing us!" Nixie backed away from the others and hovered silently in a corner of the shattered flight deck.

* * *

The drone of the jumpship's engine had lulled Molly Winters to sleep. Once again, she was floating freely in the cabin. Her eyes moved rapidly under their lids as she dreamt of running in a relay race. She was clutching the baton tightly, her legs pumping up and down. A faceless woman with copper-colored hair stood ahead of her. Her body was crouched. She was poised, ready to take the baton and begin her leg of the race.

Molly kept running as fast as she could. As she drew next to the mysterious woman, she raised the baton for the handoff. Suddenly, the woman reached out and grabbed her by the shoulder. With strength found only in dreams, the woman lifted Molly off the running track and tucked her under her arm. Molly felt herself falling as she was being carried off the track.

Her eyes snapped open. Darkness. Molly's head was still covered by the thick cloth. She pulled again at her restraints. No success. She listened to the muted rumble of the jumpship's power plant. Its pitch changed, and then the engine went silent. Molly heard the hissing of steering rockets. Once again, her body bumped softly against one of the bulkheads. There was a chunky clanking sound that resonated through the bulkhead. Molly had heard the sound before. The ship had just docked. A cramping fear clutched her stomach as she wondered what would happen next.

* * *

Norman's backup power supply ran out of juice, and his screen blinked off. Ice turned to the others, rubbing her arms in the gathering chill of the flight deck. "Two hours," she said quietly.

"That's it?" Slake pouted. The warrior-woman met his gaze with a flinty, almost statuesque expression. "We have only two hours of air left?" Ice didn't respond.

The emergency lights were growing dim. Nixie still cowered in her corner. She had been crying silently in the shadows, tormented by shame. Spif was right. She never should have agreed to smuggle contraband without the right to inspect it. Now *The Raccoon* was a goner, and it was her fault. Nixie felt like she had been hit by a psychological earthquake. A fissure of doubt opened up in her, threatening to swallow her up in its maw. A great darkness was stalking her, threatening her confidence. She should not have misled her crew. She was only a kid, and they were right to question her command authority. She was a fool.

Nixie had retrieved Captain Grit from the stateroom, and the doll now resided in a soft shoulder bag. She wanted to hug him. She wanted to close her eyes, as she had done countless times before, and pretend he was her father. However, she didn't want the others to see her weakness. Nixie hugged Grit through the cloth bag instead.

She drew in a slow breath through her nose. Mucus gurgled. Nixie wiped her nostrils on her sleeve. She felt groggy. The air was becoming stagnant; the carbon dioxide levels were rising. Ice was still hovering next to Norman's blank display. Slake was shaking like a leaf, half from the cold and the other half from fear. Spif hung on the other side of the flight deck, his back against a rack of equipment. He was staring at her with unforgiving eyes.

Nixie looked away. She took another breath. For the moment, there was enough air to survive, but not enough to satisfy. She sucked in another lungful and held it. She closed her eyes and let the air out slowly. And then, Nixie passed out.

* * *

Rough hands seized Molly Winters. She tried to fight them, but found it impossible in the zero-g. The air grew colder. She wiggled violently, and one of the hands struck her on the head. The blow startled her. It was a clear message: comply or suffer the consequences. Molly's captors pulled her through the cold space, scraping her back on what must have been a hatchway. There was the sudden sensation of gravity, and Molly felt herself falling. Her hands and feet were bound, and she could not protect herself. Her body slammed down onto a hard surface. She felt someone touching her ankles, and then her legs were free.

"Get up!" a stern voice commanded. Molly felt someone's shoe against her ribcage. She rolled over on her face and pushed up into a kneeling position. She rose to her feet on wobbly legs. Someone grabbed her by the shoulder. It was a man's grasp. He pushed her forward. She marched tentatively, still blinded by the heavy cloth over her head.

Molly heard new sounds. There was a deep thrumming in the lowest octaves of audible sound. She felt it in her bones. She had been transferred to a much larger ship. Then she heard voices. They were growing louder. She heard a girl scream and a chorus of whimpers. There were other prisoners here. They were girls like her.

Molly's legs were like rubber. She wasn't certain how long she could remain standing. The man who gripped her shoulder told her to stop. There was a click, followed by the sound of a hatch opening. The other voices grew louder. They were right in front of her. The man pushed Molly forward, and she stumbled, crashing down to the decking just inside the hatchway. She saw bright flashes of light against the darkened cloth. Molly took a breath and smelled the raw odor of fear surrounding her.

* * *

Amos Cross's office at Meridian Headquarters was the most secure room in the solar system. When the chamber was empty, only Cross could enter. When he was there, no one but top level staff could open the main door. The room was suspended in a series of vacuum channels, offering the ultimate in soundproofing. A Faraday Cage was impregnated into the walls, preventing electronic eavesdropping. Finally, Cross's dedicated comp system was essentially a standalone network, firewalled by two dedicated AIs.

The great man was surrounded by a breathtaking holographic image. Cross had called up a photo-realistic model of the solar system. The sun blazed in the center of the space, filtered down to a tolerable luminosity. Cross had overridden the geometry, shrinking the size of the sun and the diameters of the planetary orbits. Each of the eight planets hung majestically, washing the office with varying hues of reflected light.

Meredith Frank stood rigidly before Amos Cross. He could tell she was unnerved by the planetary tableau. When she entered the office, he saw her struggle to control her balance. He knew she could feel the floor under her feet, but all of her other senses had suggested she was suspended in space. She was prone to vertigo, a fact which had prompted Cross to program this particular holographic effect. Needless to say, Cross liked his visitors off balance.

The woman was dressed in a brand-new carmine business suit with a low-cut blouse. Her hair had been cut to medium length and expensively styled to keep its shape in the low lunar gravity. She had the subtle odor of custom body wash, which was tuned to her skin chemistry, offering a unique olfactory signature. Although he would not show it, Cross was impressed.

"Do you like my solar system?" he asked her.

"Yes, sir!" Meredith did not hesitate. "It's awe-inspiring, sir."

There was a catch in her throat, a sign of anxiety not lost on Amos Cross. His eyes lingered on the woman's cleavage. Her breasts reminded him of his mother, an unpleasant memory. "I want you to organize a meeting with Ryan Davies and his people. Do you know who he is?"

"He is the head of your AI research team."

"That is correct. I want to meet with him and three of his top design people this afternoon. Have them clear their schedules and set up the holo-conference for two o'clock."

"Yes, sir."

"And Miss Frank..." Cross could see the woman tense. He felt a rush of satisfaction, enjoying his sense of power. "You are wearing too much eye-shadow. Make sure you fix yourself up before you come in here again." The woman's shoulders sagged slightly. Cross knew he was breaking her down. "Now go and earn your pay!" He said it sternly, like a rebuke. Meredith Frank pivoted carefully and then made her way toward the door, crossing the dark holographic void that surrounded her.

Cross smiled to himself. She had submitted to his game. He had her right where he wanted her. Meredith Frank would do his bidding without question. Her psych profile had predicted it. A soft chime resonated in the office. Cross touched his comlink. "What?" he barked impatiently.

"It's Remson Burke, sir."

"Connect."

A portion of space began to glow where Meredith Frank had stood. A man with a swarthy complexion coalesced. He was seated in a sauna with his legs crossed. He was naked, except for a towel wrapped around his waist. His skin glistened with sweat as steam wafted around him.

"Kind of informal, wouldn't you say Mr. Burke?"

"To each his own, Cross." Remson Burke was not easily intimidated. "I take you to be a formal man who is fastidious and proper. I, on the other hand, go with the flow. Life is too short to stand on formalities." Burke uncrossed his legs, revealing his manhood in the shadows under the towel. "I like to relax when I can."

"I can see that." Cross didn't like the man. "What do you have for me?"

"I have good news. Everything has worked according to plan. Your man, Jedro Skye, gave Miss Drake the package. She squawked about not inspecting it, but she did what she was told. The device detonated right on time. The ship was destroyed. No one could have survived."

Cross permitted himself a smile. "That is very good news, Mr. Burke."

"This Nixie Drake was just a kid. She was a garden variety smuggler."

"I'm well aware of that. A few years back, she and her friends provided aide to an enemy of mine. I never forget, Burke. That's something you should consider when you deal with me."

"I catch your drift, Cross. I'm a straight shooter. You can count on me."

"It appears that way, so far." Cross ran a hand across his scalp. "What about Mr. Skye?"

"He had an accident on his way home from the spaceport."

"We have containment?"

"Absolutely. Nothing will lead back to me, much less to you."

Cross nodded, then abruptly terminated the holo-link.

* * *

Raven and her crewmates gathered around the forward viewport on *The Celestial Ghost's* flight deck. Before them, perhaps a dozen kilometers away, floated the mangled tail section of an aging transfer ship. The stern was dark. Her engines were offline. A twisted mass of wreckage marked where the propulsion deck had once been mated to the rest of the ship. Flames were still erupting into the vacuum of space, fueled by the out gassing of hydrogen and oxygen. The fire roiled and boiled in the zero-g, burping spherical plumes of liquid plasma.

"Something blew up in her hold," Eagle surmised.

"Seems so," muttered Raven. "All of her cargo is lost."

William "Hawk" Ashbury fingered the inside of the viewport. He looked like a wrestler from the waist up. His arms bulged with muscles, and his neck was short. His head seemed to be attached directly to his shoulders. Hawk had no legs. "Once the fires burn out, we can take the stern for scrap. The engine didn't blow, so some of the power plant might be salvageable. There could be fair money in that," he observed. Eagle nodded in agreement.

Raven unconsciously reached down and scratched the skin where her left leg had once been. Her eyes were locked on the severed tail section of the dismembered transfer ship. The tangle of twisted pipes and conduits reminded her of blood vessels and sinew. The fire triggered a visceral response, reminding her of the burning pain she had felt when *The Astral Explorer* had crashed, and her legs had been shattered.

"The rest of her is a fair distance away to the starboard." Falcon was squinting at the sensor display positioned above the helm.

"Take us there, Falcon." Raven pulled her hand away from her empty hip socket, her eyes still glued to the burning wreck. "Let's take a closer look." Her voice was soft, but her words were woven with a solemnity born of suffering. She hoped the victims of this ship had died quickly. She felt Eagle's hand on her shoulder, and she gave him a sideways glance. He knew exactly what she was thinking, and she appreciated it.

"Aye, ma'am. Prepare for maneuvering, everybody." Hands snaked through gripping points as Falcon fired the steering thrusters. *The Ghost* yawed to the starboard and accelerated toward the second piece of debris. As expected, it was the forward section of the stricken transfer ship. The battered mass of wreckage was tumbling on all three axes. Falcon brought the ship to a standstill, perhaps ten klicks away from the gyrating hulk.

"No doubt about it," Hawk concluded. "The blast was in the hold. Look how the nose was ripped away."

Unlike the stern section, there was no fire. The bow of the transfer ship was dark. Her hull was ripped and torn where the forward bulkhead of the hold had been. "There might be something in the forward compartments," offered Falcon. She scratched her left shoulder. "The flight deck seems intact. The viewports aren't broken."

Raven's eyes narrowed. "You could be right. Let's grapple her and see what she's got."

"Her tumble is too severe," Eagle observed. "We'll have to stabilize her first."

Hawk grinned. "Looks like I'm going on a field trip!" He rubbed his hands enthusiastically.

Raven nodded. "Okay. Falcon will stand watch at the helm, and Hawk will suit up for the EVA. We'll focus on the forward compartments first. There's room for her in outrigger hold C. Once the fire goes out in the stern, we'll bring the rest of her on board."

"Aye, Captain," Falcon intoned seriously. Raven gave her friend a knowing smile, then pushed off a nearby handhold and disappeared through the flight deck hatch.

* * *

Nixie stirred, her body bitten by the chill that was permeating the darkened flight deck. She looked at her crewmates through bleary eyes. Spif was still floating on the other side of the compartment. He was in a fetal position, and his eyes were shut. Slake was to her left, his motionless body suspended in the overhead spaces. Nixie couldn't see his face. She didn't know if he was alive or dead.

Ice looked blue. She had sprayed on some liquid clothing before their meal. The thin coating over her body couldn't be offering her any protection against the cold. Her face was as stolid as ever. She was gripping a handhold by the viewport, gazing out at the stars. Nixie thought she saw the woman's body tremble. The younger woman felt a sympathetic chill caress her, and she pulled her knees up to her chest and squeezed them tightly. Nixie closed her eyes, and consciousness slipped away as the mists of sleep permeated her mind. She was back in her childhood home. Nixie was six years old and in her bed. The room was cold, and she pulled the covers under her chin. It didn't help. She shivered uncontrollably.

There was a creaking sound, and the bedroom door opened. The chamber was dark, and she couldn't see who it was. Then she saw a shadowy figure in the doorway. It was the silhouette of her father. She froze, pretending to be asleep. She didn't want him to come in. The shadow moved. Her father had entered the room.

Nixie pulled her head beneath the covers and held her breath. She heard approaching footsteps, and then a heavy weight on the mattress as her father sat down on the bed. She could smell alcohol and sweat. A meaty arm reached across her head and pulled back the blanket.

"Are you cold, little girl?" He said it like a drunken lover. Nixie dared not open her eyes. She instinctively squeezed her legs together and pulled her arms across her chest. Her father's voice frightened her. It was deep and resonant, a big man's voice. Her father was strong and powerful, able and willing to do terrible things to young girls. "Why don't I warm you up?" he breathed. Nixie felt a tugging on the blanket. She wanted to scream, but could not. Something told her it was only a bad dream, but she couldn't wake up.

CHAPTER FIVE

A hand grabbed a fistful of the cloth bag and yanked it from Molly's head. A dozen strands of hair were ripped from her scalp, and she recoiled from the sudden pain. She was blinded by the sudden light. The hatch slammed shut behind her. Molly rolled onto her side, her cheek flat against the cold decking.

As her vision cleared, Molly saw at least a dozen pairs of feet. They were bare and dirty. She looked up. A group of young girls encircled her. They were wearing wrinkled smocks. The meager garments were filthy. Molly saw their arms. They were thin and spindly, with pale skin. Some of the girls had slender fingers with nails chewed to the quick. Molly saw their faces. They were stained with tears, framed with unkempt hair. Each one looked terrified. Even worse, they looked defeated. The children gazed at her suspiciously, their eyes darting back and forth, measuring her. She was another confirmation of their hopelessness.

No one spoke. After studying her for a moment, the children moved back along the walls of the hold. The bulkheads seemed to offer safety, like a tree line along the edge of an open field. They retreated from her and cowered there, some standing, others crouched on their haunches.

Molly didn't try to stand. She remained seated on the decking, fighting back the needles of terror pricking the inside of her chest. She was a prisoner, and her sister inmates had delivered an unspoken message. It was as clear as a clarion call on a frosty winter's night.

Molly's life would never be the same again. Her hope would fail, as it had for each of the children in this place, and she would become like them: a frail harbinger of despair. She was doomed.

* * *

Hawk was in his e-suit, floating outside *The Celestial Ghost*. He was tethered to the ship's grappling arm, a long telescoping fin that hung from the belly of the vessel, between the flight deck and the four outrigger holds. Raven and Eagle were observing him from the grappling pod, a nacelle attached to the end of the arm. Hawk wore a personal mobility unit, or PMU, which enabled him to steer through space on jets of compressed air. He held an odd device in his left hand.

The remains of *The Raccoon's* nose section pitched and rolled, perhaps fifty meters away. There was a jagged tear around the circumference of the hull. A few meters of bent and warped decking were all that remained of the ship's massive hold. A mangled exercise bike dangled from a broken brace. The forward bulkhead of the hold was torn free from the curved skin of the ship. A myriad of pipes and cables hung out of every crevice.

"Damn!" Hawk muttered through the comlink. "It's a wonder anything is left of her."

Raven peered at the wreckage through the grappling pod's viewport. She tugged at Eagle's arm while pointing to a flat section of hull near the forward hatch. "The airlock looks okay. Let's attach the stabilizer just aft of it." Eagle nodded. They had done this kind of thing many times before.

"I was thinking the same thing," Hawk concurred offhandedly. He maneuvered toward the wreckage, then launched the strange-looking apparatus. The portable stabilizer unit whisked out of his hands, propelled by streams of compressed gas. Its AI analyzed the perturbations of the shattered hull and tracked its gyrations. Within seconds, both were pitching and yawing in lockstep, like two synchronized swimmers.

The stabilizer was now in the hull's frame of reference. Hawk held a control unit in his hand. All of his attention was focused on the unit's small screen. The image of the wreck before him was steady. *The Celestial Ghost's* hull occasionally flashed by in the background, the only evidence of the rapid motion. Hawk flew the device to the forward hatchway and landed it on the hull, just aft of the airlock. Locked in place, the stabilizer's AI took command, firing its thrusters to counteract the tumble of the wreckage. Within moments, the jagged hulk floated motionlessly next to *The Celestial Ghost*.

"Nicely done, Hawk," Raven said warmly. "Come on back and we'll snag her with the grapple."

Moments later, Hawk was floating next to his friends in the grappling pod. He remained in his e-suit, but had removed his helmet. Falcon transferred control of the *Ghost* to Eagle, and he began the delicate task of maneuvering the grappling pod over *The Raccoon's* airlock. Once in position, the pod's docking collar was mated to the hatch.

Hawk waited impatiently while his companions donned their e-suits. Once the safety checks were complete, they floated into the grappling pod's airlock. With the hatch secured behind them, they pressurized the docking collar and entered the space just outside the wreck's forward hatch.

"It's got standard manual overrides," Hawk observed.

Eagle had his face to the small viewport in the airlock hatch. "The inner hatch is shut."

"Okay." Raven shared their excitement. Entering a derelict spacecraft was always thrilling. "Let's open the hatch and see what we've got."

Hawk pulled a crank handle from its cradle and inserted its business end into a socket next to the hatch. He glanced at his crewmates and then began to open the hatch. There was a slight hiss as the seal was cracked. "It's got pressure," he announced.

They entered the airlock, leaving the outer hatch open to the docking collar. They didn't want to risk the hatch jamming shut. Eagle fished a gun-like device out of his tool belt. He secured the muzzle to the inner bulkhead with a magnetic clamp and pulled the trigger. A probe penetrated the wall, immediately sealing the puncture. "Well, what do you know? There's standard pressure in there." He turned to his crewmates. "Carbon dioxide levels are pretty high."

Eagle stepped aside, and Hawk inserted the manual crank. Seconds later, they stood on the flight deck of The Raccoon. There were four bodies floating amidst the tangle of broken equipment. A woman, who was wearing nothing but a layer of liquid clothing, was gripping a handhold near the forward viewport. Ice looked up at them with dead eyes. "Welcome aboard," she whispered.

* * *

Molly Winters squatted on the deck near one of the bulkheads. After the initial shock of her arrival, the other girls withdrew into themselves, each perched on a razor's edge between horror and hopelessness. There was quiet sobbing in the cabin, but little conversation.

Molly thought of her father and mother. She had grown up in a comfortable home, with loving parents and clear expectations. Hers had been an intellectual family that wasn't afraid of ideas and enjoyed a lively debate. She could hear the echo of her father's voice, telling her to keep thinking. "When you stop thinking," he would say, "you start reacting." He had told her that thoughtless reaction was the unsteady foundation for disaster. Thinking in times of crisis enabled a person to sort out real dangers from the imagined ones.

Molly knew this was a real danger. A horrible knot constricted her gut and cinched her stomach. She felt the urge to vomit. Keep thinking! Some things are beyond your power. Some things are not. Molly shivered from the effort to keep her composure.

The girl next to Molly had pulled herself into a ball. Her arms and legs were drawn tightly against her body in an attempt to shield herself. Molly leaned toward her until their heads were centimeters apart. "My name's Molly. What's yours?" she whispered. The girl's body jerked. Her arms tightened around her, but she cocked her head slightly, her eyes wide with fear. It was as if she had been trying to hide in plain sight, desperate to avoid notice. Molly's question had struck her like the bright beam of a headlight. She was discovered, singled out. "I won't hurt you," Molly said softly. "Tell me your name." The girl recovered slightly. She didn't move her head, but Molly saw her eyes shift briefly in her direction.

"Susan Sullivan." Her voice was so thin and quiet, Molly couldn't understand what she was saying. Then, before Molly could ask the girl to repeat herself, she said, "My friends call me Suzy."

"That's a beautiful name." Molly felt the fingers of hopelessness loosen their grip on her. The simple act of reaching out empowered her. "Can I call you Suzy?" The girl nodded as she shifted her weight and turned to face Molly. She wore a mask of dread, which made her seem much older than she was. Molly realized at once that her companion had seen things that had scarred her for life. "Where are you from?" Molly asked.

Susan looked down at the deck. "Wichita."

"Kansas?"

The girl nodded again. "I won a prize." Molly was confused. "I was the millionth visitor to the state fair." She still didn't understand. Suzy read her face. "I went to the Kansas State Fair in Hutchinson with my parents. When I went through the entrance, a bunch of lights went off. I was the one millionth visitor. They gave me a prize." Molly almost laughed at the thought. Surely being kidnapped couldn't be the prize. The girl continued. "I won a ride on one of the space elevators. I was supposed to go up and spend an hour on the observation deck." The girl's voice cracked. "Then I was going to go home." The young girl's shoulders sagged, and she tightened her arms around her chest, digging her chin down behind her forearms.

Molly understood. "That's what happened to me," she whispered. Susan looked up again. "I was on Space Elevator Four with my mom and dad. Somebody grabbed me. Now I'm here."

"I want to get out of here," the girl mewed.

"Me, too." Molly felt a trembling in her bones.

* * *

The sweet smell of pine filled her nostrils. Nixie had sequestered herself in a small stand of evergreens in the Copernicus Base Commons. She pulled the ragged piece of cloth she was using for a blanket up to her chin and flinched in her sleep as the nightmare played itself out in her mind. Her father was hovering over her bed. She could smell his excitement as he poised himself for his hideous assault on her girlhood. She looked down at his waist, expecting to see his swollen manhood. Her father had no legs.

Nixie jerked awake, expecting to find herself beneath the sheltering limbs of the scotch pine where she had dreamt of falling asleep. Instead, she was floating in a strange cabin filled with soft white light. A woman with a kind face was hovering over her. Nixie pushed her away in fright, and the woman grabbed a handhold to stabilize herself. Nixie went tumbling backward from the sudden movement. With reflexes honed from years in zero-g, she snatched another handhold and brought herself to a stop.

"Sorry to startle you," the woman smiled. "It looked like you were having a bad dream."

Nixie's eyes narrowed as she took in the stranger. The woman was a double amputee. Her legs were completely gone, truncating the base of her torso. "Maybe still dreamin'," Nixie gasped.

Raven laughed. "You're awake." She spread her hands. "Welcome aboard *The Celestial Ghost*."

Nixie's eyes darted back and forth, as if she was expecting a ghoul to leap out at her. "Don't like ghosties."

Raven could have laughed again, but she saw the fear on the girl's face. "It's our ship. That's her name. It has nothing to do with the supernatural. We're just good at keeping a low profile. We stay in the shadows." The woman stuck out her hand. "I'm Sarah Miles. My crew calls me Raven. I guess you could call me the captain of this vessel."

"Nixie Drake, ma'am." Nixie couldn't take her eyes off her host's missing legs. "Looks like yer missin' somethin', if you don't mindee my sayin' so."

Raven could always tell when people fixated on her missing limbs. Sometimes they stared at her, like Nixie. Others did the opposite, refusing to look at her. Some tried to hide their discomfort, but she could always see it in their faces. She read Nixie easily. There was no judgment in her, only curiosity. "I'm surprised you noticed," she deadpanned.

Nixie looked up sharply at the strange woman, caught off guard by the remark. Then she saw the twinkle in her eyes, and Nixie grinned.

Raven gestured to her left shin. "Speaking of legs, you've got a bad bruise there. It'll be sore, but it's not serious."

"Whaker-dackered it when the 'plosion hit us," Nixie offered. Raven studied her for a moment, deciphering the girl's curious dialect. "Where's the resty-rest of my crew-cuts?"

Raven hesitated. "How many of you were there?"

The color drained from Nixie's face. "Me and three more." She gave Raven a panicked look.

"You were all on the flight deck?"

Nixie tried to clear her mind. She still felt confused from the lack of oxygen. "Yessim."

Raven sighed with relief. "They're fine. They've got an assortment of bumps and bruises, but everyone survived."

"*The Raccoon?*" Nixie knew the answer to her question.

"Your ship?" Nixie nodded solemnly. "The explosion took place in her hold. It ripped her in half. She's beyond repair."

The sound of Spif's voice echoed from beyond the cabin hatchway. "Get away from me, you freak!" There was the muttering of a man's voice, mellifluous and indistinct. Raven turned toward the hatch, excusing herself as she pushed away from a gripping point. She shot out of the cabin. Nixie followed close behind her.

The two women swam down an access corridor and came to rest at the entrance to another cabin, identical to the one they had just left. Two men were holding Spif's arms as he squirmed and kicked in the zero-g. A bandage covered his nose and was held in place with two pieces of surgical tape, forming an X on his face. His captors were strong. Each had one hand through a handhold and gripped Spif with the other. It was as if Nixie's crewmate was shackled with iron chains. The two men were calm. While Spif pulled with all his might to get away from them, the men didn't appear to be exerting themselves at all.

Spif jerked as he saw Raven appear in the hatchway. "Oh my God! There's another one!" His eyes narrowed as he caught a glimpse of Nixie behind her. "Nix! What's going on? What are all these damned freaks doing here?"

Eagle sighed as he gave Spif's arm a yank.

"Ouch! What are you trying to do? Pull my arm off so I can be like you?"

"If that's what you want, sir." Eagle pulled a little harder.

"No! Goddamnit! That's not what I want!"

"Are you going to behave yourself?" Hawk asked quietly. Nixie recognized his deep voice as the one she had heard from the other cabin.

"Yeah!" He gave Nixie a pleading look. "Tell 'em Nix! I won't hurt them."

Raven couldn't suppress a laugh. She turned to Nixie, who now was floating next to her in the hatchway. "What do you think, Nixie? Is this man a danger to us?" She turned back to Spif without waiting for an answer. "You got a nasty bump on your nose, buddy. Did you piss off somebody?"

It was Nixie's turn to laugh. She gave Spif a knowing look. He plead with her silently to keep quiet about the source of his injury. If the two legless men found out that she had hurt him, it would inflict a mortal wound in his manhood. "He's okee-dokee, Raven. Spiffer won't hurt a fleesy-wheezy. He hits his noggen on a bulky-head when *The 'Coon* went splewy, buts he's movin' back into his brain now, ain't ya Spiffy?"

Spif glared at Nixie. He was still angry with her about Captain Grit, but she had kept their secret, and he was grateful for that. He gave Raven a tiny nod.

"Okay," Raven said warmly. "Let him go, guys." She translated across the cabin until she was a handful of centimeters from Spif's face. She wore a customized jumpsuit which fit her body like a glove. Raven was a sexy woman, and Spif noticed. She was much too close to him. He tried to back away and bumped against the bulkhead. He bounced and almost collided with her. "Your name is Spif." Her voice was quiet, throaty.

"Yes, ma'am," he stammered.

"Let me introduce you to my mate, Eagle." She took the hand of the man floating to her left. Spif nodded to him nervously but said nothing. "And this is Hawk." Raven gestured toward the powerful man on her right. Spif glanced at him and the second man. Hawk gave him a wide grin. Spif was unnerved by him. Raven continued. "This is our ship, and you are our guests. All of us are able-bodied folks in zero-g. We can do anything you can do. Don't forget that. We also saved your asses, so a little respect would be appreciated."

Spif was like a cornered rat. He wanted to escape from the misshapen people who surrounded him, but they had him boxed in. He looked into Raven's eyes, and she held him in her gaze like a teacher waiting for her student. "Yes, ma'am," he said finally.

"Good!" Raven pivoted away dismissively. "Your friend Ice is in the multi-cabin. Hawk will show you where she is. The other member of your crew is in the sick bay. It looks like he hit his head pretty hard when your ship exploded. Our crewmate Falcon is keeping an eye on him. He has a slight concussion, but he'll live."

"I gots to seeze 'im," Nixie squeaked.

"Certainly," Raven replied. She swam to the hatchway. "Follow me."

Spif hesitated. "You go ahead, Nix. I want to see Ice."

Nixie turned away from him without a word and followed Raven down the corridor.

* * *

The Ankrum Platform, Cornell University's orbital campus, hung at the Earth-Moon L1 point, about 326 thousand kilometers from the Earth's surface. It resembled a hemispherical spider web, with nodes and long slender corridors arranged in a complex geodesic pattern. Living quarters for students and researchers were arranged around the perimeter of the web. Class rooms and laboratories occupied the center portion of the structure. A ring of docks was attached to the outermost nodes.

Sprite Logan was brimming with anticipation as she glided through the docking collar that attached her jumpship to the platform. She squinted into the brightly-lit docking bay, its floors and bulkheads gleaming white. A lanky man with a shock of unkempt red hair floated near one of the bulkheads. He wore wire-rimmed glasses and had a kind face. A younger man, obviously the older man's son, hovered next to him. He was thin and athletic. His eyes were bright, and his hands were as delicate as those of a surgeon. Tyson Edwards was her father's closest friend. He and his son Kell both wore big smiles. Sprite grinned broadly as she swam across the dock.

"It's great to see you, Sprite!" Tyson exclaimed as he gave her a warm hug. "What's it been? Three years?"

Sprite nodded, momentarily choked up at the sight of her friends. "About that," she managed.

Kell touched her on the shoulder. Sprite pivoted toward him and slid her arms around his waist. "Hey," she murmured. "You look good."

"You're not bad, yourself," he replied. Kell pushed away from Sprite. He slid his fingers down her arms until he was holding her hands. The young man nodded as he took in her form. "You're even more beautiful than I remember."

Sprite glowed, her eyes twinkling at her old friend. She and Kell had spent a lot of time together on the Moon and then at Meridian 6, a research settlement in the Asteroid Belt. They both had been kidnapped by Amos Cross a few years before, in an attempt to force their parents to recreate dangerous nanobots.

"My skin is a lot better," Sprite told him. "The nanoskin healed the scar tissue. I don't even wear makeup anymore." Sprite was badly burned during an attempt on her life. Her parents developed a synthetic skin to save her. Based on advanced molecular engineering, the nanoskin was a permanent part of Sprite's body. The tiny nanomachines constantly serviced her skin cells, creating an optimal microenvironment for them. A keypad membrane was located on the inside of her left forearm. With it, Sprite could control the temperature of the n-skin, its hue, and its hardness. The skin could be soft and supple or as hard as diamond.

"I still feel bad about that day in the infirmary," Kell said. Sprite remembered the look on her friend's face when he had first seen her after her injury. His look of horror had stung her to the bone, but she had long since forgiven him. Kell sighed. "I shouldn't have reacted that way when I saw you."

"It is all forgiven and forgotten." Sprite pulled Kell toward her and gave him a playful peck on the cheek. The young man blushed, his face wreathed with a smile.

Tyson cleared his throat. "Welcome to Ankrum Platform!" he interrupted. "Let's get you to your quarters, shall we?"

Sprite nodded enthusiastically, as Kell and his father led her out of the docking bay.

* * *

Nixie followed Raven to *The Celestial Ghost's* sick bay. Slake floated in the center of the small cabin. His head was bandaged, and his eyes were closed. Nixie was startled by the thin woman who was studying the cerebral scans of Slake's head. Her left arm was missing, as well as her left leg. Her flight suit was tailored to her body. There were no empty sleeves or pant legs where her missing appendages might have been. Her skin was pale, and her eyes were set deep within their sockets.

The emaciated woman looked up from the diagnostics screen and gave Nixie a hesitant glance. She had noticed Nixie's reaction out of the corner of her eye. Nixie recovered quickly and offered the stranger a nod in greeting, but the woman looked away with a pained expression. Nixie scolded herself silently, wishing for a second chance to give a first impression, but the woman didn't look at her again. She was immersed in the results of Slake's brain scan. "There's no brain damage, sir," she said crisply to Raven.

Raven nodded to her crewmate with a smile. "Excellent!" She pivoted sideways in an attempt to include Nixie. "Falcon, this is Nixie Drake. She was the skipper on the disabled ship."

"No, ma'am," Nixie was trying desperately to avoid staring at the women. "Firsty-matey. Our skips was Cap'n Grit."

Raven grabbed her arm, a look of alarm on her face. "Is he still on board your ship?"

"Gritty's dead, ma'am." Nixie's voice was thick with grief. She studied Raven's long, graceful fingers.

"I'm sorry to hear that." Falcon's voice was almost a baritone. Nixie looked up, not expecting such a rich sound to come from such a thin woman. She looked directly into her eyes, in an attempt to ignore her body. Her gaze was met with shy compassion.

"Thankee," Nixie muttered before looking away.

"Were you close?" Falcon asked.

"Yupper."

"He was a frickin' doll," Slake whispered. The color drained from Nixie's face as the two women turned toward him. The man's eyes were still closed. He brought both hands up and pressed the bandage on his forehead. He pulled them away with a grimace. Falcon moved closer to make sure the bandage was still securely in place. Slake opened his eyes. "What the fuck? Get away from me!" He grabbed her arm and pushed. Both of them began to move apart in the zero-g.

Falcon was shaken by the invective. She grimaced painfully at Raven, then turned back to Slake. "I'm trying to help you."

"Don't need your damned help!" Slake's eyes darted around the compartment, unsure of where he was.

"C'mon, Slakee!" Nixie moved closer to her crewmate. "Wheeze almost kickered the deadly doornail. *The 'Coon's* a goner. These peeps keptered our lights from blinkin' out."

"Where are we?" Slake was calming down.

Raven gave him a commanding glare. "You are on board *The Celestial Ghost*. I'm the captain. We're a salvage ship. When your ship exploded, it lit up our sensors, so we rendezvoused with your ship to see what had happened."

Slake's eyes were fixed on Raven's groin, where her legs used to be. "What's the matter with you people?"

"There's nothing wrong with us. Why do you ask?"

Nixie shot Raven a sideways glance. The woman was completely serious. Slake hesitated, then began to smile. "You're pulling my leg, aren't ya?"

"I am always serious about legs." There was a twinkle in Raven's eyes.

Slake shook his head and then broke into a discomforted laugh. "You folks are different. I'll say that much."

"So are you," Falcon interjected. "Your brain, however bigoted, seems to be fine."

"Be kind to our guests, Falcon." The captain of *The Celestial Ghost* said evenly. "We will accept them as they are." Falcon gave her a sour look and a small nod. Then Raven turned to Nixie. "Is this one related to the other guy?" she asked quietly.

Nixie grinned broadly. She was going to like these peeps.

* * *

Molly Winters sat on the edge of an examination table in what appeared to be a ship's infirmary. An ugly-looking man stood nearby, watching her with a smirk. Molly didn't like the way he was looking at her. Her mother had warned her about such men, but this was the first time she had been near one. She could almost see the wheels turning in his head, how he was looking at her and imagining bad things. She considered leaping from the table and escaping from him, but even if she could get out of the cabin, there was nowhere to go.

The hatch opened, and a woman entered. She had copper-colored hair. Molly recognized her immediately as the woman who had taken her from her parents. The man glanced at her and then straightened up. The woman was his superior.

"I want to go home," Molly stated flatly. "You took me from my parents, and I want to go back."

The woman ignored her. The ugly man chuckled under his breath. It was a deep and malevolent purr.

"Take me home!"

"Be quiet, girl!" The woman's voice was like a piece of broken glass. "Take off your clothes."

Molly's heart skipped a beat. A chill shot down her spine. She glanced at the man. A broad smile had bloomed on his face, and he was licking his lips. She gripped the sides of the table with trembling fingers. "Why?" Her voice cracked.

"I have to examine you. Take off your clothes before I have Mo do it for you." She gestured toward the ugly man.

"Don't touch me!" Molly squealed. She reached down and slipped off her shoes, keeping her eyes on the man every second.

The woman stood at a small counter attached to the bulkhead. She reached up and opened one of the cupboard doors, which lined the wall at eye level. Molly glanced away from Mo long enough to see her remove an odd-looking device that resembled a pistol. A glass vile of dark blue liquid was attached to the top of it. Instead of a barrel, it had a tip filled with metallic bristles. Molly's pulse accelerated.

"Hurry up!" The woman held the device in front of her like a weapon.

Molly pealed off her socks and started to unfasten the cuffs of her blouse. "I want him to leave."

The woman laughed. "You're a modest one, aren't you? You'll get over that soon enough, child." She watched as Molly fumbled with the Velcro on her wrist. "Guess you better help her out, Mo."

Molly jumped as the man stepped to her side enthusiastically. He grabbed the cloth of her blouse in a meaty hand and gave it a jerk. The cloth tore violently, and the blouse disintegrated into strips of ragged material. She screamed as sharp threads cut into her underarms. The man reached behind her and pulled away the rest of the blouse. Molly covered her chest with her arms and began to sob. The man grabbed her pant legs, and once again, he pulled with ferocious strength. The trousers slid down her legs. Molly felt her underpants slipping and grabbed them. "She *is* kinda shy, Star," Mo laughed.

"Stop!" Molly pleaded. She could feel her ears burn with embarrassment. Mo reached toward her bra, and she pulled away. "Don't touch me!"

The woman called Star gestured toward Mo, and he took Molly's left wrist. He pulled roughly, raising it over her head and exposing her bare underarm. Molly tried to free herself, but his grip was like iron.

"Don't move, kid," he grumbled.

Molly's eyes narrowed as she saw Star bring the metal pistol toward her exposed underarm. Before she could react, the woman plunged it into her armpit. Molly felt a burning sensation and a thousand needles pricking her skin. She screamed.

"You'll live," Star said unsympathetically. She withdrew the device, and Mo let go of Molly's arm.

"What did you do to me?" she squealed. Molly winced as she peered at her tortured skin. The tattoo of a barcode was inked into her armpit. "You have no right to put marks on me!" she shouted.

Star placed the gun-like instrument on the counter and stepped directly in front of Molly. "There are two things you need to get through your head, kid." Her eyes were cold and hard. "First of all, you don't have a family anymore. They are gone, and you will never see them again." Molly held her breath. "Secondly, you belong to us now. You are no more than this piece of furniture." The woman ran a finger along the edge of the examination table, brushing the skin of Molly's leg with her nail. "That barcode is your inventory number. We put them on all of our property. You now exist for our pleasure and profit, and we can do whatever we want with you." Something girlish and innocent died within Molly. She believed the woman, and that was the most terrifying thing of all.

CHAPTER SIX

The crew of *The Celestial Ghost* provided modest cabins for their guests. The explosion on board *The Raccoon* had destroyed everyone's possessions, leaving Nixie and her crew with scarcely more than what they were wearing when they were found. Hawk scavenged some clothing from somewhere in one of the outrigger holds. The sizes weren't quite right, but no one complained. Nixie exchanged her torn and soiled clothes for a baggy jumpsuit. She zipped it all the way up, but the neck was large, and her shoulders practically slid through the opening. She found a piece of cord and tied the loose cloth around her waist to hold everything in place.

Nixie floated in the closet-sized stateroom she had been assigned. There wasn't a mirror, and she was glad. Nixie wasn't vain, but she knew the jumpsuit didn't flatter her one bit. She let out a big breath of air, grateful to be alone. She had spent most of her life hiding in nooks and crannies on Copernicus Base and was the most comfortable in small, solitary spaces. A light tapping on the hatch interrupted her brief hiatus. Nixie took one last pull on the knot in her rope belt and invited her guest to enter. It was Raven. She had Nixie's bag in one hand. Captain Grit's arm and broken sword were hanging out of it. Nixie blanched when she saw it, but Raven seemed unconcerned.

"You were clutching this when we found you," the older woman offered. "It was left in the airlock when we brought you on board."

Nixie took the offered bag and stuffed Grit's arm deep into the recesses of the cloth. "Thankee dankee." She was embarrassed and quickly stowed the bag in a nearby locker.

Raven floated effortlessly across the cabin and swung herself to a stop across from her younger counterpart. Nixie stared at her unabashedly. Raven returned her gaze with a curious smile. "You have questions."

Nixie nodded her head, now hesitant. "Yupper."

"Go ahead. I'll tell you anything you want to know."

"How'd yer legs fall off?"

Raven unconsciously reached down and scratched her left hip socket. "I was assigned to *The Astral Explorer*. It was twelve years ago last month. We were docking with an orbiting platform over the Martian South Pole, and our engine throttled up unexpectedly. We crashed into the platform, and everything in our ship started bouncing around. My legs were pinned between two beams. The hull was ruptured, and it took all hands to stop the ship from pissing air. If they had saved me before they sealed the breach, I might have kept my legs, but we all would have suffocated. When they got to me, the legs were dead. I spent two months in a hospital on Mars. They issued me a wheelchair, told me about robotic options. I didn't like either one. The thought of being half-machine or dependent on a set of wheels didn't appeal to me."

"Musta hurt like a sunny beach." Nixie winced at the thought of having her legs removed.

"Sunny beach? Oh, yeah. It was a bitch, but the physical pain was nothing compared with what it did to my head. I wanted to die. I was a spacer. That's where I belonged, and they told me I would never ship out again. Those were the darkest days of my life."

"Howdy you getcha out here?"

"I met Eagle and Hawk. They were getting ready to drink themselves silly at a local bar. I had the same idea, thinking a drunken stupor would numb my pain. The three of us hooked up. We bought the first round and started talking. We got along real well, since we had similar problems." Nixie nodded gravely. "We were tired of people telling us what we couldn't do, so we decided to find a ship and head back into space. If we died, we figured at least we'd be where we wanted to be. Hawk knew a guy, and we found *The Celestial Ghost*. She had been abandoned in Mars orbit. We pooled everything we had and bought her. We gassed up the main cabin and moved on board. It took us three years to recondition her. As soon as we could get her under way, we started our salvage business."

Nixie's jaw dropped open. Raven read the incredulous expression on her face and gave her a stern look. "Don't be so surprised, rug rat! Just because we don't have any legs doesn't mean we're helpless. In fact, we love zero-g. We have less mass, consume less oxygen, and can fit in tight places. We don't have legs to get in the way. And in case you hadn't noticed, Eagle and Hawk are very strong men." Nixie had caught herself admiring the men's powerful arms and torsos. She smiled and nodded appreciatively. Raven beamed. "We are free out here, and we're not disabled."

Something in Raven's tone made Nixie look into her eyes. She saw flinty determination in them. She was a powerful woman, and Nixie liked that. "You's the skip-dipper of the ship?"

"Yes, I am. Eagle and Hawk say I'm more even tempered than they are, but we generally collaborate on all the important decisions."

"How's about the one-legged lady?"

Raven nodded. "You mean Falcon. She's our pilot and medical specialist. She's only been with us for about a year. She's still getting used to everything." Nixie could tell there was a lot that Raven wasn't telling her about Falcon. She didn't pry.

The two women were silent for a moment, the center of gravity of the conversation shifting from one to the other. Raven studied Nixie intently and then spoke with a soft voice. "If you don't mind my asking, how was it with you on *The Raccoon*?"

Nixie shrugged. "Lots easy wheezier than whats yooze been through."

"Every challenge is unique," Raven countered. "It's easy to judge someone else's situation as easier or harder, but unless you are in their shoes, you can't know." Raven paused. She glanced over her shoulder to make sure they were alone. "It must have been hard trying to lead Slake and Spif."

Nixie folded her arms and eyed Raven suspiciously. "Captain Grit diddly did the leader-work, ma'am."

"Be honest with me, Nixie. I'm Raven, okay? I saw the doll in your bag. I heard what Slake said as he was coming to. Unless I'm wrong, you were pretending that there was a Captain Grit. Right?" Nixie was silent, but Raven was insistent. "Am I right?"

Nixie dropped her arms, surrendering her pride. "Yes," she said simply.

"How long have you been together on *The Raccoon*?"

"Five years, gives or takes."

"I've heard rumors about you and your crew, Nixie. There are stories about how a nine-year-old young girl won a transfer ship in a game of poker. Somehow she assembled a crew and set up a team of smugglers. Mostly small-time jobs, although there were rumblings about Meridian Corporation taking interest in *The Raccoon* a few years ago."

Nixie's eyes grew large. She blushed, uneasy with being known by strangers. She began to tremble; a single tear inched its way down her cheek. She quickly wiped it away, embarrassed by the display of weakness. Raven continued. "I take notice when I hear stories like that. I like underdogs and unlikely success stories. They prove to me that willpower and ingenuity can overcome the greatest obstacles." Raven let the silence hang between them again. "My guess is that you knew you wouldn't be taken seriously. You conjured up Captain Grit in order to command your crew."

Nixie let out a long breath. How could this woman be so smart? It was like she had read her mind, had been an observer throughout Nixie's deception. She reached up and rubbed the stubble that was emerging from her scalp. A part of her felt exposed and embarrassed, but a larger part of her felt relief. She was released from the burden of hiding. "Hows you nose it all?" she asked honestly.

"It was pretty obvious, Nixie. I watched how your crew reacted to you. Slake's comment about the doll confirmed my suspicions. Frankly,

I'm impressed. It's taken a lot of guts and brainpower to do what you've done."

Nixie felt a wave of anxiety course through her. She felt emotionally naked, and she didn't like it. This stranger knew too much about her. Nixie fell silent and folded her arms. The older woman took the hint and pushed herself toward the hatchway. "We'll eat in about an hour, Nixie." Raven left and closed the hatch.

* * *

Sprite Logan closed the door on one of the lockers in her tiny dorm room. The space was scarcely larger than a closet. There was no need for a bed or desk in zero-g. She slept in a bag attached to one of the bulkheads, and she assembled a floating armada of items around her when she was working on a project. Kell Edwards had told her that there were plans to install synthetic gravity in the common areas within the next few months. Her dorm room would still be in a zero-g zone, but the gravity would permit jogging and less rigorous exercise, to avoid the ill effects of weightlessness.

Sprite pushed away from the rank of lockers and steadied herself in the middle of her new home. She felt a thrill of excitement. She was on her own and ready to delve into her school work. She would be studying advanced digital intelligence, steeping herself in the intricate nuances of synthetic beings. For as long as she could remember, Sprite had associated with Wiley, her personal AI. They had grown up together. Now, Wiley was concatenated with Athena, a former core intellect from the Meridian 6 Research Settlement. She was deeply fond of them both and trusted them with her innermost thoughts. She respected them as life forms, living intellects with opinions and wisdom.

Sprite's empty transit bag floated nearby. She hooked a finger through the strap and pulled it toward her. She opened a narrow locker to her left and slipped the shapeless mass into its interior. She gripped a handhold to offset the Newtonian forces and clicked the door shut on the locker. Then she damped out the oscillations that trembled through her body and hovered motionlessly. She was a woman at peace.

Each of the student cabins on the Ankrum Platform had a small viewport. Sprite's cabin was on the lunar side of the complex, and the cratered landscape filled her field of view. Being at the L1 point, the platform stood before the near side of the Moon. She could see the Copernicus Crater in the distance. Memories of her family's entanglement with Meridian Corporation flooded into her mind. Her body flinched slightly, setting off another series of perturbations in her arms and legs. She remembered Amos Cross and how he had held her hostage three years earlier. She was grateful that Meridian Headquarters was on the far side of the Moon, even though the massive bulk of Earth's natural satellite wasn't enough to shield her from the thought of him.

A soft chime announced a visitor outside her cabin. Sprite was grateful for the distraction, not wanting to dwell on dark memories. She opened the portal and found Ty and Kell Edwards floating in the companionway. "Hi!" she offered warmly. Sprite nodded at Ty and gave Kell a smile, her face flushing slightly. Kell blushed in return. "Come in. There's not much room, but if we don't all breathe in at the same time, we'll be okay." They shared an easy laugh as father and son transited across the threshold.

"Would you close the door, Sprite?" Tyson's voice had taken on a serious tone.

"Sure, Uncle Ty." It was a term of endearment, not relation, Ty being her father's best friend. She snapped the hatch shut and turned, taking care to avoid bumping against her guests. She was keenly aware of Kell's body and even more so of his father's presence.

"First of all," Ty began, "Kell and I aren't using the name Edwards anymore. We are Tyson and Kell Emerson, okay? Ever since our run-in with Meridian Corporation, we've been trying to stay under the scanners. Ankrum Platform is officially United States territory, but we still don't want Amos Cross to find us."

Sprite nodded. "Ty and Kell Emerson. Got it."

"Do you think anyone followed you here?" Tyson's eyes were piercing, his face reflecting the seriousness of his question.

Sprite shook her head. "Uncle Prescott booked my flights with different names. I've been on the lookout but haven't seen anyone."

"Good. Wiley and Athena reported the same thing. You're safe so far, but it's time for another new name." Sprite felt an unexpected comfort from the thought. Tyson pulled a plastic card from his pocket and handed it to her. "This is your student ID. You are registered as Sprite LeRoc."

"LeRoc?"

"It's French for 'the rock.' It's an homage to that special skin of yours."

Kell touched her forearm. "Tough skin, soft heart," he said. Sprite blushed.

* * *

Nixie's thoughts were a jumble as she floated in one of *The Celestial Ghost's* outrigger holds. The shattered remains of *The Raccoon's* forward compartments were strapped down in the cavernous chamber. While the nose of the ship appeared undamaged, the hull just aft of the multi-cabin was splayed like the exploded barrel of an old cartoon musket. Long rectangular sections of titanium plating were bent outward at odd angles. The interior bulkhead that once separated the hold from the multi-cabin was dished in from overpressure.

Nixie curled herself into a fetal ball as she floated next to the lifeless hulk. A horrible emptiness filled her, and she closed her eyes tightly in an attempt to shut out the painful reality encompassing her. She relived the moment when the shock wave had shaken Captain Grit's cabin. She could still feel the sharp g-forces that slammed her body back and forth as *The Raccoon* was torn apart beneath her. The emotional battering was even worse. Nixie's life had exploded with the ship, and her energy had vented out of her as surely as *The Raccoon's* propellants had flooded into space.

Nixie had always been good at improvising. The months she had spent on her own in the recesses of Copernicus Base had built her self-confidence. She had come to rely on her instincts. As a smuggler, she had used her age and girlish persona to mislead clients and take advantage of opportunities. Tenacity and individualism had always been her strengths. For the past five years, she had held her crew together with an elaborate ruse. Now, faced with the hobbled wreckage of her beloved ship and the awkward revelation of Captain Grit's true identity, she felt empty and embarrassed. Even worse, she felt the cold, nagging fingers of doubt gripping her, squeezing the life out of her. She felt the fabric of her confidence unraveling.

Nixie pushed away her doubts, refusing to succumb to their siren call. What was she going to do? The ship was beyond repair. Maybe her crew could haul cargo for a third party. They could smuggle contraband on the side and build up their savings until they could afford another ship of their own. It might work.

Nixie thought about Spif and Slake. She had some fence mending to do. They were still pretty angry about the Captain Grit situation. Nixie uncoiled her body and turned away from the remains of *The Raccoon*. She resolved to find her crew and make things right. Then, she'd tell them about her plan.

* * *

Sprite Logan, a.k.a. Sprite LeRoc, floated alone in a study cubby in one of the research nodes of the Ankrum Platform. A holo-conference was slated to begin in a few moments, and she had arrived early. The walls of the cubby glowed with soothing blue light. The space made her feel like she was suspended in an endless azure sky. A virtual desk was suspended in front of her. The image of a sheet of paper lay on the flat surface. It contained an outline for the session. Sprite was certain it would be an interesting discussion. She wanted to drink in every drop of knowledge offered to her.

The whirring of an electric motor cut through Sprite's daydream. The study cubby hatch slid to one side, and a young girl floated in through the opening. She grinned at Sprite as she instructed the door to close. "Hi! Sorry to bother you. I'm Addison Traynor." She stuck out her hand.

Sprite was startled, but recovered quickly. She shook the girl's hand. "I thought I was the only one assigned to this cubby." She didn't want to sound territorial, but she was disappointed by the intrusion.

"I'm surprised too. They didn't tell me you would be here." Addison pivoted like a ballerina and slid next to Sprite. They were literally hip to hip. Sprite could feel the girl's body heat. She had the faint aroma of perfume, not unpleasant. The girl shrugged her shoulders and offered Sprite another sheepish grin. She was dressed in a utilitarian jumpsuit and had stubbly red hair. She wore a silver charm bracelet on her left wrist, and her feet were bare. The girl seemed younger than Sprite by perhaps two years, and she had a boyish figure. Her face was strewn with freckles, and her ears hugged the sides of her skull. A small hairline scar bisected her right cheek. She cleared her throat. "Ah, I missed your name."

Sprite blushed. "I'm sorry! My name is Sprite LeRoc. I'm new here."

"Me too," the girl answered. "LeRoc. Isn't that French?"

"On my dad's side," Sprite lied. "I don't know much more than that."

"That's a shame. Knowing where you come from helps teach you who you are." Addison recited the expression with a singsong voice, completely draining the moment of seriousness. Both girls laughed.

"This is the holo-conference on advanced synthetic intelligence," Sprite offered. She was fairly certain her young visitor was in the wrong place.

"That's right," Addison nodded. "And this is cubby R-27."

Sprite glanced at her course schedule. She was in the right place. She sighed, resigning to the fact that her new companion was where she was supposed to be. No one had told her that she would be sharing the cubby. She had assumed she would be alone in the small booth-like compartment. She remembered her mother teaching her to be cordial. "Where are you from, Addison?" Sprite asked politely.

"It's Addy. That's what my friends back home in Pasadena used to call me. My parents work at Caltech. I applied for a semester up here at Ankrum. They were against it, but when I was accepted, they gave in. They're such worrywarts."

"Parents always worry about their kids."

"Yours too, huh?" Addison gave Sprite a penetrating look.

"Yeah. I guess it's a side effect of pregnancy."

Addison laughed again. It was a pleasant sound. Sprite couldn't suppress a smile. The younger girl grew serious, locking Sprite in an intense gaze, as if she were some kind of laboratory specimen. "Where's your home?"

The smile froze on Sprite's lips. She felt a twinge of anxiety, as if a little voice in the back of her mind was warning her to be careful. Her guard went up. "Boston." Sprite didn't want Addison to know the truth.

"Cool!" The girl's grin blossomed on her face again. "I went to Boston once. I went up to the top of the New Hancock Tower. The view was amazing! Did you grow up in the Back Bay?"

Sprite hesitated. The girl was asking far too many questions. "Cambridge," she said finally, offering her best artificial smile.

There was an awkward silence, as though Addison was waiting for Sprite to tell her more about her girlhood in Massachusetts. Then she shivered. "Is it cold in here?" The girl rubbed her bare arms.

Sprite could see goose bumps appearing on the girl's skin. She paused, realizing that her nanoskin prevented her from ever feeling chilly. "Could be," she said finally.

"I hate getting cold. Southern California spoiled me. I hear it gets cold and damp in Boston. Is that true?"

"I don't get cold easily," Sprite countered defensively. "You had better log in."

"Oh yes! I keep forgetting that." Addison waved her hand, and a login panel appeared in front of her. She spread her fingers and placed her hand on an authenticator. Immediately, the panel faded away, replaced by another virtual desk. "There we go," she said triumphantly.

Sprite smiled, willing herself to relax. She wasn't used to making new friends. She had been cloistered for years with the other scientists in her parents' Institute. Kell Edwards had been one of the other researcher-brats and was her closest friend. It was time for a change. Addison was nice enough, she thought. The girl was chatty. She could befriend her easily. However, Sprite would have to be careful. She could not reveal her true identity to anyone, lest Amos Cross find her again. Addison turned to her, a question forming on her lips, but the blue panorama dimmed around them, and the holo-conference began.

* * *

Stephen Winters sat in his office, staring at his holo-display. It was his first day back at work since his daughter Molly's disappearance. Rene had urged him to get out of their quarters and surround himself with people who weren't saturated with crises. He had a superb staff, all polished professionals who were filled with humor and kindness. His was a great place to work.

He could not get Molly out of his mind. His heart ached for her. As a father, he feared for her safety. She was an amazing young girl, and he would give his life to protect her. He felt guilty because he had let her out of his sight at the space elevator. He knew in his mind that parents could not guarantee their children's safety in every circumstance, but his gut accused him of neglect.

Stephen looked up at the wall across from his desk. Molly's image was displayed there. She was in a field of golden wheat, backlit by the late-afternoon sun. Her arms were outstretched, and a look of pure joy was on her face. She was so innocent and beautiful.

"Where are you, Molly?" he whispered. Stephen Winters put his head down on his desk and wept.

* * *

Nixie Drake left the outrigger hold and floated through the main passageway toward the forward part of *The Celestial Ghost*, where her stateroom was located. Raven had explained to her that they occasionally booked passengers and had outfitted the spaces for paying customers. The accommodations were luxurious compared to *The Raccoon's* cramped quarters.

A deep-throated hum resonated through the ship as the main engines flared to life for a midcourse correction. Nixie saw the passageway shift around her, and one of the bulkheads slid toward her as the ship's attitude changed. She flinched, remembering again how *The Raccoon* had jerked from the explosion. She snatched a handhold and fought to steady herself as she caught up with the ship's frame of reference. The engine noise damped down to silence, and the perception of motion disappeared with it.

As she neared her cabin, Nixie heard the sound of Slake's voice murmuring from the adjacent stateroom. She was drawn toward the sound. She reached the open hatchway and paused by the threshold.

"...freaks me out." Slake was trying to talk quietly, but his voice still carried. "I'd rather be dead than lose my legs."

"Got that right." Spif was in the cabin with him. "Take away a man's legs, and certain things tend to hang out like they shouldn't, you know?" Nixie peeked into the cabin just in time to see Spif gesture toward his crotch.

Both men were facing away from the hatch and had no idea Nixie was behind them. She entered the cabin silently as Slake laughed. "These guys sure do let the women order them around."

"Woman, you mean." Spif's voice grew serious. "That Raven calls the shots around here. She seems even tempered enough."

"For a legless cripple." Slake was unimpressed.

"No, Slake. She does okay out here. She's got command presence. Pretty smart, too." Slake snorted, but Spif continued. "I'd ship out with her."

"You'd take orders from a half-bodied chick? Better check between your legs, Spif; I think you lost something, too."

"It would be better than being ordered around by a punk kid like Nix." Nixie's heart skipped a beat. She felt like she had been smashed between two rogue asteroids. "I can't believe I was fooled by that Captain Grit shit. She's made fun of us for years. I'll never put myself in that situation again."

"A little child shall lead them." Slake mocked his crewmate.

"Then why is God an old man in a rocking chair?" Spif countered. "We've been at a snot-nosed kid's tea party all along without knowing it. She's a little brat bitch."

A wave of hot shame flowed over Nixie as her doubts resurfaced. She knew that Spif would never ship out with her again. Slake was spineless and would follow Spif's lead. Her crew was shattered, and it was all her fault. Nixie pivoted around, hoping to escape without the men noticing her. As she turned, she came face to face with Ice, who had been hovering in a corner near the hatchway. Ice's jaw was set, chiseled and hard, her mouth drawn into a thin horizontal line. There was no sign of compassion from her. Their eyes met, water against stone. Nixie wiped her tears quickly, and then without making a sound, she propelled herself out of the cabin.

CHAPTER SEVEN

Nixie Drake swam through the connecting passage that ran down the center of *The Celestial Ghost's* grappling arm. She came to a stop in the small docking pod at the end of the slender appendage. A strip of viewports encircled the pod, offering a three-hundred-sixty-degree view of the stars, but Nixie paid no attention to them. Her usual bravado was gone. She was pouty and tearful, the little girl inside her screaming for comfort. Spif was right. She didn't deserve to be a skipper. Her lack of judgment had resulted in the destruction of her ship and should have killed them all. It was pure chance that Raven and her crew had come along when they did.

A montage of troubling recollections flooded her mind. She was seven years old, hiding in the Commons at Copernicus Base. She was surrounded with beauty: soft green grass, trees decked with verdant leaves, pools of water fed by a whispering stream. Nevertheless, Nixie was afraid, alone. She saw a girl twice her age sitting on a bench near the garden's waterfall. She was dressed in a brightly-colored jumpsuit, reading an ebook.

Nixie's attention was drawn to a half-eaten sandwich which lay next to the girl on the bench, along with a bottle of lunar water. Her stomach growled. Hunger overruled her sense of caution, and she approached the girl. "Howdy Doody, there!" The girl looked up. Her eyes narrowed, sizing up her visitor. Nixie could tell she was displeased.

Nixie was beside her before the girl could react and sat down on the bench, the food between them. "Likey the looky-book?" she asked.

The girl snorted in derision. "What's a 'looky-book,' kid? Are you some kind of ignoramus?" The older girl stretched out the word as if she had just learned it, luxuriating in the sound of it.

"I gots a name!" Nixie snapped back defiantly.

"What?" The girl thought for a minute, then laughed. "You are a stupid one! Not anonymous. Ig-nor-a-mus. It means stupid, uneducated. You are a brainless brat, aren't you?"

Nixie felt ashamed. The girl's words sliced through her like a stiletto. When she first saw her, Nixie had imagined the girl to be like an older sister, someone who would befriend her and offer her some food. However, this girl was from another world, a place where Nixie wished she might live, but could not. She was well dressed and well spoken. Nixie wore tattered rags. The older girl knew fancy words and had the freedom to sit out in the open on a park bench without the fear of being taken back to a bad home and hurt by horrible people. Nixie realized that she could never bridge the vast divide that separated her from proper young women like this one.

The older girl made a face and wrinkled her nose. "You stink."

Nixie blushed, accepting the condemnation and embracing the obvious. She would never be a good person. She gazed unflinchingly into the girl's arrogant face and, with a quick sweep of her arm, snatched the sandwich and water bottle off the bench. Before her older nemesis could react, Nixie disappeared into a grove of pine trees.

* * *

A subtle current of air blew against the back of Nixie's neck. She snapped out of her daydream, turning quickly to see what had caused the disturbance. Raven hung motionlessly in the hatchway, her body having been a human piston as she transited through the grappling arm passageway. Nixie frowned at the intrusion, hoping her display of disapproval would make her unwanted visitor leave, but Raven was undaunted. The woman pushed away from the rubber seal that encircled the hatch opening and glided to a stop in front of her.

Nixie braced herself for some meaningless platitude, empty words meant to offer easy answers to painful questions. Instead, Raven hung mutely before her. She gazed out of the viewports for a moment, and then she turned her attention to Nixie. Her eyes twinkled with warmth and acceptance. Her body was relaxed, her face serene.

Nixie wasn't ready for a battle of silence. She braced herself for a loud argument, her anger seething just below the surface. She was ready to push back at anything and everyone, but Raven offered her nothing to oppose. The woman seemed unhurried. Raven's attention was focused completely on Nixie. The younger girl glared back at her visitor, but Raven seemed more amused than put off by it.

Finally, Nixie reached her breaking point and spoke. "Watcher lookin' at, Ravee?"

"I'm looking at my new friend," the captain responded. "She's in a lot of pain."

Here it comes, Nixie thought. She's going to offer me advice.

Raven sighed. "When I lost my legs, I had a lot of visitors. Every one of them had something to say. They wanted to tell me how God had a reason for my accident or how I needed to take courage. Some of them suggested new careers I could pursue from a wheelchair. Still others tried to convince me to fight my insurance company and convince them to pay for bio-mechanical implants. I even had some friends tell me in a roundabout way that it was my fault, that I was in the wrong place at the wrong time."

Nixie looked away, pretending to study the starscape.

"Guess what? All of those words backfired. My visitors intended to make me feel better, but they just made me feel worse. Every time a well-wisher left my room, I felt more depressed than when they arrived."

Nixie swallowed hard. She knew exactly what Raven meant.

"So I try not to make the same mistake. I won't offer you empty words. I won't try to make myself feel better at your expense. I just want you to know that I see your pain and am not scared away by it."

A tear tumbled from Nixie's eye, forming a perfect sphere in the zero-g. Raven reached out and cupped it in her hand, holding it gently, reverently.

"I ain't no Eye-knee-stein," Nixie murmured. "Kinda dumby dumb, ack-shally. Been runny running and hidee hidin' as far as memberin' goes for me."

Raven's eyes softened even more. "What about your parents?"

"Don't member momma." Nixie had never talked like this with anyone. Not even Kate Sloan, who had saved her from a rapist outside the Delta V tavern and taken her in as a daughter. "Father was a lousy-loser. Liked touchy-touchin' me where he shouldn't, you know?"

Raven nodded slowly, but offered no comment.

"Once a Punxsutawney time, I was winky dinkin' offs to my sleeps when he cames into my roomy doom." Nixie paused and took a deep breath. She didn't know why she was telling this stranger her deepest secrets, but something about Raven was trustworthy. For the first time in a long time, Nixie knew she was safe. "That bass-turd had one and only one thingee ding in his cranola..."

A deep, gut-wrenching gasp surged upward in Nixie's chest and swept through her like an outgoing tide. She sobbed uncontrollably, against her will. Nixie never cried in front of anyone. Hell, she rarely cried at all. She doubled over and began to tumble in the zero-g as pain and grief engulfed her. Raven moved toward her and wrapped her arms around Nixie's shoulders, clinging to her wordlessly and allowing the girl's poisonous memories to surround them both.

After a time, Nixie grew silent. Her breathing steadied, still ragged from her weeping. "So you ran away from home," Raven whispered. "You raised yourself."

Nixie nodded, then told her about hiding in the Copernicus Base Commons and finding a refuge in the vast service tunnels under the complex. She told her about grubbing for food in the District and how Momma Kate had saved her that night in front of the Delta V. Nixie told her how she turned her age and size to her advantage, misleading people in order to take advantage of them. She withheld nothing from her new friend, chronicling her plan to become a smuggler, the birth of

Captain Grit, and the formation of her crew. Then, having exhausted her many secrets, Nixie became quiet once more. The two women were bound together as sisters, battered by life, survivors of common pain.

"What are you going to do now?" Raven asked finally.

"Donno," the young girl replied. "'*Coon's* a gonner. I thinks Spiffy and Slakee's through and through with yours true-truly. Icee probbly gots betters things on her butt to do. Guess I starts all rover-dover again."

"You are a smart woman, Nixie."

"Nosey I aints..."

"Yes, you are. Have you ever considered doing something else?"

Nixie glared back at Raven. "You sayin' I aints cookie cuttered out for smuggin'?"

"Not at all!" Raven spread her hands. "I'm suggesting you might be shortchanging yourself. There are better things you could be doing."

Nixie began to feel uncomfortable again, the inevitable sense of overexposure that comes when deep feelings are expressed to a stranger. She began to push Raven away, forming a barrier in her mind. She had always dreamed of getting an education, of proving to that nameless girl in the Commons that she was not an ignoramus. However, she felt it was an impossible dream. Raven's encouragement was like a hot poker, searing her flesh and tormenting her with an unreachable goal. "Never-never hap-dappin, Ravee. My rut is stucky-stuck straight and narrow."

"That's not true. Look at me. I thought I'd hit a dead end. I was sure all of my options had been taken away when they cut my legs off, but I was wrong. There are always alternatives."

Raven fell silent. Nixie knew she was right. She knew how smart she was, but changing the course of her life frightened her. She was still young enough to play the smuggling game, and at the heart of it, that was all she knew.

* * *

Addison Traynor hovered next to Sprite Logan outside the study cubby where the two girls had spent the past two hours in a holo-conference. Despite her young age, Addison had demonstrated a keen grasp of the subject matter, asking intelligent and timely questions. Sprite's initial misgivings about her new friend had evaporated.

"Studying makes me famished," the younger girl said.

"I could eat," Sprite agreed. "What's the easiest way to the commissary?"

Addison took the lead, swimming ahead of Sprite through the web of connecting tunnels, which crisscrossed the Ankrum Platform. They passed through a dozen nodes that were crammed full of small research suites, where scientists and graduate students labored with scores of experiments.

"They're going to install that new synthetic gravity system up here," Addison said as they flew by yet another research node.

"Won't that hamper some of the research?" Sprite wondered.

Addison laughed. "They won't use it in areas that require zero-g. They're thinking of using it in the connectors so we can take up jogging."

"I heard about that. I'm getting tired of working out on the exercisers," Sprite mused. "Any idea when they'll put it in?"

"Not too soon, I think. It's expensive." Sprite made a mental note to speak to her aunt Maria. She owned the rights to the synthetic gravity system. Perhaps there might be a way to facilitate an anonymous donation. Suddenly, the passageway opened out into a large compartment filled with food and beverage dispensers. Addison grabbed a handhold and pulled herself to a stop. "Here we are," she announced proudly. "Let's eat!"

* * *

Kate Sloan wiped down the bar with her tattered rag. The night before had been a busy one at the Delta V tavern. Her right shoulder ached, and she paused, rubbing it firmly to ease the pain. She was getting old. Her body was sending her messages to slow down, but Kate wasn't about to retire. She had decided long ago that she would work at the Delta V until she died.

Kate was highly respected among the blue-collar workers at Copernicus Base. Her tavern was a popular hangout in "The District," the section of the base near the ore processing plant where strip joints and brothels were found. Through the years, nearly every man and woman had hung their head across the bar from her and poured out their troubles. Kate was their confessor, their mother, their friend. Kate knew everyone's secrets, and she kept them to herself.

Kate watched a woman half her age, who had just finished placing all the chairs in the tavern's serving area on top of the tables. A large bucket with casters was next to her, the long handle of a mop standing at attention in the greenish cleaning solution. The younger woman had a simple elegance about her. Her body was slender, her movements graceful. She wore no makeup, and there wasn't a single strand of hair on her head. Susanna Sloan Frost was Kate's daughter. She worked side by side with Kate, serving their guests, stocking the liquor, and cleaning the floors.

Kate smiled as she watched Susanna pull the mop from the bucket and begin to swab the polished concrete floor. She was proud of her daughter. She had come home three years earlier after a disastrous episode as Amos Cross's executive assistant. Kate knew it hadn't been easy for her to return, forfeiting her pride, losing a lucrative salary, and exchanging the expensive trappings of success for common clothes and a dishrag. Nevertheless, in exchange for all her losses, her baby had grown up, and the two women had become closer than sisters.

Kate looked out the viewports at the spacecraft perched on the landing pad. A knot formed in her stomach. Her thoughts turned to Nixie Drake. The young smuggler was like a second daughter to her. Kate had taken her in for a couple of years, until she set out on her own to make a life for herself. Kate hadn't approved of her plans to get a ship and assemble a crew, but the older woman knew how bullheaded Nixie was. She couldn't stop her.

Kate was worried. Nixie was overdue. She had left in a hurry over six months earlier. Kate remembered serving her young friend a glass of her best brandy and listening as Nixie told her about Remson Burke's job. Kate didn't trust Burke. She had heard too many rumors about the shadier side of his business dealings, but she knew times were hard for Nixie and the girl needed to take the work.

Kate was shaken out of her muse by the old-fashioned mechanical bell that rang as the door to the tavern swung open. Pepper Sweets pushed her way into the tavern. The woman was one of the hookers who plied their trade in The District. Her body was covered with a thin veneer of translucent polymer, which did nothing to mask her feminine attributes. She was out of breath, obviously in a hurry. Kate could tell she was upset, by the expression on her face.

"Katie! Have you heard the news?" Pepper threw herself at the bar, her breasts flopping down on the smooth surface. "It can't be true!"

Kate moved closer to the woman. Pepper was a friend, and she often shared information she picked up from her Johns. "What's the matter?"

Pepper pulled herself up straight, her hands gripping the edge of the counter. "Oh, my God! You don't know."

Susanna had stopped mopping when the woman had rushed into the tavern. Now, she came over to her mother and stood next to the sparsely-clad woman.

"Don't know what, Pepper?" Kate asked cautiously.

"It's *The Raccoon*." The words caught in Pepper's throat, and she choked, a river of tears coursing down her cheeks.

Kate stiffened, dropping her rag on the counter. Time slowed down, and Kate's field of vision collapsed until the crying woman was all that she could see. "Nixie?"

"There was an explosion picked up by the sensors at the spaceport. It coincided with a brief distress signal from a ship's AI. It was *The Raccoon*."

Kate's heart skipped a beat. She felt a sharp twinge in her chest. "Survivors?"

"They don't know, Katie, but it was a big explosion. They think all hands were lost."

Kate reached under the bar and pulled out three glasses. They clicked loudly as she banged them down on the counter. Then she took a bottle of her best brandy from the shelf behind her and mindlessly poured a round, spilling the expensive liquid across the surface of the bar.

* * *

The Celestial Ghost achieved lunar orbit without incident. Nixie and her crew had scavenged the remains of *The Raccoon* for whatever belongings they could find and then turned the twisted hulk over to the salvage crew, in payment for their hospitality. Now they floated in *The Ghost's* shuttle bay, each with a nylon duffel. A large jumpship was berthed there. An immense hatchway, sealed with split doors, was centered under the fuselage. Raven, Eagle, and Hawk hovered before them. Falcon was already strapped into the command seat and was prepping for departure. There was an awkward silence.

Spif and Slake were visibly disgusted. They barely made eye contact with their hosts and then boarded the jumpship without a word. Hawk shook his head. He had little sympathy and even less patience with people like Spif and Slake. Ice nodded curtly to Raven and swam over to the hatch. She pushed her duffel ahead of her into the jumpship's cabin and was gone. Nixie gestured toward the open hatch. "Sorry 'bouts my peeps," she managed. "We'd a been door-nailed dead, if you hadn't pop-popped our hatch back there."

"We're glad we happened along when we did," Raven offered with a smile.

Nixie grabbed her duffel with a frown. "Wishy-wished we coulda talky-talked some more, Ravie."

"Me too, Nixie. You are a good spacer."

The younger girl measured the expression on Raven's face. There was no deceit in it, just the honest assessment of a friend. Nixie smiled. "Nice an' tight to meecha, Ravie. Eyes won't runs tother ways ifs I seezy-wheezee ya 'gain sometime."

Raven was momentarily perplexed, then nodded warmly as she caught Nixie's meaning. "Let us know when you get another ship. We'll lend a hand outfitting her."

Nixie gave her a curt nod. "Justy might dooze that," she murmured. A deep thrumming sound issued from the jumpship as the propulsion system stirred into life. Nixie shook hands with her and disappeared through the hatch.

* * *

A steady stream of jumpships flowed into the Copernicus Base spaceport every day. Some of them came from other bases and settlements on the lunar surface. The others, like the one from *The Celestial Ghost*, shuttled crews to and from orbiting transfer ships. Falcon guided the jumpship into the queue, and within a few minutes, she set them down expertly on the landing pad.

A short while later, the four of them gathered in a sparsely-furnished boarding area. Under normal circumstances, Nixie and her crew would dine together after a long trip. They would enjoy good food and potent drink as they celebrated the completion of a job. The present circumstances were anything but normal, and there was nothing to celebrate. Nixie screwed up her courage to break the silence that hung over the group.

"Gonna needy 'nother shipper," she began. "Any nosey-hairs wheres we mights find one?"

Slake glanced at Spif uneasily. He rubbed his hands. "I guess we could look for somethin'," he said softly. "Whadda you think, Spif?"

Spif had been staring at the floor. He looked up, his eyes bright with anger. "Let me put it to you straight." Nixie flinched from the man's intensity. Spif generally looked good, but not today, not now. He was different. Like an athlete who had left the home team to join another, exchanging the colors of friendship for those of a foe. "We ain't looking for a new ship with you, Nix. We talked it over, and we're done." Spif swung his duffle over his shoulder and turned away. Slake refused to look at her, pivoting on his heel and following Spif wordlessly across the boarding area.

Nixie stood there. She knew the vein of distrust and anger ran deep in her crew, but she wasn't prepared for Spif and Slake's departure. She felt immobilized, out of control. The men were almost out of sight when Nixie regained her wits. She heard a deep guttural sigh next to her. She turned quickly at the unexpected sound and looked squarely at Ice.

The dispassionate woman's face was twisted into a hateful mask, her eyes blazing with frozen fire, her angular chin set, her fists clenched. Nixie took a step back, startled by the woman's raw emotion. Nixie gasped as waves of guilt and regret pummeled her like a tidal wave. Ice grimaced, as if her body was so unaccustomed to such a display of anger, it might split in two. Then she turned on her heel and walked away, leaving Nixie shaken and utterly alone.

CHAPTER EIGHT

S lake followed Spif through the massive supply dome and onto the central concourse, which led to Copernicus Base's crown jewel, her public green area in the Base Commons. Once there, they paused to take in the lush vegetation. They agreed to meet up again in a few days and then went their separate ways. Spif headed toward the residence domes to the north, and Slake went toward The District.

A man was sitting on one of the park benches, enjoying the fragrance of the green area, with its flowers and evergreens. He froze when he saw Slake walking toward The District. He looked down, hoping his reaction hadn't drawn the man's attention. He breathed slowly, watching the other man out of the corner of his eye. The man noticed Slake's gait. There was an eagerness in his step. The stranger was stunned. He tried to fathom the impossibility before him. The man shouldn't be here. In fact, the man shouldn't be alive. A shiver ran up his spine as he considered the implications of what he was seeing. There would be hell to pay, and he feared he was going to be the man who got the bill.

Slake had a burning in his groin. It had been too long since he had bedded a woman, and he was of a mind to buy some time with a hooker. He left the grassy carpet of the Base Commons and stepped into The District. The main corridor was awash with a soft reddish light, offering a measure of anonymity for those who wandered there.

He made a beeline to the "Head's Up," an intimate establishment tucked against the exterior wall of the second dome on the left.

Slake entered the foyer and was greeted by a sleek woman adorned with a microscopically-thin sheath that had been sprayed on her body. She was burgundy from head to toe, with flecks of reflective dust sprinkled across her breasts. Ultraviolet lamps revealed phosphorescent marks, which had been drawn on every inch of her. The glowing image of a serpent encircled her waist, and long, slender flower petals descended from her shoulders to her navel.

The woman smiled beguilingly at him, flexing her pelvis in a suggestive invitation. He felt his heat rise as she glanced between his legs appreciatively. She pirouetted slowly, allowing him to gaze at her. She was a professional, posing her body to maximize her allure. As she pivoted away from him, Slake could see the artwork on her back. The image of a man's testicular sack was superimposed on her buttocks, with an erect phallus rising up her spine.

The blood drained from Slake's mind. He forgot about Captain Grit and the breakup of his crew. He forgot about his long space voyage. He forgot about everything, except this luminescent creature who was inviting him into her lair. She smiled, and his knees buckled. He was at her mercy and was ready to die in her arms. She stepped toward him, and her scent enveloped him, the exotic pheromones working their magic on his nervous system. He breathed deeply as her hands touched his body. The room expanded as her airborne opiates coursed into him, and Slake, now aflame with passion, followed the nameless woman into the shadowed interior of the brothel.

* * *

Remson Burke hurried back to his office in the administration section of Copernicus Base. He swept past his receptionist without acknowledging her and went straight into his holo-chamber. Burke decided it was best to send a preemptive message to his boss. It would go better for him if he was the one to break the unfortunate news of his failure. He instructed the AI to open a private channel and gave the machine the code which would connect him with Amos Cross.

"What do you have for me?" Cross was perturbed by the interruption. He appeared larger than life, even though he was half Burke's size.

Remson swallowed nervously. "I just saw a member of Nixie Drake's crew in the Copernicus Commons."

Cross's eyes narrowed. "You assured me that she was taken care of."

"The device detonated. My contact at the spaceport told me their AI pulsed a distress packet and then went silent. The ship had to have been destroyed."

"Was Miss Drake with this person?"

"No, sir. The man was alone."

"Then it's possible that the girl is dead."

Remson nodded. "Yes. The man I saw might have been the only survivor."

"Question him! Find out if Nixie Drake is alive."

"I will, Mr. Cross."

"I am surrounded by idiots!" Cross sneered at Remson with disdain. "I expect you to fix this. Do you understand me? I want Nixie Drake terminated. I don't ever want to hear her name again. If she has the misfortune of being alive, I want you to kill her and dump her meaningless carcass where it will never be found."

Remson cowered under the withering diatribe. "I understand, sir."

"You had better, Mr. Burke. If you fail me again, am going to hold you personally responsible." Cross's image winked out, and Remson Burke sat in the darkness of his holo-chamber, gasping for breath.

* * *

For the first time in her life, the Cuss didn't feel like home. Nixie left the spaceport and wandered up the main thoroughfare, toward the Base Commons. The last time she had been there, she had walked with pride. She had been a businesswoman, the embodiment of the Copernican dream. She had started with nothing and had made something of herself. Although her crew hadn't known it at the time, she was the captain of a transfer ship. She had clients and a good reputation in a shady line of work.

Everything was different now. Her ship was gone. Her crew had discovered her secret and abandoned her. Her reputation was in shambles. She was going to have to start over. The last time, she had built her business on her appearance. She had been a little girl and as such, was underestimated by her competition. It had been a big advantage. Now she was getting older, and although she still looked younger than her age, she would not be able to employ the ruse much longer.

Nixie felt lost. She wanted to hide from everything. She turned left at a cross-junction that connected the base's main corridor with an older one, which ran parallel to it on the northern side of the complex. Before she had met Momma Kate, Nixie had spent a lot of time in this part of the base. There were hundreds of access shafts and tunnels which honeycombed the rock beneath the complex. Nixie knew them all like the back of her hand. In fact, she still had a hiding place near the Old Commons. The bowels of Copernicus Base were like a mother's womb, dark and safe. She was drawn to them.

Nixie reached the older corridor and turned right. It was the longest passageway in the Cuss, and foot traffic was lighter there. Far ahead of her, she could see a bright spot where the corridor ended at the Old Commons. It was a modest dome, much smaller than the new Base Commons, but the light was pleasant there. Nixie remembered running away from her childhood home, running away from her father. She had spent her first night of freedom hidden behind a vending machine in the Old Commons.

Nixie yearned to see Momma Kate, but she couldn't bring herself to go to the Delta V. Kate had warned her about doing business with Remson Burke, and she had ignored her advice. Nixie remembered a story she had heard somewhere. It was about a young man, whose father was a wealthy surface scratcher on Mare Cognitum. The boy demanded his share of his father's wealth and came to Copernicus Base to enjoy his freedom. He went straight to The District and spent all of his money on women and strong drink. Penniless, the boy ended up eating food out of dumpsters, just as she had done. The boy resisted going home because his pride wouldn't allow it.

Nixie paused on the concourse. She saw herself in the reflection of a storefront. She was still wearing the ill-fitted clothes given to her by Raven. Her eyes were sunken from lack of sleep. Her mouth had found a resting place in what seemed a perpetual frown. She realized she was like that boy. She hadn't taken anything from Momma Kate, but the storybook-boy's shame and guilt felt familiar to her.

The squeaky mewing of a child echoed down the corridor and interrupted Nixie's musings. She looked in the direction of the sound and saw a young girl, not three years old, pulling away from her father. The man reached for her, but she was too quick for him. He called her name sharply, but the child was defiant. She rushed away from him on tottering legs, running as fast as she could down the passageway. Her little feet slipped on the smooth concrete, and she crashed down on the floor, striking her head on the hard surface.

Nixie saw her hit the floor. The little girl picked herself up to a sitting position, unsure of what had happened. She screwed up her face and took a deep breath. There was a pause, and then she let out a mind-shattering scream. Nixie thought the child was calling for her father, but she couldn't quite make out the words through her blubbering. The father, who had been chasing his little charge, scooped her up into his arms. He wasn't angry. He didn't look ready to scold her for letting go of his hand and running away. The man simply held his daughter and stroked her back.

Nixie thought of her father, the beast of her memories, the monster of her dreams. An intense longing welled up inside her as she watched the small girl grow calm in her father's embrace. She yearned for a father like the one in front of her. Why had she been born into a family of abuse? Why did she have to grow up so quickly and be on her own before her time?

Nixie glanced back into the storefront reflection. She was tired of being on her own. The ending of the story came to her like the opening of a ship's hatch after a long space-flight. The boy had also grown tired of being on his own. He had returned to Mare Cognitum, to his father and his family. Instead of condemnation, the boy was greeted with tenderness and joy. In that moment, Nixie knew what she had to do.

* * *

Slake lay naked in the woman's lair, basking in the afterglow of their sex-making. His arousal had seemed interminable, and the harlot continued to stroke him, extending his ecstasy with her long, experienced fingers. Slake's world was a warm, damp fog, his mind still muddled by the woman's pharmaceutical perfume.

There was the kiss of moving air as someone else entered the room. Slake, whose attention was focused entirely on the tips of the woman's fingers and where they were touching him, felt her hand jerk suddenly. "Don't stop, baby," he managed before he heard the sound of the woman's soft skin slap against the hard floor. Rough and powerful hands grabbed Slake up off the bed. He felt a pinprick in his neck, and then he felt nothing at all.

* * *

Molly didn't like the cold metal decking of her prison. She would stand as long as she could, but it hurt her feet. She would sit on it until her bottom grew numb, the chill of the coarse metal working its way through her pelvis and into the rest of her bones. Then Molly would kneel on it, but the rough non-skid surface bit into the soft flesh of her knees. She wasn't alone. Each of her sister captives went through the same standing, sitting, and kneeling ritual.

The hatch hissed open, and there was a collective gasp. Several of the girls began to cry; others shook with fear. Two of their captors, clad only in undershorts, stepped into the hold. "We're here on official business," one of them announced. He scratched his manhood unceremoniously. Several of the girls turned their heads away. "You might call us your quality control team." The second man laughed lasciviously. "We're going to pick two of you at random and check you for quality." The hold grew silent, the girls hushed with terror.

The men roamed among the children, pausing before this one and that, touching and squeezing them without any thought for their dignity. Four girls were compelled to stand in the middle of the chamber. The men pulled off their smocks. Molly shook with fear as she watched the men examine them. The girls dared not whimper, but their tears flowed freely as the men disgraced them. They were treating them like cattle.

Finally, two of the girls were selected, and the men paraded them out of the hold. The hatch slid shut, and no one spoke as the two naked girls fumbled nervously with their discarded smocks. Molly closed her eyes and tried to forget the looks on the girls' faces, but the images would not go away. Just a few short days ago, she had been a naive little girl. She had dreamed of story-book romances and handsome princes. Sex had been a mysterious word. Now it was an unimaginable horror. In the examining room, the woman with the copper-colored hair had forced her to strip off her clothes in front of one of the men. They had touched her in ways she had never experienced before. Molly blushed at the humiliation. However, she knew that what she had faced was nothing compared to what was happening to the two girls who had been taken from the hold. A wave of cold fear, more pronounced than anything caused by the decking, swept through her marrow. Molly knew without a doubt that her time would come and the ugly men would take her, too.

* * *

When Kell Edwards had invited Sprite and Addison to his residence for dinner, both girls had wondered how they would all fit into the place. Space was at a premium on Ankrum, and everyone, as far as Sprite could tell, was issued closet-sized domiciles like her own. Sprite recalled the day when Uncle Ty and Kell had come to visit her. Squeezing three bodies into her quarters had been downright claustrophobic.

Kell greeted them at the door and ushered them into the quarters he shared with his father. There was a small foyer that opened out into a spacious multi-purpose cabin. The far bulkhead was filled with large viewports, which gave an unobstructed view of the Earth. There were no furnishings in the room, since there was no need for them in zero-g.

"This is huge!" Addison exclaimed as she swam into the middle of the chamber. Addison was dressed in a skin-tight outfit, which conformed to every curve and crease in her body. She was clearly an athlete, her body lean, her muscles toned. Sprite pivoted to smile at Kell, but his attention was elsewhere, mesmerized by her young friend. He couldn't take his eyes off her. It was as if Sprite didn't exist.

Addison paused in front of a photograph, which was attached to one of the bulkheads. It was the picture of a dark-haired woman, standing on what appeared to be the rim of a rocky gorge. A stand of pine trees was behind her left shoulder; a deep canyon fell away on her right. Her face glowed in a late-afternoon light, and her smile was full of mischief. Kell pushed away from a handhold, leaving Sprite by the door. He came to rest next to Addison. He watched silently as she reached out and touched the picture with her finger. "Your mother?" she asked.

"Yes." Kell's voice was soft, reverent. "She died a few years ago."

Addison studied Kell's face. "You must miss her terribly." She withdrew her hand from the picture and gently stroked Kell's arm.

"There was an explosion," he offered quietly. "Her death was unexpected."

Sprite remembered the story of Jo Smith's self-sacrifice. She had destroyed a Meridian security ship in order to save Kell's life. She was a brave and noble woman, although Jo would never have seen herself that way.

"That's so sad," Addison murmured. She looked at the picture again. "She was beautiful."

Kell hung motionlessly beside the girl, his eyes fastened upon her. Sprite watched as Addison turned back to him, her face wreathed in a smile. "You look like her," she exclaimed, "only taller." Kell laughed self-consciously, but it was obvious that he was flattered by the comment.

Sprite moved behind her two friends. She felt like a peeping Tom. Something was going on between them. Their shared chemistry was forming an impermeable bubble around them. Sprite watched Kell defensively as he responded to Addison. There was a certain twinkle in his eye that unsettled her. What was she feeling? Was it jealousy?

Sprite and Kell had been friends for many years, and she had always looked upon him as a brother. Kell, on the other hand, had made numerous sexual advances, and Sprite had repeatedly spurned him. She had never sought anything more than friendship, but ever since she arrived at Ankrum, she had felt drawn to him physically. The friendship she felt for him was still there, but now there was something more. She wasn't sure what she wanted, but she knew she didn't like the way he was responding to Addison.

"Show us the rest of the place," Sprite said loudly.

Kell jumped at the sound of her voice, his moment of infatuation shattered. Addy seemed unperturbed by the interruption. Sprite was pleased to see a fleeting shadow of guilt cross Kell's face.

* * *

Slake awoke in a dimly-lit room. He was strapped to a metal chair, his hands tied securely behind his back. He shivered as he felt the cold surface against his skin. Then Slake realized that he was naked. The memory of sex with the prostitute flashed through his mind. It did not arouse him but only served as an explanation for why he had no clothes. Slake was not a shy man, but even he found his present circumstances quite embarrassing. He pulled against his restraints with no effect. He was at the mercy of whoever had bound him, and it troubled him to be in such a vulnerable position.

There was a sound outside the chamber door, and Slake tensed with apprehension. The door opened on squeaky hinges, and Remson Burke stepped into the room with two other men. Burke came to a stop directly in front of Slake. His associates flanked the chair, their arms hanging loosely at their sides. Burke smiled widely at Slake, his teeth white and even, a Cheshire Cat grin.

"I hope you slept well." There was death in Burke's voice. A shiver coursed through Slake that had nothing to do with the cold metal of the chair. "I want this to go well for you, so I suggest you answer my questions." His eyes pierced Slake's soul. "Do you understand me?"

Slake was wide-eyed with fear. "What am I doing here?" he mewed.

Burke nodded at one of his associates, and the man slapped his face. Hard. Slake felt a burning tingle of pain where the man had struck him. He glanced at the man's hand. It bore a heavy ring. It must have scratched his cheek. Slake felt blood oozing out of the wound.

"Did I say anything about you asking questions?" Burke spoke in a menacing whisper.

Slake shook his head, beads of sweat forming on his brow.

"All right, then. Where can I find Nixie Drake?"

Slake was confused. "Who are you?" he managed.

As instantaneous and unexpected as a lightening bolt, the second man slammed his fist into Slake's abdomen. He would have doubled over, but the cords that held him to the chair prevented it. He felt a rib crack under the assault, and then an abrasive burning pain besieged him with every subsequent breath.

"You are a slow learner, aren't you, Mr. Slake?" Burke rubbed his hands together. "But you will learn. I am sure you are familiar with the concept of negative reinforcement. If you keep asking questions, you will find out how negative we can be." Slake's vision was blurred by the intense pain in his stomach. Burke's face was no more than a white smear against the darkened walls of the chamber. "I will ask you again. Where can I find Nixie Drake?"

Bile was rising in Slake's throat. He arched his back, then brought his knees together as he fought the urge to pee. "I don't know."

Burke nodded again to the first man. His arm and fist were like a battering ram as the man drove a punch into Slake's kidney. The man had put all of his weight behind the blow, and Slake felt a rib snap, and then something popped inside him. A fireball of pain expanded in his torso, and he screamed, biting down on the inside of his cheek with clenched teeth. Slake leaned forward, his eyes clamped shut, blood now coursing from his mouth.

"This isn't going well for you, Mr. Slake. 'I don't know,' isn't an answer." Burke seemed to be enjoying himself. "Trust me, you don't want to be hit again." He stepped closer to Slake and grabbed his chin. He tipped his head up; Burke's steel-gray eyes were centimeters from Slake's face. It was at that moment when Slake's bladder spasmed, and a stream of hot urine soiled the leg of Burke's pants.

Burke cursed and stepped back, his face twisted into an angry, loathing mask. "Fix that!" he commanded, gesturing toward Slake's groin. The second man pulled something from his pocket and reached down between Slake's legs.

"No!" Slake squealed. "I'll tell you." The man glanced at Burke, who motioned for him to withdraw. He stepped back, the sharp blade in his hand glinting in the dimness.

Burke grabbed Slake's chin again. "I'm waiting."

Slake swallowed a mouthful of blood. "The Delta V," he gurgled.

"What did you say?" Burke commanded.

"The Delta V," Slake shouted. "She always goes there." The room began to spin as another wave of pain tightened its grip on Slake's body.

Burke smiled at him. "Now that wasn't so bad, was it?" He stepped back, glancing at the two men who still flanked Slake's chair. "Gentlemen? Make Mr. Slake's pain stop." Slake watched as Remson Burke pivoted toward the door. He sensed sudden movement in his peripheral vision. Then everything went dark.

CHAPTER NINE

K ate Sloan rushed toward Nixie when the young woman entered the Delta V. She threw her arms around her and squeezed her until Nixie couldn't breathe. When the younger woman squirmed free of her friend's powerful embrace, Kate paused self-consciously, unaccustomed to such displays of emotion. She returned to her place behind the bar. Kate pulled two small glasses from under the counter and poured shots of her best brandy, sliding one into the waiting fist of her visitor.

The older woman took her brandy in one swallow, slamming the empty shot glass on the countertop. "You gave us a real scare, Nix," she breathed. "Got word that *The Raccoon* sent out a distress call and then went silent."

Nixie's drinking hand froze halfway between the bar and her lips. She lowered the glass and rocked herself onto one of the barstools, putting both elbows on the counter. She stared morosely at Momma Kate, as a tear eased its way out of her eye and dribbled down her cheek. "I screwy-screwed the puppy," Nixie began. "Shoulda 'spected the cargo Remson Burke had us snaggy-snag from Mars. Spiffer told me so, but I twasn't in a listenin' mood. Told 'em that Gritty was coolly-cool as a colander 'bout it. So we tuckered it down in the hold and bouncy-bounced back." Tears were streaming down her face, now. "*The 'Coon's* gone. We's all livin' and stuff, but my crew's doornail-dead. Splintered up like an old piney-board. And it's all on meezy-wheezy."

Kate poured herself another shot. "Spif blames you for what happened?"

"All threes of 'em do, Momma." Nixie hung her head in shame. "Even Icy."

"I find that hard to believe." Kate held Nixie with a steady gaze. "Ice isn't one to overreact."

Nixie snorted. "Shoulda noticed the looky-look on her faceplate, Katie. She was diss-gusted. She was..." Nixie paused, her emotions taking an upper hand. "She was ass-shamed of me." Her voice trailed off.

"I hate being the bearer of bad news," Kate sighed. She glanced around the empty bar, then lowered her head and leaned forward until she was a few centimeters from Nixie's face. "But you've got bigger problems than losing your ship and your crew."

Nixie's eyes grew wide. "Howsy that?"

"Remson Burke has been on the prowl. Folks have seen him and his men all over the Cuss."

"He livey-lives here," Nixie opined. "Gots a big dome-home over in the oldy section."

"I know that," Kate hissed. "But he's been looking for something. Someone. I think that someone is you."

Nixie nodded, accepting the possibility. "Maybe he wants some pay-backer for his fee."

"Could be, Nixie." Kate frowned at her young friend. "But what if that cargo was meant to blow up?"

The color drained from Nixie's face as she grasped the implications of what Kate was saying. "Old Burkey's out to doornail me?"

Kate nodded. "It's possible. He's a very dangerous man."

"Your old brain-bulb come up with a reason for that idea?"

"I can think of someone who wants to settle a score with you."

"Lots o' them type peeps," Nixie laughed.

"I mean someone very powerful. Someone who was after the people you smuggled back from Rinker's Knot a few years ago."

"Cross? You's thinkin' Boss-Cross might have an inny for old Nix?" Nixie picked up her drink and gulped it down nervously.

"I don't know, but you'd better be careful, Nixie. If I were you, I'd find a safe place and hold up there for a while."

Nixie pushed her empty glass across the bar. Kate could see the fear in her face. Remson Burke was bad, but Amos Cross was diabolical. She poured her young friend another drink and then goaded her out of the tavern.

* * *

Remson Burke cursed as he pulled off his soiled pants. He wadded them up and threw them angrily into a disposal unit. He hated the smell of urine and was disgusted by Slake's cowardice. He peeled off the rest of his clothes and stepped into a steaming hot shower. Slender jets of water massaged his skin, spraying his body with nano-detergents. The shower could cleanse the body, but it could not cleanse the man. Burke emerged from the stall, his life still stained by hatred and greed.

He opened an immense walk-in closet and took a deep breath. He loved the smell of fine clothing. He ran his fingers across the fabrics and then paused to look in the full-length mirror that was built into the wooden cabinetry. He liked looking at his body, but he never looked at his face. Burke pulled on a thin pair of trousers and a dress shirt. He paused in front of his impressive collection of shoes and selected a pair of soft, slipper-like loafers. He hated the feel of stiff, formal shoes. Then, he left his bedroom suite and took his place at the polished stone desk in his private study.

"How may I serve you, Mr. Burke?" His AI purred with a husky feminine voice.

"I want to speak with Rattler," he commanded.

Within a moment, a man appeared before his desk. His image shimmered in the hologram. He was dressed in a sleeveless vest and expensive silk pants. A narrow strip of curly chest hair erupted between the unfastened breast panels of the man's upper garment. The image of a snake meandered up his left arm and disappeared beneath the faux leather of the vest. The serpent's body continued unseen across the man's shoulders and then slithered down his right arm, its ugly head enshrined on the back of the man's hand. The snake's tongue erupted threateningly from its mouth and was inked in fine detail along the top of the man's middle finger.

"Mr. Burke." The tattooed man frowned.

Remson was pleased to see the man tense in deference to him. "Rattler. I have a job for you."

"Anything you want, Mr. Burke."

Burke paused. He enjoyed making the man wait. Rattler stared at him through the holo-display and then looked down, shifting his weight to his other foot. Burke smiled in satisfaction, choosing that moment to speak. "Do you know what Nixie Drake looks like?"

"Yesser. I've seen her around."

"How about the rest of her crew? Do you know them?"

"I seen Slake around The District from time to time."

"Don't worry about him," Burke offered benignly.

"I can pick Spif out of a crowd, but I don't know him. The other woman on her crew is hot. She doesn't wear much for clothes, you know? She makes an impression. I think her name is Ice."

"I want you to find Nixie Drake and bring her to me. If you see the others, I want them too."

"Any idea where she is?"

"Go to the Delta V. If she's not there, she'll show up eventually."

"I've seen her there before." Rattler rubbed his chin.

"And do it quickly."

"You got it, Mr. Burke." The tattooed man nodded curtly, and the image faded from view.

* * *

Nixie's senses were on high alert as she left the Delta V. She took a circuitous route through the industrial quarter to avoid Remson Burke and his associates. When she got to the Blue Collar Commons, a lower-class center of activity located near the ice mine, she kept to the perimeter of the dome, moving stealthily from kiosk to kiosk. She ducked down the corridor that led into the cavernous industrial center.

There, loud machines and relentless robotic arms toiled endlessly, fabricating everything from clothing to high technology. She wove her way through the aisles, careful to hide her face from the array of surveillance cameras, which monitored everything in the concrete structure.

Nixie emerged from the industrial center and took a right in Copernicus Base's central corridor, keeping her head down as she wandered slowly toward the Old Commons. She took a side passage toward the north and slipped into a recess in the concrete wall. The nook was much deeper than it appeared from the hallway, its walls narrowing. Nixie wedged her way to the back of the niche and squeezed through a narrow air vent. The metal screen was loose, enabling her to move it easily. Nixie could tell she was getting older. Her hips weren't as narrow as they once had been. Before long, she would not be able to use this entrance to her secret lair.

A slender ladder fashioned out of flattened iron bars descended through an opening in the floor. Nixie wasted no time and swung herself onto it, eager to find safety in the bowels of the labyrinth below. Forgoing the last rung, she dropped to the floor of a long tunnel, her feet slapping against the hard stone. She did not hesitate as she set off down the passage. This was familiar turf.

Nixie paused by a large circular pipe. It was almost three meters in diameter. A door-shaped hatch was cut into the curving metal. She tightened the shoulder straps of her backpack and then undogged the access panel. She smiled to herself as the hatch swung inward. She stepped into the giant duct. A great wind whipped at her collar as she closed the hatch. This had always been her favorite moment. She stood still in the gale-force wind, fresh air coursing around her body. She took a deep breath and exhaled slowly. The breeze was neither cold, nor hot. It caressed her like a giant hand, pressing against her, whipping her clothing. Nixie spread her arms and opened her fingers, allowing the Cuss's breath to engulf her.

There was a noise outside the duct. Nixie heard it above the rush of wind. As a young girl, she had learned the sounds of the base. She knew the location of every pump and blower. Every hatch had its own auditory signature; every passage resonated with a different hollow pitch. Someone was standing outside the hatch. Perhaps they had seen her enter the duct. Nixie clenched her fists and pulled her arms back to her sides. Then, she made her way swiftly and silently through the pipe, each step taking her deeper into the wind. She came to the first junction and glanced behind her. The cylindrical cavity was empty and dark. She dodged to her left. Now the wind was to her back, and she let it carry her like a leaf scuttling across a late-October road.

Nixie took yet another fork in the aqueduct, the pipe now less than two meters from top to bottom. She came to another hatch and opened it carefully, making sure no one was waiting for her on the other side. Stepping through, she secured the portal behind her and took another passage that was chiseled into the native lunar rock. The air was musty there, and the floor was strewn with rocks the size of her fist. She walked carefully, avoiding the stones, creeping silently through the ancient rubble. She passed through an opening in the rock wall and then found another ladder, which she descended to yet a deeper level of the catacombs.

The air was fresher there. Metallic conduits emerged from unseen chambers behind the stone walls and threaded their way down the long corridor ahead of her. Nixie unslung her pack and ducked behind one of the large rectangular chases. There was an opening, perhaps waist-high in the wall, that could only be found if one knew where to look. Nixie dropped to her knees in front of the opening and pushed the pack into the dark opening. Beyond the innocuous aperture was a room.

Nixie stood up and reached out in the darkness. Her fingers found a roll of cloth above the hole she had just wormed through. She let it fall, its upper end fastened to the transom. The thick, dark cloth covered the entrance. Instinctively, Nixie reached to her left and found a switch. She pressed it, and soft, dim light flooded the chamber. Everything was as she remembered it, and Nixie smiled.

An old crate sat against the far wall of the room. A tablecloth was draped over it, and a half-empty bottle of clear liquid stood at attention on its surface. A plastic cup was its only companion. A smaller crate, obviously a makeshift chair, knelt at the side of the table. A series of metal boxes was stacked neatly in a corner, each adorned with a faded paper label, announcing its contents. A ragged blanket cast across an inflatable bladder was Nixie's bed. A faded pink pillow rested at one end.

Nixie moved the bottle and cup. Then she laid her backpack on the table. She ripped open the hook-and-loop fastener and withdrew the Captain Grit doll. She cradled it in her hands, examining the broken sword and the thread-worn seams.

"Watch we gonna do now, Gritty?" she asked. "I gots the pooch all screwy-screwed. The 'Coon's a goner. I gots peeps after my butt. My crew... I gots no crew no more." She gestured toward the humble furniture. "Wheeze backs to whereas we wuz, Gritty. An I got no frick-fracken notion what to dooze next."

Nixie propped the doll on the old bed, its back against the faded pillow. She smoothed a wrinkle in the captain's jacket. The Davy Jones hat was at an odd angle, so she adjusted it. She turned to the table and was about to empty the rest of her pack when she heard a sound from the passageway outside her door. Nixie froze. She heard it again, the sound of cloth rubbing against metal ductwork. Someone was nearby.

Nixie stole silently to the entrance of her hideaway and flicked off the light. She stood in the darkness, not daring to breathe. Her heart was pounding in her chest, and she was certain her unwelcome visitor would hear it. For several long minutes, she didn't move, listening for any further sound. Finally, there was a scuffing sound some distance away. Someone had kicked something with their foot. Nixie estimated that whoever it was had moved on and was no longer a threat.

She waited another thirty minutes and then carefully removed the blackout curtain from the entrance of her den. She got down on all fours and poked her head through the opening. As she suspected, no one was there. She was about to retreat back into the chamber when something caught her eye. It was a piece of paper, no more than eight centimeters long. It was lying on the floor of the passageway, directly in front of the hideaway. It had not been there when she had arrived. A chill coursed through Nixie's bones. She reached out and snatched the scrap of paper. It was a gum wrapper.

* * *

Kate Sloan could see every table in the Delta V from behind the bar. She was a watcher, reading her clients, knowing when they wanted refills on their drinks, sensing when things were about to get out of hand. She kept a stout titanium club under the bar for the latter situations. At the moment, she was keeping an eye on a man called Rattler. The man had drifted into the Cuss a few years earlier, and Kate had been told about him. He was an occasional customer, usually after one of the bawdy celebrations in The District. Rattler was sitting alone at a table near the viewports. There were two gorgeous women nearby, but he paid no attention to them. Rattler's eyes were locked on the entrance. He studied every person who entered the tavern.

Kate knew of the man's connection with Remson Burke, and she had a good idea that he was waiting for Nixie. She slid out from behind the bar and wandered through the tables, schmoozing with her regulars, wiping an occasional empty tabletop. She took her time, not wanting to raise Rattler's suspicions. Finally, she approached his table, her attention fixed on the landscape beyond the viewport. She paused, then glanced down at the tattooed man. "Nice tats, buddy," she offered. "Where did you get the snake?"

Rattler glanced down at his right hand, the head of the snake caught in the cold lunar light. "Proclus Base," he replied without a smile. "You like snakes?"

Kate gave him a disarming grin. "I deal with them all the time."

Rattler nodded, oblivious to her meaning. "Busy night, tonight."

"Usually is, though it seems everybody's been in here today."

"Popular place."

"Been here a long time," Kate responded.

Rattler thought for a moment, then pushed his glass away from him. "Do you know a girl by the name of Nixie Drake?"

Kate was expecting the question, but she felt her heart skip a beat, nonetheless. "Sure. She's a regular, when she's on base."

"Have you seen her?" Rattler's eyes narrowed.

"Sure have." Kate knew the man could tell if she lied about that. Sometimes it was best to wrap a lie a cloak of truth.

"Where can I find her?" The man looked hopeful.

Kate leaned over and wiped the table with her rag, removing a wet ring left by Rattler's glass. "She was in here about an hour ago." Kate tried to look thoughtful. "She was talking about getting laid over at the G-Spot."

"That whorehouse for lesbians?"

"That's it." Kate was the epitome of nonchalance. "She just got back from deep space and had a need, you know?"

"Been there," the man nodded.

"Hope you find her," Kate offered smoothly. "Have a good evening." She wandered past his table, greeting the two women she had seen earlier. Kate heard Rattler's chair scrape against the concrete floor. She stole a glance over her shoulder. The man was already halfway to the door.

* * *

Sprite Logan was hovering in the Ankrum Platform commissary, trying to decide what to have for lunch. Her morning seminar had run late, and most of the other students had already eaten. She held an insulated bag of hot coffee in one hand and was thumbing through the virtual menu of the automated dispenser. She had a hankering for tomato soup and a peanut butter sandwich.

Addison Traynor came up behind her and brushed against her shoulder. Sprite jumped. She let go of the bag of coffee, and it tumbled away from her. "Don't do that!" she scolded her new friend. "You scared the daylights out of me."

Addison snatched the beverage bag in midair and handed it back to her. "Have you been avoiding me?" she asked abruptly.

Sprite blushed. "No!" she lied. She was still angry at her for showing too much interest in Kell.

"Don't lie to me." Addison smiled at her disarmingly. "I know something is bothering you. What did I do?"

Sprite cleared her throat. "It's not your fault, Addy," she said finally. "I'm being petty."

"Was it something that happened the other night when we were at Kell's place?"

Sprite couldn't hide her surprise. Addy must have known from the beginning about her jealousy. "Maybe," she offered meekly.

"Tell me what it is! I can't fix what I don't know about." Addison spread her hands.

Sprite looked at her friend. She was beautiful. Her body was perfectly proportioned, her muscles toned, her breasts shapely, her hair as smooth as silk. The memory of her floating next to Kell was seared into her mind. They made a terrific-looking couple, and it bothered her.

"I know that look," Addison said with sudden recognition. "You're mad at me because I showed interest in Kell." It was a statement, not a question.

Sprite blushed. Her ears burned. She nodded slowly to her friend. Addison laughed. "You don't have anything to worry about, sister! I like Kell. I really like him, but he's not my type."

"He's not your type." Sprite echoed.

"No! And you know what? He kept looking at you all evening. He was very dashing and courteous, a perfect gentleman, but I could tell he was more interested in you."

"He was?" Sprite felt her heart leap.

"Yes," Addison paused dramatically, "he was. So you don't have anything to worry about and hopefully no other reason to avoid me." The two girls giggled, their bond of friendship drawn tighter.

* * *

Spif stepped out of a clothing shop in the commercial section of Copernicus Base. It felt good to be in new clothes. He was a man who put a high value on his appearance, and the clothing provided by Raven and her crew had not come up to his standards. He was glad to dispose of the ill-fitting hand-me-downs.

He walked southward toward the Base Commons, thoughts of a good meal and a pretty woman filling his mind. He emerged from the connecting passageway and paused to enjoy the light which filtered in through the aluminum-silicate glass panels of the massive dome. A play area was tucked into the edge of the grand gardens with swings and slides and a dozen more of the usual playground accoutrements.

A gaggle of children was squealing with delight, rushing back and forth on the soft rubberized pad that covered the hard concrete flooring. Little boys tussled with one another for the top spot on a jungle gym. A little girl peered at Spif from the bubble window of a tree house nestled in the branches of a metallic oak. Still more children were riding teeter-totters and fussing with toys in a sandbox.

Spif didn't care much for children, but he enjoyed watching the young women who were with them. He found an unoccupied bench and wiped his hand across the seat before sitting down. A young woman with brownish hair caught his eye. She was pushing a small boy on one of the swings. Her arms were raised up, grasping the chains. Spif sighed at the sight of her bosom. He had been in space for almost eight months and was hungry for sex. Some mixed-gender smuggling crews were famous for their endless sexual escapades during long space flights, but Spif's crew wasn't one of them. Although Ice wore liquid clothing, or nothing at all, she was an unapproachable warrior-woman. She never shared her body with anyone, male or female. Nixie was young and attractive in a tomboyish way, but she had a streak of modesty that ran counter to her bawdy language. While Ice was stoic and withdrawn, Nixie was burdened and sexually aloof.

Spif's attention shifted to a woman with copper-colored hair, who was strolling slowly near the playground. She moved like a cat, and Spif appreciated her hips. He undressed her in his mind, imagining the ecstasy they could share in front of a synthetic fireplace on a soft gel-mat. The woman was walking away from him, and Spif was disappointed that he could not catch her eye. He felt a burning urge to woo her with his new clothes and good looks.

The woman, oblivious to Spif's scrutiny, scanned the mass of children and adults in the playground. A young girl with dark hair had separated from the group and was lurking behind a stand of short, bushy pine trees, which skirted the inbound edge of the play-space. The woman saw her and adjusted her step, intercepting the child where they could not be seen by the others in the playground.

Spif watched as the woman knelt down and spoke to the girl. Then, in a single fluid motion, the woman swept the child off her feet. With an arm wrapped around the girl's waist and her hand over her mouth, the copper-haired woman carried the squirming child behind the trees. The two were gone in the blink of an eye.

Spif rose from the bench to follow them, his attention more on the voluptuous woman than on the welfare of the child. He had made love before in the dense foliage of the Base Commons, and the memory of it stirred in his loins. Spif never did his best thinking when his libido was in command. As he weighed his odds at getting lucky with the copper-haired woman, his body took over from his brain on several levels, and he began to follow the woman into the garden glade.

Spif did not notice the two powerful men who had come up behind him. He took two steps toward the trees, and they grabbed him by the arms, tearing a shoulder seam in his new shirt. Spif winced in pain, momentarily disoriented.

"What in hell are you guys doing?" Spif demanded.

"Our boss wants to talk to you," one of them said with a gravelly voice.

"Take your hands off me!" The men ignored him, gripping his arms even tighter.

"Don't give us any trouble," the talkative thug grumbled. All thoughts of the copper-haired woman were swept from Spif's mind as the men led him out of the Base Commons.

* * *

The original design of the Cuss had called for a Base Garden, which still occupied the northwest corner of the base, and the Old Commons which once served as the center of commerce. The latter still hosted a small green area with real grass and foliage. An orrery was suspended in the circular dome, the mechanical device reproducing the orbits of the planets. A large glowing sphere representing the sun hung in the center, with a statue of the astronomer Nicolaus Copernicus standing in the middle of the green area directly beneath it.

After the new Base Commons was added to the Cuss in the mid twenty-second century, its older counterpart was re-purposed to serve the needs of the upper-crust of Copernican society. A luxury hotel was built into one of the smaller satellite domes, and the Old Commons became the home to a score of trendy cafes, whose dining areas spilled out into the green area. There, the well-to-do often sat, drinking their coffee under the verdant canopy of trees and discussing the weighty concerns of the day.

Remson Burke took a sip of his hazelnut mocha latte, allowing the warmth of the cup to permeate the palm of his hand. The sounds of artificial tropical birds filled the air, along with the gentle murmur of a brook that was nestled beneath the feet of the statue in the center of the dome. Pierrè Antoine sat across from him, a glass of red wine in his fist.

Burke gestured toward a waitress with his cup. She nodded and promptly refilled his coffee. Pierre admired the young woman, but she ignored him. He began to reach for her, but Burke stopped him. "This isn't The District, Pierre. We are more dignified here."

Pierre shrugged, a wicked smile on his face. His eyes followed the young woman as she made her rounds among her customers. "She's a fresh one," he murmured, his words full of desire. "I could make a lot of money with her."

"She's the daughter of a security officer."

"You know her, Rem?"

"I'm one of her regular customers."

Pierre gave Burke a lascivious glance.

"Not that kind of customer, you pervert! I take my morning coffee here almost every day."

Pierre chuckled silently, enjoying his insinuation.

Burke took another sip of coffee. "When will the shipment be ready?"

"We are picking up our last item as we speak." Pierre raised his glass. "Your customer is going to be very pleased. We have filled our hold with very fine stock."

"So you will be ready to depart soon."

"Within a day or so..."

"I'll want to inspect the product before you leave."

Pierre grimaced. "So you said before. We will be delighted to have you. You can even take a taste, if you like."

"That's not the deal, Pierre! My client wants unused goods. Is that clear?"

"Sure, sure. I get it. Clean and fresh, all the way." Pierre spread his hands.

"I know it's a long trip to Rinker's Knot. You better get a few companions from the District to provide entertainment along the way. My shipment has to be off limits. Otherwise, the deal is off."

"You got it, Rem." Secretly, Pierre wasn't about to spend any of his profit on traveling prostitutes. His men would skim off the top of the cargo and frighten the girls into keeping their mouths shut. After all, they were his property until Burke's man took delivery.

Burke studied Pierre from across the table. The man didn't belong in a fine cafe. It was a place for leaders like himself, not men of Pierre's ilk, who got their hands dirty. He knew full well that Pierre's crew would sample the merchandise, but he had done his due diligence. Now he could tell his client that he had done his part in insuring the purity of the shipment, and he would be telling the truth. A thought struck him. It was a moment of inspiration, and Burke could not hide his epiphany.

"What is it?" Pierre asked.

Burke placed his coffee cup gently on the table. "There's one more favor I'd like to ask, and it will be of mutual benefit to us both."

Pierre smiled broadly. He enjoyed granting favors. They put others in his debt, which was always a good thing. "What do you need?"

"I am in the process of securing one more package. I have orders from Meridian to dispose of it."

"I don't care too much for Meridian." A shadow crossed Pierre's face.

Remson laughed. "There's nothing to worry about. My instructions come from the very top. Do you understand me?"

"The very top?"

"No one higher."

"And you need this package to disappear."

"Without any trace. Your crew can have as much fun with her as they like. That should solve their hunger for entertainment on the way to the Knot. Just make sure the body is jettisoned into the void before you arrive."

"Sounds easy enough." Pierre was licking his lips in anticipation. "Does the package have a name?"

"She's a small-time smuggler. Her name is Nixie Drake."

Pierre Antoine's eyes narrowed. "How old is she?"

"About seventeen. She helped some people a few years ago and made some powerful enemies. You heard of her?"

"The name rings a bell." Pierre hadn't heard the name for a long, long time. Granting Remson's favor was going to be a pleasure.

Burke's comlink whispered in his ear. He tipped his head. "Hold on for a minute," he hissed at Pierre. He listened to the voice in his ear bud, a smile forming on his lips. "Very good. Take him to the place. I'll meet you there." Burke took a big gulp of coffee. "That was good news," he said smugly. "We are one step closer to getting Ms. Drake. I'll contact you when we have her."

"I can't wait," Pierre purred.

* * *

Nixie emerged from the service tunnels beneath Copernicus Base. She slipped through a grating near the Old Commons and walked stealthily toward a small stand of trees, which flanked the statue of Nicholas Copernicus. She paused behind a low-hanging branch and surveyed the people who were meandering through the public space.

A slender woman with a fresh coat of liquid clothing was strolling effortlessly on the other side of the dome. It was Ice. Nixie surmised that she had emerged from one of the cafes lining the perimeter of the dome. Nixie felt the urge to join her, when she suddenly remembered the gum wrapper she had found outside her lair. It had come from a stick of Fruity-Juice gum, Ice's favorite. Was Ice up to something? Nixie felt a wave of anxiety fill her chest. Something wasn't right. Her survival instincts kicked in, and she stooped down, tracking behind the tree branches to make sure Ice could not see her. Nixie looked more closely at the woman. Her hand was to her ear, and her lips were moving, obviously engaged with someone on her comlink. Ice disappeared from view, and Nixie sighed with relief. She found solace in being alone. Trusting people didn't come easily for her, and the breakup of her crew had reinforced her desire for self-reliance. She straightened up and looked back toward the cafes, feeling hungry. She knew one of the cooks who would give her a meal.

A man emerged from behind a tall bush. He was following the same path Ice had just taken. Nixie shuttered at the sight of him. It was Remson Burke. She stooped down again, this time pressing herself into the low branches of the tree. Her eyes were locked on the man. He seemed happy, as if he had just heard some good news. Nixie wondered if there was some connection between Ice and Burke. What were the odds of seeing the two of them at the same time? Was Ice working for Burke? Nixie hardly breathed until Burke disappeared from view, then she slipped away cautiously. She was no longer the smuggler with a ship of her own. Once again, she was a lonely beggar filled with paranoia and dread, a child of the corridors, whose wits were her only comfort.

CHAPTER TEN

A filthy black bag was pulled over Spif's head. His hands and feet were bound, and he was taken to a dark place that stank of blood and decaying flesh. Spif remembered finding a dead mouse in the hold of the Raccoon. The musty odor had been unpleasant, but the present stench was much worse. Spif's stomach convulsed. He tasted bile. A dribble of vomit erupted from his lips, staining his new shirt.

Spif was thrust into a chair; his hands jabbed him in the back. Someone ripped the sack from his head. A frayed edge caught one of his ears, ripping the lobe and drawing blood. Two very serious men towered over him. Spif looked down to the floor, not wanting to see their faces. It was then when he saw Slake's lifeless body.

Slake's throat had been cut. His corpse was naked, his hands and feet still tied by coarse brown rope. His friend's body lay in a puddle of bloody urine, an expression of terror etched on his face. Spif was startled and drew in a quick breath, the full bouquet of death accosting his nostrils. He pulled at his restraints as what remained in his stomach rose up in his throat, and then he vomited all over his new pants.

Remson Burke stepped into the room, holding a white handkerchief to his face. He stepped carefully to avoid the blood and waste. He glanced at the corpse before turning to Spif. "Your friend wasn't cooperative," he began. "I asked him a simple question, and he failed to comprehend the consequences of resisting me." Burke waited, allowing his words to have their desired effect. Spif's eyes were locked on his crewmate's swollen cadaver. "If you want to live, you will give me the information I require." Spif continued to stare at Slake's body. "Spif!" Burke shouted. "Look at me!"

Spif was shaking uncontrollably. His chin came up, and he gave Burke a cowering look. "Yessir," he mumbled.

"Where is Nixie Drake?"

Spif's mind was in overdrive as he measured the harsh reality set before him. Although he was angry with Nixie for deceiving him, he had no desire to harm her. Nevertheless, sitting before Slake's bloodied corpse drove home the consequences of the decision which now confronted him. It was his life or Nixie's. Spif found the choice easy.

"I can get her for you," he managed.

One of the men raised his fist, ready to strike Spif. Burke shook his head, and the man relaxed. "And how would you propose to do that?"

"I can get word to her. She'll meet me, and then you can have her. Just don't kill me."

Burke smiled. "You are a wise man, Mr. Spif. Set up the meeting and let me know when and where it will be. If you play your cards right, this will all be a passing nightmare." He gestured toward Slake's body. "If you try to run, I will find you, and you will join your friend in hell."

* * *

Ice sat quietly in the automated surface transport, watching the bleak terrain of Mare Insularum inch past the viewports. She had dialed in the latitude and longitude of her destination by heart and was letting the onboard AI navigate around the occasional obstacles that appeared in her path. The small vehicle lumbered past a cylindrical structure. Ice stared at it intently, making out a lone figure in an e-suit. The person was a surface scratcher, a miner who harvested thorium from the lunar seas surrounding Copernicus Crater.

It was fitting that this place was called Mare Insularum, the Sea of Islands. The lunar plane had an over-abundance of tiny, isolated settlements occupied by stanch loners and individualists. Each man and woman was an island. It was a hard life, filled with risk and disaster. If a surface scratcher succeeded with Thor, the ungodly side effects of radiation exposure would surely collect their toll sooner or later. The men and women like the one who toiled anonymously outside Ice's viewport eked out their livings with no illusions. Life was a desperate struggle with little or no reward, except the hope of a better life for one's offspring.

Ice felt a faint quiver of discomfort. She had been told never to return to this place. She had watched her father and mother scramble for survival when Meridian had shunned them, leaving them to die beyond the comfort and safety of the Cuss. She remembered their difficult journey to an abandoned habitat, the desperate early days when survival had been their only goal. She had helped her dad mine Thor long before she knew what she was doing.

It had been a great and fearful day when her mother had put a tattered bag in her daughter's hand and sent her to live with an old friend. Ice had looked in the bag and found everything of value that her parents possessed. They had left nothing for themselves, so great was their desire to send their beloved away from the hellish life they had to endure. Ice was told to forget them, to wipe the coordinates of the little concrete dome from her memory, but she could not. And now she was returning, a homecoming that would signify a failure to those who had desired much more for the child they loved beyond measure.

The vehicle crested a small rise. Beyond it was a tiny concrete pustule, nestled in the vast wasteland of Mare Insularum. There were no signs of life around the dome, only a dilapidated shed housing a broken-down lunar-plow and a small funereal mound a hundred meters to the north of the habitat. The sun was baking the surface, making exterior work almost impossible without a well-insulated e-suit. Ice knew her father couldn't afford such a luxury.

The surface transport trundled to a stop outside the dome, a scant five meters from the airlock. Ice fastened the seal on her helmet and powered up her suit's environment system. She dismissed her misgivings and decompressed the cabin. Within a few moments, she was inside the airlock.

A chime rattled through a broken speaker, announcing the equalization of lock pressure with the interior atmosphere of the dome. Ice pulled off her helmet and unslung the life-support system. The inner door swung open on squeaky hinges, and a gaunt man with the face of a skeleton stood before her. His eyes were tired, but his face was like flint. His grin was a thin line on dried lips. He spread his arms wide, and Ice could hear his shoulders pop. "Welcome home, girl," he said softly.

* * *

Nixie breathed a sigh of relief when she finally entered the immense Base Supply dome. She had returned to the service tunnels under the base to get there and had taken her time, doubling back several times to insure no one was following her. When she emerged in the supply center, she kept her head down to avoid the security cameras. She wove her way through the seemingly endless aisles of crates and shelves.

The AI, which monitored the warehouses, seldom flagged lone individuals. Workers came and went all the time. Security at Base Supply was focused on inventory, not people. Every item in the vast stores was impregnated with a smart tag, allowing the comp system to track its location to within a few centimeters. Everything was checked in and out meticulously, making theft very difficult.

There was, of course, a black-market supply business. Not everything on the shelves was tagged. Hidden among the millions of items was contraband, tracked with equal care in a separate, stand-alone database. The Meridian supply comp didn't know about what came and went under the table. Nixie had been part of this "unofficial" supply business for years, ferrying illicit goods from base to base and beyond.

Robert Mann was an appropriator at Base Supply. He had been Nixie's first customer, and the two had become fast friends over the years. If Momma Kate was her surrogate mother, he was her kindly uncle. The Delta V and her hidden lair were no longer safe, so Nixie gravitated to "Uncle Bob." She found him sipping a cup of hot brew in his tiny office. The place looked like a junkyard, but it was a disaster by design. Stacks of comps and spare parts littered the floor, and his desk was awash in synthetic paper and bottles of spray cleaner.

"Hey, Unka Bobbo. Sluff-a-duffing, I seezy-wheezy."

Robert jumped, spilling his drink on the desk. "Whoa! Nixie! Don't surprise me like that!" He grabbed a handful of invoices and wiped up the mess. "I just cleaned my office." Nixie ignored her friend's attempt at humor and plopped herself down in a molded plastic chair next to the desk. "You are in one pile of do-do, kid." Robert spun around in his swivel chair and grabbed a bottle and a pair of shot glasses from a shelf behind him. "This calls for something stronger than coffee," he announced as he poured two fingers of amber liquid into each glass.

Nixie took a swig, enjoying the liquid fire as it coursed down her throat. The drink took the edge off her fear. "I's dumped as a rump-on-a-stump, Bobbo."

"Sorry to hear about *The Raccoon*. She was a good ship."

"Shad her moments, but she flewy truee."

"I hear Remson Burke's men are asking around for you."

"Yupper." Nixie finished her drink and presented the empty glass to her friend for another shot. "Lost his biggy-blue fancy flight-case with secrets in it. Wants Nix's butt in a sling-shot."

"It's more than that, Nix." Robert glanced at the door to his office and gestured for Nixie to close it. She did so. "I hear that Burke has been told to make you go away. The explosion on *The 'Coon* was no accident."

"Momma Kate is thinkin'-dinkin' the sames as you." Nixie shook her head.

"My sources are quite good." Robert handed the glass back to her. "Seen Spif around?"

"He's gots a painus in the anus 'bouts me. The whole crewy is screwy. Wheeze busted up."

Robert considered Nixie's words carefully and then put down his glass, clicking it loudly on the desktop. "He's looking for you, Nix. I saw Spif a little while ago, and he told me he wants to apologize."

Nixie was crestfallen. "Spiffer all 'poligetic?"

"That's what he said."

"Nosey wheres I's can fine-diner him?"

"No, but I think I can get a message to him."

Nixie squirmed in her chair. She looked up at the ceiling, trying to decide on her next move. "Okee-dokey, smokey," she said finally.

"Tells him twos meets meezy ats the Oxy Farm tomorrow ats oh ten-hunnered."

* * *

Amos Cross stood next to a stone altar. It looked like something from Stonehenge. Virtual reports were strewn across its surface. Cross had programmed his office to resemble a medieval castle, complete with harsh stone walls and musty tapestries. A huge fireplace stood solemnly against one wall, with an immense inferno blazing within it. The office windows, which normally revealed the sprawling Jackson Base, now displayed pastoral scenes from an old English countryside.

Cross was waiting for his new assistant to respond to his summons. He wasn't used to waiting and was becoming more agitated with each passing moment. Finally, a faint chime resonated in the Spartan chamber, and Meredith Frank appeared. She paused, disoriented by the primitive decor.

"It's about time!" Cross thundered. "When I call for you, I expect you here without delay!"

The rebuke snapped Meredith back to reality. She took a breath and strode across the office, her shoes clicking loudly on the cold stone slabs beneath her feet. Her hair was coiffed in the latest professional style. Her carmine suit was tailored to her slender frame and looked brand new. Her shoes were dark, with hints of gold banding across the toes. It was obvious that she had tended to every detail of her appearance.

"I'm sorry, Mr. Cross. It won't happen again."

Cross wasn't satisfied. "What took you so long?"

"I was in the bathroom, sir."

"And what were you doing in there?"

The question caught Meredith by surprise. "What was I doing, sir?"

"That's what I asked you."

"I was using the bathroom."

"Specifically, Ms. Frank. What were you doing in the bathroom?"

Meredith blushed. She had never been asked to report on such personal activities. "I, I was sitting down, sir." She prayed that Cross wouldn't ask her to elaborate.

"If you want to remain in your position, Ms. Frank, you will learn to spend less time in the lady's room." Cross glared at her, daring her to question his statement. As outrageous as it was, Meredith remained silent. "Has Remson Burke reported in?"

"No, sir."

"I want you to track him down. I want to know if he has found Nixie Drake." Cross pounded the stone altar. The holo-system emitted an ominous sound, like a hammer hitting a slab of granite. "Tell him to contact me immediately!"

"Yes, sir." Meredith began to shake, but she used all of her strength to steady herself, refusing to let the great man see her nervousness. "Is there anything else, Mr. Cross?"

"There is." Cross stepped out from behind the stone table. Meredith cowered as he approached her, unsure of what he would do next. "I am astonished by your feeble attempts at professionalism, Ms. Frank. I couldn't help but notice your nails. They offend me. Don't you know enough to have them manicured? A little polish would help, too. How can I have an executive assistant who doesn't know how to look presentable?"

"I'll try harder, sir." Meredith stared at the flagstones in the virtual floor. She wanted her job, and she wanted desperately to make her boss happy. She was like a moth drawn to a candle. She was mesmerized by Amos Cross, drawn to him by some inexorable force, but her individuality was evaporating in the flames of his criticism.

"See that you do," Ms. Frank. Cross turned his back without dismissing her. The meeting was over.

* * *

The interior of Jacob and Katherine Karlsen's tiny dome was a single colorless room, its furnishings worn from years of use. One quadrant of the circular enclosure was littered with tools and nondescript apparatus. Another was adorned with a small flat-screen and a couple of tattered chairs. Two beds occupied a sleeping area, with two chests of drawers, their tops cluttered with toiletries and the minutia of life. A kitchen of sorts completed the domestic tableau, with a wave oven and refrigerator. An empty aluminum sink punctuated a worn countertop, a rack of dishes by its side. A small table with four chairs stood within reaching distance of everything. The entire place reeked of hopelessness and neglect, save the dishes and the kitchen counter. It was as if the inhabitants had given up, resigning themselves to the necessities of living without any signs of self-respect or care.

Ice sat at the kitchen table in the chair she had always occupied as a little girl. She wore a thin jumpsuit, in deference to her parents' sensibilities. They did not know of her penchant for nudity. Ice looked at the empty chair across from her. Ever since her twin sister Holly had died, Ice hadn't liked anything covering her body. She disliked blankets and coats. She had always hated the coarse garments her mother had made for her. They never fit, and the cloth chafed her skin uncomfortably. She preferred liquid clothing because it seemed a part of her body. It was also much easier to pack, and Ice liked traveling light.

When Ice left her parents' home, her only passion had been to become a warrior. She enlisted in the Terran Special Forces and underwent rigorous physical conditioning. She excelled, becoming a member of an elite team. TSF troops were groomed for battle. Although they were taught to use all kinds of military hardware, they were programmed to rely solely on their bodies and minds. To that end, Ice spent years of training in the neo-gymnasia, where men and women spent months in the nude, becoming desensitized to sexuality and emotion. She had found a home there, learning to face her enemies with nothing but her wits and her raw physicality.

Katherine Karlsen poured three cups of day-old coffee from an old porcelain pot and placed them on the kitchen table. Then she pulled a basket out of the wave oven and offered it to Ice with a wan smile. Inside it were three toasted biscuits. Ice accepted the food and looked into her mother's face. Her eyes were sunken, and her hair was thinning, giving her the appearance of someone who had recently undergone cancer treatment. She was a pale woman who looked perpetually undernourished. Ice could tell the woman was in pain, but she also knew her mother would never complain. She had never heard the woman complain about anything.

Ice took one of the biscuits and handed the basket to her father. Jacob Karlsen sat stoically on her right, his back bowed from hard work, his hands twisted from wrestling levers and wrenches. The index finger on his left hand was bent at least thirty degrees, the result of a broken bone that was never set properly. He gave Ice an almost imperceptible nod as he took one of the biscuits. Ice set the basket down in front of her mother. Only then did the woman retrieve the last one for herself.

They ate in silence, because that was the way Ice's family had always been. They were a stoic lot, not accustomed to idle chatter. Although they had been separated for a long time, there was no small talk about the intervening years since their last meal together.

Ice put the last piece of her biscuit in her mouth and washed it down with the rest of her coffee. She knew it was the only meal they would eat that day. Ice's mother stirred in her chair; half a biscuit still lay on the plate in front of her. Her fingers trembled around her coffee cup as she lowered it to the table. "Good to see you, child," she murmured. She withdrew into herself, her five affectionate words left hanging in the silence.

* * *

Nixie arrived at the Oxy Farm an hour before her meeting with Spif. The sprawling complex dwarfed even the large dome over the Base Commons. Copernicus Base's Ice Mine had been established over one hundred years earlier and fed an immense photo-oxidation farm, which melted the ice for drinking water and electrically divided the water into oxygen and hydrogen for breathable atmosphere and fuel. Two massive storage chambers held the harvested gasses.

Nixie stood watch behind a large pump housing. She was on edge. It wasn't like Spif to offer apologies, and her sixth sense was tweaked by his uncharacteristic behavior. A steady stream of automated carts laden with large chunks of ice entered from the service tunnel, which led from the mine. Workers scurried about, tending to various machines as the ice was deposited into gigantic vats for melting. Nothing seemed out of the ordinary.

Spif arrived shortly before ten o'clock. He wandered into the complex alone. Nixie watched as he lingered in the open. He was a man obviously searching for someone, his eyes scanning every person as he slowly turned on his heel. She let him grow uncomfortable. She wanted to make him pay for the terrible things he had said. After a few more minutes, she could tell Spif was exasperated.

Nixie emerged from her hiding place and walked slowly toward her former crewmate. Spif's back was turned, and he didn't see her at first. She glanced at the workers around them. No one was paying attention to them. Spif practically jumped out of his shoes when Nixie tapped him on the shoulder.

"Where did you come from?" he gasped. "Scared me half to death!" Spif laughed nervously. "I thought you were going to stand me up."

"Noper-doper, Spiffy," she shot back. "I makes my 'pointments." Nixie noticed something in Spif's eyes. He was particularly apprehensive. "Unka Bobo says you wants to 'pologize."

Spif hesitated for a fraction of a second, enough to signal his deceit. Nixie frowned, her eyes narrowing. "Ain't no 'pology comin' my way, is there, Spiffy?" Nixie heard a sound from behind her. She started to turn as two men grabbed her arms. She struggled but was no match for them. They hustled her behind a massive machine, out of sight from the workers.

Spif shook his head slowly. "Sorry, Nix. I had no choice." She gave him a hateful look.

"He's telling you the truth." It was a familiar voice. Remson Burke circled around her, a wide grin on his face. "He didn't have a choice, so don't blame him. When he saw what happened to Slake, he realized the futility of resisting me."

"Whats 'bouts Slakee?" Nixie hissed. Spif diverted his gaze, unable to look her in the eyes. "Spiffee? What the duck's up with Slakee?"

Spif shook his head. "He's dead, Nix. They were going to do the same to me if I didn't help them."

"You dumb-ass dodo! They's still gots ya and meeze twosome. You're doornail-dead too!"

Spif suddenly realized the truth in Nixie's words. He pivoted angrily toward Burke. "No! We made a deal!"

"Relax, Mr. Spif. You will be rewarded for your part in this."

A look of confusion spread across Spif's face, and he started to reply, when a woman with copper-colored hair appeared behind his nemesis. Two mean-looking men accompanied her. She stepped in front of Nixie, dissecting her with her eyes. "This the one Pierre told me about?" she asked Burke.

Burke nodded. "One and the same. The great Nixie Drake. I hope you and your crew enjoy her on your way to Rinker's Knot."

"We will," she replied enthusiastically. "It's a long trip." Burke's men dragged Nixie over to the other pair of thugs. Spif stood by, his face flush with shame. Nixie pulled one arm free and pounded the face of one of her captors. "Run Spiffy!" she shouted. Spif didn't hesitate. He turned and ran as fast as he could from the Oxy Farm.

The man Nixie had struck cursed at her and brought his fist down on her head like a sledgehammer. She fell to her knees, dazed. "Little bitch!" the man hissed as he handed her off to the other men.

"Make sure she disappears," Burke told the copper-haired woman.

Nixie felt a pinch in her arm. She turned quickly and saw the hypodermic needle. Her vision blurred, and she felt her legs buckle. Strong hands gripped her. Then all feeling drifted away, and a deep fog surrounded her.

CHAPTER ELEVEN

The impressions of a thousand boot prints, silent witnesses to sacred moments and deep human pain, surrounded the mound of lunar regolith. Ice stood with her back to her parent's dome, her hands hanging helplessly at her sides. Day had passed, and she was encircled by the darkness, the crystalline stars overhead. She turned down the temperature in her e-suit, and almost immediately, the deep chill of the lunar night permeated her gloves and boots. Ice closed her eyes, allowing the falling temperature to wash over her like an avalanche of snow. She embraced the cold, daring it to overcome her, to kill her. Her teeth chattered as the frigid sensation spread to her neck and back. Then she felt the glacial enemy in her bones. The chill in her e-suit was like a slithering snake, winding itself around her body, tickling malevolently at her skin. She felt its unwelcome caress but shunned its deadly embrace.

The cold transported her to another time, to the early days of her family's exile in this god-forsaken stretch of lunar dust. She had been twelve years old when she first stepped foot inside the abandoned habitat. It was dark and frightening, the atmosphere barely breathable. There was a patina of frost on everything, and she could see her breath in the frigid air like puffs of wispy smoke. The Moon did her best to kill them, as her father scrambled to bring the habitat back to life.

The Karlsen family had not been prepared to live in such isolation, in a broken-down shanty of a dome. They had moved to their tiny oasis during the lunar night, when the surface temperature averaged minus 153 degrees Celsius. Their struggle to survive had demanded everything they could give and more. It was during their fifth sleep period when the dome's dilapidated heating system failed. They were asleep, and the temperature inside the habitat plummeted. Ice was the first one to wake. She found her twin sister Holly's frozen body lying on top of her. She had died, shielding Ice from the cold. She could still feel the awful chill of Holly's body, her lifeless eyes keeping watch over her. Ice was never the same after that. The bitter cold had not killed her, but it had frozen something deep within her soul.

Alone in her e-suit, her comlink muted, her face unseen, a single tear meandered down Ice's cheek and froze. She looked at the mound in front of her, remembering the day when she and her parents had buried Holly beneath that barren knoll. Her sister had been her friend and confidant, the only person Ice had ever trusted fully. Ice cursed the cold for taking her. She bowed her head, thanking Holly for saving her life. Then Ice increased the temperature in her e-suit and turned back toward her parents' habitat.

* * *

Kate Sloan sat near the bar, taking a load off her feet after a busy evening at the Delta V. Wimpy McGee, a grizzly old dockworker, sat across from her, sipping a Forty-Two, the tavern's most popular drink. Kate fidgeted with her napkin, twisting it unconsciously in her fingers. "Rumors have been flying all night about that incident over at the Oxy Farm," she told him.

"You talkin' about that girl bein' kidnapped?" Wimpy had wiry, unmanageable hair and four days of stubble on his pock-marked face. He was strong as an ox but gentle as a lamb. Kate had known him and his family for twenty-five years. She could name his children.

"Yeah. Some folks tell me it was Nixie." Kate picked up her glass, but her hand was shaking, and she had to put it back down.

"Nixie was taken? That's bad, Katie. That's real bad. I heard Remson Burke was there."

"Burke has been looking for her." Kate kept her suspicions about Burke's connection to *The Raccoon's* explosion to herself.

"I hear there was another group involved." Wimpy stole a glance around the tavern, making sure no one could overhear them. "Burke and his men were there, and so was Spif. Do you know him?"

Kate nodded. "He was a member of Nixie's crew before her ship blew up."

Wimpy shook his head in wonderment. "They were damned lucky. People generally don't survive explosions in space." He glanced across the barren lunar surface to the spaceport. A massive transport ship squatted on one of the pads. "Anyways, I saw Spif on the docks. He was in a big hurry; looked scared, too. He hightailed it over to where Nixie keeps her jumpship and took off."

"This was right after the abduction?"

"Must have been."

"Where do you think he was going?"

Wimpy gave Kate a sly smile. "I was curious 'cause he was so worked up and all." The old man waited.

"Tell me!"

"He went to Einstein Base."

"That's clear out on the limb, almost to the far side!"

"He's running from something."

"Or someone," Kate added, thinking of Burke again. "You were saying there was another group at the Oxy Farm?"

"Oh, yeah. Sorry." Wimpy gave her a nod and returned to the subject. "There was a woman with copper-colored hair. She and two other men, took the girl away."

Kate's heart skipped a beat. "The woman had copper-colored hair?"

"That's what I'm told."

"She's one of Pierre Antoine's people."

"Oh, shit."

Kate choked up, overwhelmed with fear. "Nixie's in a helluva lot of trouble if she's with them. They're sex traders."

"There's been a lot of kids snatched the last couple weeks." Wimpy scratched at his stubbly chin. "Antoine must be getting a big shipment ready."

Kate nodded. "I've heard of at least three abductions in the Cuss."

"There have been others. I heard about three more at Proclus Base, a couple at Plato, and even some from Earth orbit."

Kate twisted her glass. "Where do you think they're taking them?"

Wimpy shrugged. "No idea, Kate. But I'd put my money on the Ice Line."

Kate had a sinking feeling. No matter where they were going, Nixie would never make it. Cross wanted Nixie dead because she had helped the Logans return to the Moon from Rinker's Knot. Burke was one of Cross's men and had cut some sort of deal with Pierre Antoine. A pang of guilt swept through Kate. She had recruited Nixie to help Hunter Logan's family. The abduction was her fault. "We've got to do something," she whispered pleadingly.

Wimpy set his glass down on the table. "Lots of luck with that one, Katie. These are bad people. You don't want to get involved."

"I'm already involved."

Wimpy sat back in his chair, astonishment on his face. "What did you do?"

Kate shook her head. "I'm not involved in sex trafficking, you idiot! I can't tell you any details, but I feel responsible. About three years ago, I asked Nixie to help some friends of mine, and now she's paying for it."

"What are you going to do?" Wimpy gave her a concerned look.

"I think its time for me to call in Nixie's guardian angel." Wimpy was mystified. "Are you willing to take a little trip to Mare Insularum?"

"Wow, you sure know how to pick exciting destinations!" The old man shook his head. "That's a godforsaken stretch of moon-dust."

"I'll give you the coordinates. I need to get a message to Ellie Karlsen. She has to come here right away."

"Why don't you use the comlink?"

"It might not be safe."

Wimpy's eyes narrowed. He could tell Kate was deathly serious. "I'll leave right away."

Kate reached across the table and touched the old man's hand. "I owe you, Wimp. Your first drink is always free, from now on." Wimpy gave her a huge grin as he stood up and left the Delta V.

* * *

Meredith Frank was on the comlink as Remson Burke was entering his office. Amos Cross's diffident assistant told him that her boss was expecting a report on his latest assignment. Remson frowned, displeased by his superior's nagging. "Put him on!" Burke's tone was dictatorial.

"I will see if he wishes to speak with you," she replied.

Burke swore under his breath. Why wouldn't Cross want to speak with him? He was the one who wanted the report! Burke stared petulantly into the holodisplay. He could feel his anger rising. He realized it was unwise to challenge Amos Cross, so he took a long breath and tried to calm down.

Meredith Frank appeared once again. "Mr. Cross will be with you momentarily," she said. The woman was gone before Burke could reply. He pounded his desk.

Cross was frowning when he finally appeared. "Give me your report," he demanded. "Tell me the Drake woman is dead."

Remson Burke did not like lying to Amos Cross. As ruthless as he was, Cross was much worse. Nevertheless, the man seemed out of sorts, and Burke didn't want to present himself as a target for his wrath. "She's dead, sir. I'm having Pierre Antoine dispose of her body in deep space."

The great leader of Meridian Corporation smiled. "Very good. And the rest of her crew?"

Burke was caught off-guard. He should have known better, since the explosion on Drake's ship was meant to kill everyone on board. He cleared his throat nervously. "Ah, one of them is dead, sir. The other two are still at large, but we will find them."

"See that you do, Mr. Burke. I expect good news from you by the end of the week."

Cross's face winked out in the holodisplay, and the comlink was severed. Burke's heart was racing. He pulled a bottle from his desk drawer and poured himself a drink. Then he summoned his henchmen.

Moments later, the alcohol had taken the edge off Remson Burke's anxiety attack. The two men who had accompanied him to the Oxy Farm were standing before him. "Do we have any idea where Spif went?" he began. One of the men told him that Spif had departed for Einstein Base shortly after his escape. "He's a loose end. I want you to find him. Make him disappear." The men nodded enthusiastically. It was the kind of work they enjoyed.

"There's one person left." Burke ran his fingers through his hair. "Her name is Ice. She's some kind of Amazonian nymphomaniac. You can't miss her. She doesn't wear clothes." The two men grinned broadly. One of them gestured toward his crotch. Burke shook his head. "None of that, Frank. Just find her and kill her. I want them both taken care of right away." The men nodded and left the office. Burke's chest ached as his anxiety returned. He pulled out the bottle again and poured himself another drink.

* * *

Wimpy McGee piloted his borrowed jumpship low over the lunar landscape. His destination was a little over three hundred kilometers from the Cuss, a short trip for the speedy little craft. The nav-AI gave a proximity warning, and at once he saw the old dome. "What a dump," he muttered. He took manual control of the jumpship and settled down near the airlock.

If the Karlsens were surprised to have a visitor, they didn't show it. Wimpy pulled off his helmet and stuck out his hand. "You the Karlsens?" he asked warmly.

"Maybe," the man replied.

Wimpy was familiar with the stanch reticence of surface scratchers. Thorium mining was not for soft and squishy folks. He smiled disarmingly. "I'm a friend of Kate Sloan's." The older of the two women nodded. "She sent me out here to find Ellie Karlsen. Is that one of you?"

Ice stepped forward. "That's me," she offered.

Wimpy shook her hand eagerly. "Great! Kate wants you to come back to the Cuss with me. It's about Nixie Drake." Ice stepped over to her e-suit without saying a word and started to put it on.

* * *

Nathan Trent was in his early thirties, a small-framed, expressionless man with a muscular body and steel-gray eyes. He was a member of the Terran Special Forces, on leave after three years of brutal training. Trent was on board *The Martian Princess*, a modest passenger ship that was about to leave lunar orbit. He was going to Mars, where he would visit his brother at Aonia Terra.

Trent scanned the other people in his compartment, reflexively making a threat assessment of his surroundings. Nathan was always on alert, even when he appeared at ease. The element of surprise was the enemy's greatest weapon. Constant vigilance was a trooper's best defense. He leaned down and touched his go-bag. It was situated between his feet, always within reach. Hidden within its unassuming folds was his pulse-pistol, chemical heaters, a small oxy-mask, and four compression grenades.

Trent was one of a special breed. He had been conditioned mercilessly until he was in top physical shape. Highly intelligent, he had a mental toughness that was practically unshakable. He excelled in hand-to-hand combat in all gravitational environments, and was a master of improvisation. He could take a handful of innocuous items and turn them into a lethal weapon.

To the casual observer, Nathan Trent was just another sleepy businessman. His head was tipped back against his seat's head-cushion. His eyes appeared to be closed. No one fathomed his thoughts or knew of his substantial abilities. Children squealed as *The Martian Princess* came to life, her main engine accelerating her smoothly to lunar escape velocity. Nathan took note of the g-force; the ship's power plant was functioning correctly. He stole another glance at the woman seated next to him and then slipped into a shallow sleep, ready to respond at any sign of danger.

* * *

Wimpy McGee settled the jumpship expertly on one of the outlying pads at the Copernicus spaceport. Ice sat silently in the copilot's seat, intent upon the ground transport vehicle which lumbered toward them. The old man had called ahead for it, but Ice was still wary. She unlatched her harness and swiveled out of the seat. Wimpy glanced at her out of the corner of his eye, appreciating her slender form.

Ice waited by the hatch, listening to the clanking sounds as the transport soft-docked and then secured itself to the side of the jumpship. She could hear the hissing of air as the coupling pressurized. Wimpy had powered down the ship and joined her as Ice swung the hatch open. Kate Sloan stood in the threshold.

"Sorry to cut your vacation short, Ellie." Kate Sloan was the only person beside her parents who used that name. "We've got a problem." Kate boarded the jumpship, then turned back toward the transport. "Mike? I'll be a few minutes. Just hang tight."

"Sure thing, Kate," said a disembodied voice from beyond the docking collar.

Kate swung the hatch closed. "Let's have a seat, shall we?"

The three settled into the jumpship's passenger cabin. "First thing's first. Were you hurt when *The Raccoon* exploded?" Kate asked softly.

Ice shook her head, and Kate smiled. "Good! I was so worried about you and Nixie. Ever since your mother asked me to take you in, I have felt responsible for you. I know you've been trained in the special forces, but mothers still worry, you know?" Kate patted Ice's knee. "When I asked you to join Nixie's crew and watch over her, I never imagined I would be putting your life in danger." A tear traced its way down the older woman's face. Ice stared at Kate intently, gripping every word. "Did Wimpy tell you what has happened?"

"You told me not to, Kate." The man gestured apologetically to Ice. "Sorry, Ellie."

"It's Ice," she corrected him. Then she turned to Kate, "What's happened?"

Kate told Ice about her visit with Remson Burke's man Rattler and the reports of Nixie's abduction. Her voice trembled as she mentioned Burke's connection with Pierre Antoine's sex trafficking ring.

Ice's eyes narrowed when the older woman told her about Spif being seen at the abduction and his sudden departure for Einstein Base. "Where did they take her?" Ice asked. Her voice was hard, businesslike.

"We don't know," Kate sighed, "but Spif might." She turned to Wimpy. Could you take Ice to Einstein Base?"

"Sure thing, Kate." The old dockworker turned to Ice. "When do you want to leave?"

Ice slid back into the copilot's seat. "Now," she said.

* * *

Stephen and Rene Winter were not religious people, but they prayed daily for their missing daughter. Molly was their first thought every morning and their last every night. And it was the thought of her that made it impossible to sleep. The couple lay together in their bed, wrapped in a blanket of silence. Stephen reached out and grasped Rene's hand. It was ice cold. He cleared his throat. The sound echoed in the bed chamber.

"I wonder where she is?" he asked for the millionth time.

Rene squeezed his hand. "I had a dream last night," she whispered. "I dreamt that a great bird flew to a far-off island. Molly was there, marooned on the beach. The bird swooped down, and she climbed up on its back."

Stephen sat up in the bed. The Moon hung low in the sky over Cayuga Lake, and its cool light shimmered on the waters. "Did the bird bring her back to us?" he asked wistfully.

"I don't know," she replied. "I woke up, and the dream was gone."

* * *

Nixie slowly came to her senses, the blackness surrounding her pierced by a foggy light, which resolved into a nondescript cabin. She felt like someone was pounding rocks in her head. Harsh tingling was marking the return of sensation in her hands and feet. She was lying on an examining table. She could tell it was a shipboard infirmary. There was a pungent odor, but she wasn't sure what it was. There were people near her. She coughed and tried to sit up, only to find her hands strapped to the sides of the table.

"She's coming around." It was a woman's voice. Nixie looked in the direction of the sound. She saw a flash of copper-colored hair, and then the woman's face came into focus. She had cold eyes and chiseled features. Nixie had seen her somewhere before.

"Did you have a nice sleep, Miss Drake?" The woman did something to the table, and the section under her back came up, bring her to a sitting position. Nixie drew in a sharp breath as she looked down at her body. Someone had removed all of her clothing while she was unconscious. She blushed. A rough-looking man was in the room, and he was staring at her. She strained against her bindings in an attempt to cover herself, but she could not move. The man laughed.

"Modest, are we?" the woman cooed. "That will change."

"Let me go!" Nixie shouted.

The woman touched Nixie's shoulder with her forefinger and traced an imaginary line down her arm. "We can't do that. You belong to us now, and we have a use for you. In fact, we have many uses for you."

"I have rights!" Nixie squealed.

"No, you don't." The woman grinned sardonically. "You are no longer a person. You are a plaything, an accessory. You only exist for our pleasure. The quicker you accept that, the better it will be for you."

The man ran his hand up Nixie's leg, and she shuttered violently. "No!"

"Oh, yes," he said malevolently. Nixie clamped her eyes shut, retreating into herself. His fingers were at her knee, then her thigh. Dark memories of her father flooded into her mind as she jerked at her bindings again.

CHAPTER TWELVE

Ice had been to Einstein Base many times and knew that Spif would likely be in one of the bars in the red-light district. She didn't find him at first, but luck was with her when she scanned the clientele of the fourth drinking hole. It was a dark, low-class place. The bar surrounded an elevated platform in the center of the room, which was decorated with a couple of artificial palm trees. An exotic dancer gyrated emotionlessly around the faux oasis, halfheartedly wooing the bleary-eyed men who stared at her through the bottles that lined the edge of the platform. Ice caught sight of Spif, hunched over a drink on the far side of the dance floor.

She circumnavigated the bar and settled down on the stool next to her old crewmate. Spif pivoted his head toward her and then practically fell off his chair in surprise. "What in hell are you doing here?" his voice was thick with intoxication. "Go away!"

Ice held her ground. She had always found Spif an irrelevant twit. The man had some skills, but he posed no threat to her, especially in his present state. "What happened with Remson Burke?" she asked coldly.

Spif stumbled to his feet, and Ice grabbed his arm in an iron grip. "Ouch! That hurts!" He tried to pull away from her but could not. "I'm just goin' over there." He gestured toward a booth in the back corner of the bar. "More privacy, you know?"

Ice let go of him, and Spif took his beer off the counter, slopping some of the liquid on the sticky floor. She strode ahead of him to the booth and took the seat facing into the room, enabling her to keep an eye out for anyone who wanted to eavesdrop on their conversation. Spif sat down across from her. "It wasn't my fault," he mewed pitifully. "Burke's men killed Slake." Ice's eyes narrowed, but she showed no signs of surprise or grief. "They were going to kill me too, if I didn't deliver Nixie." The man looked ruined. He finished his beer in one long pull and slammed it down on the table. "Barkeep!" he bellowed hoarsely.

"The Oxy Farm?" Ice asked.

"Yeah," Spif nodded mournfully. "She wanted to meet me there. I told Burke, and he was waiting for her."

The bartender brought Spif a fresh beer and asked Ice if she wanted one. She shook her head and waited for the man to return to the bar. Ice wasn't surprised by Spif's behavior. She had sized up the man years ago, and he was everything she had imaged him to be. He was a gutless prattler, an ugly coward in a pretty package. His betrayal of Nixie was to be expected. Ice could not elevate the man to the level of her contempt. "The copper-haired woman," Ice stated flatly.

"Now, I didn't know anything about that!" Spif replied defensively. "She was there with a couple of thugs. Burke must have made a deal with her."

"With Pierre Antoine," Ice corrected him.

Spif choked on a mouthful of beer. "Well, yeah. I guess so."

"Where did they take her?" Ice didn't like conversations, and she was growing quite weary of this one.

"I don't know!" the man pouted. "They made a move on me, and I hightailed it out of there."

"Think." Ice gave him a cold, hard stare. "Remember."

"I've been trying to forget!" he whined. Ice gripped the edge of the table and shoved it forward. It scraped across the concrete floor and cut into Spif's chest. His drink tipped over, the liquid coursing into his lap. "What did you do that for?" he shrieked. The bartender looked in their direction but did nothing.

"Remember," Ice's voice was pitched lower, threatening.

"Okay! Okay! They said something about Rinker's Knot."

"You are sure?"

Spif was running out of air. "Of course I'm sure, Ice! Stop crushing me!"

Ice let go of the table, and Spif took a deep breath. "Nixie's jumpship," she demanded quietly.

"Come on, now; Nix don't need it no more." Spif was rubbing his chest where the table had pinched him.

"I'm going to take it," Ice stated simply.

"What am I going to use?" Spif grimaced as she started to push the table toward him again. "Take it!" he surrendered. "It's in bay twenty-six at the spaceport."

Ice slid out of the booth without a word and left the bar.

* * *

Molly Winters pulled her smock tightly around her legs as she sat down on the coarse decking. Over the last few days, the conversations among the girls had dwindled, and now a hopeless silence had settled over the group. She thought of the two girls who had been taken away. They had come back lethargic and hollow-eyed. They did not speak, but cowered silently in a corner of the hold. One of the girls had blood on her leg. The sight of it had frightened Molly. The girls' removal had caused a tidal wave of fear to engulf the hostages. Their return had driven home the hardened truth of what was in store for all of them. Everyone's fear was now superseded by stark terror.

There was a sharp metal click that issued from the hatch, and a collective gasp rippled through the children. Those nearest to the large doorway scurried as far away from it as they could. Molly squeezed her knees to her chest, trying to remember the bedtime prayer her mother had taught her. She tipped her head down as the hatch opened, unable to face the obscene horror that could be waiting for her.

* * *

Remson Burke stood next to Pierre Antoine, near the hold on the slave-trader's ship, *The Cassiopeia.* "You've got the new synthetic gravity system!" Remson Burke remarked. "Very impressive."

Pierre chuckled. "One of the benefits of a lucrative business, Remson. It's a long way to the Ice Line, and it makes the trip more tolerable."

Burke's host stabbed the hatch actuator, and the large titanium panel swung open. A fetid breeze issued through the opening. Burke quickly pulled a handkerchief from his pocket and put it to his nose, grimacing from the vile odor. "Pretty ripe, Pierre!" he muttered. "I hope you clean them up before delivery."

Antoine nodded. "We're professionals, Remson. We'll prep them all for the buyer when we get close to Rinker's Knot. We've inoculated them against disease. We're feeding them on schedule. The hold is crowded, but it's warm, and there's plenty of air." Remson stepped into the hold, the cloth still at his nose. His eyes wandered from girl to girl, each in turn looking away from him. "Would you like to sample one, Remson?"

There was a muted gasp from somewhere in the hold, then a whimper. Burke walked closer to a small gaggle of children who were clinging to one another. One of them shushed her neighbor. He reached out and touched the girl's shoulder, and she stiffened. "No," Burke said finally. "I've seen enough. They're fine."

Burke was glad when the hatch closed. The ship's life-support system filtered the air quickly, removing all evidence of the foul odor. He stuffed the handkerchief back into his pocket. "What about the Drake girl?"

Antoine smiled broadly. "She's in a separate compartment. Would you like to see her?"

"Please."

Pierre gestured toward the woman with copper-colored hair, who was standing behind Remson Burke. "Star will take you to her. I have some business to attend to on the bridge." He nodded to his subordinate and then disappeared into the forward compartments of the ship.

Star gave Burke a hubristic grin. "Right this way, sir," she purred. Burke followed the woman aft. They paused in front of a hatch near the propulsion deck, and the woman pressed her thumb against a biometric sensor mounted in the jamb.

Burke wasn't prepared for what he saw. Nixie Drake was naked, and the woman named Star made no attempt to cover her. She was tied to her bunk, her face a mask of despair. Burke remembered the last time he had seen her. She had been a spitfire, a cocky, animated young smuggler. Now she was laid out like a piece of meat, more an object than a human being. Nixie blushed as he stepped to the side of her bed. She pulled half-heartedly at her restraints and then lay still. She didn't utter a sound.

"Well, Miss Drake, I wanted to wish you bon voyage," Remson offered sarcastically. "You should never have helped Hunter Logan and his family. Amos Cross doesn't take kindly to people who get in his way."

"Sticky your stick in a meaty-grinder," Nixie hissed.

Burke leaned forward, his face hovering over her tiny breasts. Then he moved closer to her face. He could see the shame in Nixie's eyes. "I have half a mind to do you with my stick right now!" he growled. Nixie cowered, pure fear blanching her complexion. "Here's what's going to happen to you, Miss Drake. You are going to service everyone who wants you on this ship. You're going to spend the next four months doing whatever they desire. Then, my friend Miss Star here is going to eject your worthless little body out into space." Nixie trembled. "You are nothing but a lump of expendable skin." Remson Burke smiled victoriously. "I want you to remember that." He poked at her breast with his index finger. "You are nothing!" Burke turned his back to her and left the cabin.

* * *

Ice found Nixie's jumpship and launched immediately. She flew almost due East, toward Copernicus Base. Within moments, she was on an encrypted comlink with Kate Sloan. "Burke's men are watching the Delta V," Kate reported. "I think they are still looking for you." Ice told her about Slake's death and Spif's accounting of the abduction. Ice could hear the guilt in the older woman's voice.

"Can we get a bearing on *The Cassiopeia*?" Ice asked coolly.

"Wimpy ought to be able to do that," Kate responded. "Hold on."

The connection grew silent as Kate made contact with the old dockworker. Ice brought the jumpship down low, scarcely three meters from the unforgiving lunar surface. The ship had no beacon and had been modified to remain invisible to standard sensors. Nevertheless, she wanted the ship to stay lost in the ground clutter. Amos Cross was behind Nixie's abduction, and her friend's life depended on Ice avoiding Meridian complications.

A few moments later, Kate's voice whispered in Ice's ear. "I've got some bad news, Ellie." Ice's lips were set in a hard thin line. She knew what Kate was going to say. "*The Cassiopeia* left orbit four hours ago. We're too late."

* * *

Nixie felt the ship's thrusters accelerate *The Cassiopeia* out of lunar orbit. She was still tied to her bunk, but mercifully, she was alone. No one was staring at her exposed body, taunting her with promises of violation and death. Nixie reached back into her memory, calling forth images and feelings surrounding her father. He had been an evil man, a danger to children, especially little girls. Somehow in her child-mind, Nixie had recognized the perilous situation she was in and had fought against him.

She remembered him climbing into her bed one night. Something in his eyes frightened her. She remembered lashing out, refusing to succumb to his desires. She remembered his anger. She could still hear his voice, cursing her in the darkened bedroom. Nixie was no match for him, but she had fought back with every ounce of her strength. She ran away that night, preferring to be on her own than abused by such a monster.

Nixie had survived by the shear force of her will. She had hidden in the Copernicus Base Commons. She had stolen food. She had tunneled into the duct system and set up her safe room. She had taught herself to read, expanding her vocabulary by listening to videos on a flat screen that she had found in a dumpster. The odds had always been against her, but she had prevailed, until now.

Only a few short weeks had gone by since the explosion on *The Raccoon*. It was like a moonquake had thundered through Nixie's life, shaking her meager foundations and shattering the things she had worked so hard to build. She had lost her beloved ship. Her crew had uncovered the myth of Captain Grit, and each of them had turned away from her. She had responded with her signature bluster and bravado, but then Spif had betrayed her to Remson Burke. Now she was strapped to a bunk, naked and alone on some sort of pirate ship.

Nixie felt the ship's engines throttling up. Lateral g-forces told her they were changing course, lifting out of orbit. She had no choice but to go where the spacecraft was taking her. It seemed a cruel metaphor. She had spent all of her life battling against things much bigger than herself, but all of her struggles hadn't changed the fact that she was still at the mercy of life's penchant for natural selection. She could kick and connive and scheme all she wanted, but she would never be in control of her destiny. She would still be a grain of sand caught in an immense gravitational field, a young woman strapped to a bunk in a spacecraft whose trajectory she could not change.

An emotional numbness settled over her, and Nixie closed her eyes. She no longer cared what happened to her. She felt no hope, no shame, no sorrow. Remson Burke was right. She was nothing.

* * *

Ice settled the jumpship down on the lunar surface near Rima Manus. She needed to think. Catching up with *The Cassiopeia* was going to be difficult, almost impossible with a jumpship. The little ship's safe operating range was limited to perhaps two million kilometers. She would have to move quickly.

At the moment, Ice had two immediate needs. She had to stock the jumpship with extra supplies, and she had to find out where *The Cassiopeia* was. The supplies weren't a problem. She knew a place where she could get extra oxygen, a portable grappling kit, and other sundry accessories she would need once she rendezvoused with the slave ship. Tracking Pierre Antoine's ship was another matter. *The Cassiopeia* would be stealthy, almost impossible to find.

A memory flashed into Ice's mind. She had been in this very same jumpship with Nixie a few years earlier. They were chasing another ship. Hunter Logan, a scientist who had developed a lethal nanobot, was trying to prevent his creation from being used against the Earth. Ice remembered Logan's daughter. The girl knew a powerful AI in the Meridian network. The AI had been able to track their foe.

Ice keyed her comlink, and Kate Sloan's worried voice filled the small cockpit. "Do you have a plan, Ellie?"

"I'm going to get her back." Ice said simply. "Do you know where I can find Sprite Logan?"

Kate hesitated. "Are you thinking she might be able to help you track Antoine's ship?"

"I am," Ice replied.

"How secure is this link?"

"It's safe," the younger woman assured her.

"Go to the Ankrum Platform at the Earth-Moon L1 point. Ask for Tyson Emerson."

* * *

Sprite Logan, a.k.a. Sprite LeRoc, whisked through the interconnecting passageways that webbed the Ankrum Platform. Kell Edwards (Emerson) had found her in her study cubby and told her that his father needed to see her right away. His voice was thick with worry. Thinking that something had happened to her parents, Sprite had checked in with Wiley/Athena, but her synthetic friends were not aware of any emergencies related to her family.

Sprite whipped through several laboratory nodes. Students looked up from their work, startled by the human projectile that was hurtling through the passageway. She grabbed a handhold outside Tyson's residence and swung to a stop, her body bouncing off the padded wall of the corridor. She pressed the door chime breathlessly, anxious to find out why Kell had been so worried.

Tyson opened the hatch and greeted her with a smile. "That was fast, Sprite! Did you run the whole way?"

"Can't run in zero-g," she gasped.

"Well, you must have almost reached escape velocity. Come on in." He gestured for her to enter the cabin.

Sprite transited across the threshold and hooked a handhold to break her velocity. She came to a stop in front of a slender woman in a thin, dark-blue jumpsuit. She looked familiar.

Tyson closed the door. "Sprite, this is Ice. I think the two of you met a few years ago."

Sprite studied the woman closely. "You were on the jumpship that took us to the Space Elevator," she said slowly. "You're Nixie Drake's friend."

Ice nodded curtly. "Yes," she said. "Nixie needs your help."

Sprite nodded enthusiastically. "Of course. You folks saved our lives."

Ice explained how Nixie was taken hostage on board *The Cassiopeia*. She asked her if her AI friend might be able to find the ship and track it. Sprite pulled her card comp from her pocket and posed the question directly to Wiley/Athena.

Sprite's synthetic friends had been hidden in the Meridian network, that is to say, the backbone of all digital services in the solar system. They had been there for three years and had become very powerful. The comp scientists who ran the network did not know of their existence. They had played a pivotal role in saving Sprite and her family from the clutches of Amos Cross and, since that time, had learned how to navigate through the immense network at will, leaving no trace of their activities.

"*The Cassiopeia* left lunar orbit twelve hours ago," Wiley/Athena began. "The ship has no beacon, but we are able to detect gravitational fluctuations caused by her passage through space. Her course is generally consistent with a transfer orbit to the asteroid Vesta, where Rinker's Knot is located, but she seems to be headed toward a waypoint that will place her in temporal proximity with another spacecraft, *The Martian Princess*."

Sprite grinned at Wiley/Athena's choice of words. "So you are saying that they are going to rendezvous with this *Martian Princess* before continuing on to Rinker's Knot."

"That is correct, Sprite. They will reach the *Princess* in four days."

Sprite scratched her head. "Tell us about *The Martian Princess*, Wiley."

"She's an excursion-class passenger ship, bound for Mars orbit. She has a crew of eight persons, and there are sixty-seven passengers on board. Her manifest indicates there are forty-one adults and twenty-six children, excluding the crew."

"That's a lot of kids," Sprite breathed.

"Why would *The Cassiopeia* want to rendezvous with her?" Tyson pondered.

Ice sniffed unceremoniously. "She's a sex trader. They're after the kids."

Tyson dropped his jaw in disbelief. "What can we do?"

Ice straightened her back, her face set like flint. "I'm going to stop them and get Nixie back."

"I'm going with you," Sprite said. Tyson objected, but she would have none of it. Sprite turned toward Ice. "You're going to need Wiley/Athena to track that ship. Anyway, I owe Nixie."

"You might get hurt, kiddo," Tyson pleaded.

Sprite pulled up her sleeve and touched the controls of her n-skin. Her body turned a silver-gray color; her skin became as hard as diamond. "I can be useful in a fight, Uncle Ty." She dialed the skin back to normal. "Seriously Ice, you could use me out there."

Ice nodded almost imperceptibly, and the decision was made. "Get your things," she said simply. "We'll leave as soon as you can be ready."

* * *

Sprite rushed to her quarters and had just pulled a small flight bag from her locker when Addison appeared in the doorway. "What are you doing?" she asked innocently.

"I've got to go away for a few days," Sprite replied. "It's a family emergency."

"Can I help?" Addison's eyes were full of panic.

Sprite let her flight bag hover next to her viewport and took her friend by the shoulders. She was touched by the concern on Addison's face. "There's nothing you can do. I won't be gone long." Sprite turned away and hooked the handle of her flight bag with her index finger.

"I'm sorry to be in such a rush," she apologized. Her girlfriend didn't answer her. Sprite glanced back at the doorway. Addison was gone.

Sprite shook her head, but had no time to think. She stuffed a couple changes of clothes into the bag, then some toiletries and the mask for her n-skin. Her father had fashioned the device during their struggle with Amos Cross. With it, Sprite could withstand the vacuum of space for almost twenty minutes. Sprite zipped the flight bag shut and secured the thin door to her quarters.

Moments later, Sprite entered the Ankrum dock. She passed by the dock master's office. Ice's back was to the hatch. She was listening intently to the man. He was outlining the safety procedures related to their departure. Sprite kept going, crossing the large room where she had arrived a few weeks earlier. The only open hatch led to Ice's jumpship.

Sprite floated through the docking collar and gazed into the interior of the jumpship. It was the same ship she had ridden in years before. The cabin was filled with an odd collection of gas canisters and flight cases. She was amazed by what Ice had been able to gather in such a short amount of time. She was strapping her flight bag into an empty passenger seat when she heard a familiar voice through the hatch.

Sprite exited the jumpship and saw Kell hovering nervously on the dock. She pushed away from the hatchway and swam toward him. She reached out for a handhold and came to rest in front of him. Kell did not hesitate. He put his arms around her and pulled her to his chest. He buried his head in her shoulder, his lips a scant centimeter from her ear. "I love you, Sprite," he whispered. "I don't want to lose you ever again."

Sprite brought her knees up, straddling Kell's waist. She let go of the handhold and gently pushed his head back, cradling his face in her hands. Then she kissed him. She had always loved him, and this was the moment of her dreams. No longer were they children. No longer did she have to hold him at bay. This was their time, their instant. Their lips parted, and she was breathless. "I love you, too," she whispered.

"Sprite!" Ice was standing by the hatchway, beckoning her to board the ship.

Kell's eyes fell. "You've got to go," he murmured.

Sprite nodded, pulling back from their embrace. "I'll come back to you," she promised. And then she turned quickly and followed Ice through the hatch.

CHAPTER THIRTEEN

Nathan Trent wandered through the passenger spaces on board *The Martian Princess*. There was a synthetic gravity system on the ship, although it was not a strong one. Nathan estimated its force to be about half of that found on Earth. Nevertheless, he appreciated it, preferring to get his exercise roaming the cabins than strapped into a stationary zero-g cycle.

Nathan stood amidships, by a closed hatch emblazoned with a "Crew Only" sign. His training in the TSF had included the study of spacecraft designs, and he knew the layout of the ship. Aft of the hatch were the galley, ship's stores, crew quarters, and the propulsion deck. He turned his back to the hatchway and looked forward. A wide corridor lay before him, punctuated by doorways every three meters, which provided access to small passenger staterooms. He jogged past them and paused as the passageway widened out into a comfortable lounge filled with tables and soft chairs. There were people everywhere. An older couple sat together, reading. A young man stood by a pleasant-looking girl, trying to impress her with his banter. A family was seated around one of the larger tables, playing a game.

Nathan had been taught memory tricks to develop mental dossiers on potential foes. He had applied those skills to his fellow passengers, amassing a catalog of traits associated with each person. He could build his knowledge base each time he encountered one of his traveling companions. He walked slowly through the lounge, measuring the emotional tone, watching for telltale signs of danger, assessing who represented the greatest threat.

"Hey, Trent!" It was the teenaged boy he had spoken with the previous day. Trent smiled and nodded, noting the boy's posture. He was an athlete, perhaps a swimmer or a runner. Trent tagged the information in his mind and tucked it away.

"Solve that puzzle, yet?" Nathan replied easily. The boy had told him about his penchant for crossword games.

"Not yet, but I will!" The boy grinned, pleased that Trent had paid attention to him and cared enough to comment on his interests. Little did the young man know he was the subject of a constant threat evaluation. Nathan smiled and kept walking.

A small exercise cabin was located forward of the lounge. Nathan glanced at the handful of lean men and women who occupied the space. Three were on treadmills, and a couple of others were pumping away at stationary bicycles. He spent a lot of time here, usually during the sleep period when he could be alone with his body and his thoughts.

The main airlock was just past the exercise area on the port side of the ship. Across from it was the e-suit storage-locker. Nathan paused in front of the airlock. The inner door was closed, and the lock chamber was pressurized. He turned to the right and stole a quick glance through the transparent panel in the e-suit locker hatch. He could see six suits, hanging neatly along the bulkhead. Helmets and extra life-support packs were stowed away on shelves. Obviously, the suits were there for show and perhaps an occasional extra-vehicular repair job. He remembered reading about great disasters on ancient ocean-liners, which had failed to provide enough lifeboats for their passengers. If the ship ever decompressed, everyone would die, Nathan surmised. There would be an ugly battle for the e-suits. The mob, clamoring for survival, would kill anyone who tried to put one on.

Nathan took several steps further. A truncated spiral staircase descended through the decking to a large observation cabin and recreation space below. He remained on the main deck, passing a cluster of restrooms. Beyond them was a sealed hatch, bearing another "Crew Only" sign. The flight deck and officers' quarters lay beyond it.

He turned back the way he came. This time, he gripped the railing and took the staircase to the lower compartments. There was no gravity there. The staircase ended as soon as he descended through the opening, and he floated the rest of the way.

* * *

Sprite Logan felt like she was hitching a ride on a cargo carrier. The interior of the jumpship was cramped. Most of the cabin was cluttered with cases of pre-processed food, oxygen canisters, and rigging equipment. Something that resembled a small rocket motor mounted on stout gimbals was lashed down to the decking in the rear of the compartment.

She couldn't imagine why Ice had chosen to bring such an odd assortment of things, but she understood the need to be prepared for any challenge that might face them. They were on an unarmed jumpship with a limited range, chasing a full-sized transfer ship on its way to the Asteroid Belt. They were going to have to sneak up on the sex-traders' vessel, which was probably outfitted with enough firepower to blow them out of the galaxy. Then, they would have to devise a plan to rescue Nixie. Sprite burst out laughing. The whole enterprise seemed perfectly stupid.

Ice pivoted in the pilot's seat, giving her a quizzical glance. Sprite shook her head and made a gesture with her hands, indicating that it was nothing. However, Sprite knew their mission was no laughing matter. She had stared death in the face before and knew that it was possible they would not return from this fool's errand. She thought of Kell. Their moment on the dock had made life infinitely more precious to her. When Ice had summoned her into the ship, she had almost changed her mind. She wanted to stay with Kell forever, but years before, she had been kidnapped. Being a hostage had changed her, and she could not stand by, no matter what the cost, and do nothing when a friend was taken against her will.

"When will we catch Nixie's ship?" Sprite asked.

Ice didn't take her eyes off the controls. "About two hours," she murmured. "This is a fast ship."

"Fasty-fast," Sprite intoned.

Ice flinched, turning suddenly to face her. "What?"

"This jumpship is fasty-fast," she repeated. "That's what Nixie said when we were on our way to the Earth." Ice nodded slowly, wordlessly. For the first time, Sprite saw a minute crack in the woman's emotional armor. A look of profound concern flashed across her face and was gone.

* * *

Remson Burke leaned back in his chair. He had just received a report from Rattler. His subordinate had found Spif in a drunken stupor at Einstein Base. The tattooed man had assured him that Spif's death would never be questioned. The man had been well on his way to alcohol poisoning, and Rattler had just helped him over the threshold by adding a little something to his last drink. Only the woman called Ice was left.

Rattler reported that the bartender had seen a woman matching Ice's description come into the bar. She and Spif had taken seats in a booth in the back corner of the tavern. Their conversation had become animated, and the bar-keep had noticed the woman pushing the table against Spif's chest. She had left a short time later.

Burke wondered if Ice was worth his trouble. Amos Cross had been very specific about Nixie, but less so concerning the rest of her crew. He had told Rattler to keep looking for Ice, but Burke held no hope of finding her. It didn't matter, anyway. He had done his job. Nixie's crew was shattered, and the young firebrand would never be seen again.

* * *

The Cassiopeia was a small glowing dot of light against the vast black curtain of space. Sprite could hardly take her eyes from it. Nixie was now within sight. Wiley/Athena had led them directly to her. Sprite pulled her card comp from her pocket and linked with her digital friends. "Will the ship be able to see us?"

"You are within sensor range, but *The Cassiopeia's* ion trail will mask your presence. As long as you stay directly behind her, she will not see you." Wiley was speaking this time.

"What about the network sensors?" Sprite was referring to the web of sensors that were distributed throughout the inner system, which tracked space-traffic, asteroids, and man-made floating debris. Any ship linked to the Meridian network could screen up a global view of the space surrounding their craft.

It was Athena's turn to answer. "We are actively editing the sensors, Sprite. We have deleted your ship from the data. They cannot see you."

Ice grunted. "Nice work," she muttered.

"Thank you, Ice," Athena purred. The stoic pilot didn't respond to the AI.

Sprite turned to Ice. "How close are we going to get to her?" she asked.

"Very close," Ice answered. "We're going to stick our nose right up their butt."

Athena's voice lilted from the small speaker in Sprite's card comp. "We recommend you keep your distance, Ice. The ion flow from *The Cassiopeia's* engines could play havoc with your systems."

"We've got extra shielding on this boat," Ice snapped back.

Athena paid no attention to the woman's rejoinder. "We recommend keeping a klick or two between the vessels."

Ice grunted again.

* * *

Pierre Antoine sat in the captain's chair on the bridge of *The Cassiopeia*. His pilot lounged at the controls, his head bobbing as he fought against the urge to sleep. There was little to do. The intercept course had been laid into the nav-AI, and only a few hours remained before they space-jacked the passenger ship. "You'd better not fall asleep, Driver. I'm going to need your best pretty soon."

"Aye, sir," the man replied.

"Why don't you perform a pitch maneuver to check our baffles?"

"There's nothing on the network sensors, sir." The pilot sounded bored.

"Do it anyway. I don't trust those damned things. Take us through a gradual 360-degree pitch maneuver. I'll expect your report when I get back."

"You're leaving the bridge, sir?"

"Captain's prerogative, Driver. Carry on."

* * *

Nixie was lost in a daydream when she heard footsteps outside her cabin door. She could tell from the sound that it was a man. The hatch clicked open, and Nixie turned her face to the wall. If she closed her eyes and turned away, she could pretend that she was dressed. She willed her senses to shut down, retreating into her mind, into a self-made alternate universe where her body was properly covered and her hands unfettered. Nixie separated herself from the naked body on the bed. She told herself that it wasn't her, that she wasn't there, that what was about to happen was going to happen to someone she didn't know.

The hatch clicked shut. She heard the rustle of clothing, fabric rubbing against fabric. There was another footstep. It was beside the bed. Then Nixie heard the voice.

"Nixie Drake. It's been too long, girl." The voice was familiar. She had heard it in her nightmares. "Look at me, child. I've missed you."

Nixie's eyes opened wide. She dared not move. A gut-wrenching fear erupted in her stomach. A hand touched her head, and she grimaced. It was a rough hand, an unkind hand. She tried to resist, but it was very strong. Her visitor turned her head, and she saw his face. It was her father.

Nixie gasped. Pierre Antoine let go of her and stepped back. His lips were curled into a sneer of primal celebration. His eyes wandered from her face, taking in her exposed body. "You remember me, don't you?" he asked. Nixie nodded, silently pleading for this present nightmare to evaporate into the kind morning light, but there was no daybreak, no escape from her present horror. "Do you remember where I was when you ran away from me?" Pierre's voice was pitched low. He whispered like a demon muttering in a crypt.

Nixie nodded again. She couldn't speak. "I was in your bedroom, wasn't I?" he asked. "I had come for you. I wanted you, and you struck me. You ran away."

Tears erupted from Nixie's eyes. She drew in a quick jagged breath and held it. She trembled uncontrollably.

Pierre began to unbuckle her restraints. "You are on board my ship. This time, there is nowhere for you to run." Nixie's leg was free. She flexed her knee unconsciously. "I am going to take off these straps, but you better not run from me again." Her other leg was released, and Nixie brought her knees together, attempting to shield her womanhood. He laughed, running his hand up her leg. He touched her pubic hair with his fingers. Nixie flinched. His hand moved to her belly, then her breast. "You have grown into quite a young woman," he cooed malevolently. He released her left hand, and she lashed out, but he was too quick for her. He easily deflected her blow. "None of that, child. This is going to be a long journey, and it will be better if you cooperate." Nixie's other hand was free. She pushed against the bed with her feet and jammed her back against the bulkhead, wrapping her arms tightly around her knees.

Pierre Antoine stepped back and looked at her. "Now I'm going to finish what I started with you," he vowed menacingly. He began to unzip his jumpsuit. Dark, greasy hair erupted from the opening. Nixie was terrified, but she couldn't take her eyes from him. He slipped the suit over his hips, his member swelling in anticipation of their union. Nixie held herself as Pierre flopped across the bed, his strong arms pushing her legs flat against the mattress. He lay on top of her, and she felt him against her leg. Nixie suddenly felt the urge to vomit. Then his rough hands were on her knees, scratching her skin and forcing them apart. She wasn't strong enough to stop him. She felt his hairy leg slide down between her thighs as he positioned himself for his thrust.

CHAPTER FOURTEEN

I ce had disregarded Athena's advice and had brought the jumpship within fifty meters of *The Cassiopeia's* tail. She was in a state of constant vigilance, stalking her prey like a panther in the night. Ice was not prone to idle conversation, so the two women had fallen into a silent reverie. Sprite studied the outline of the larger ship, imagining Nixie somewhere within its charcoal-black hull. She wasn't surprised at their ability to find the ship, but she had no idea how they were going to rescue her young friend.

Suddenly, Sprite tensed as *The Cassiopeia's* vernier thrusters flared. The jumpship's AI responded immediately, its laser ranging system reporting the change in their target's attitude. The jumpship's breaking engines came online, ready to apply opposing thrust if necessary, to prevent the little ship from colliding with its prey. Ice's fingers hovered over the flight console, fully prepared to take manual control over the ship.

The two women watched breathlessly as the transfer ship began its pitch maneuver. Gradually, they saw its aspect change as her nose came up, revealing the ship's spine.

"They're going to see us!" Sprite shouted.

Ice remained calm. "No avoiding it. If we run, Nixie is doomed." She had a way of cutting to the chase.

Sprite's fingertips bit into the soft armrests on her seat. "Can we slip under her belly and stay out of her line of sight?"

"She already has us on her sensors," Ice whispered.

* * *

Driver watched the star field drop away as *The Cassiopeia* pitched up. Her nose hadn't risen twenty degrees before the sensor system came alive, reporting an object in close proximity to the ship. He glanced at the tactical display. It was a jumpship. "What in hell is he doing way out here?" he muttered.

The ship continued its somersault, the synthetic gravity system masking any sign of movement. Within seconds, the small silvery craft was framed in the forward viewport, upside-down and very close. Driver halted the pitch maneuver; the two ships were nose to nose. Then he punched the Master Alarm, and an electronic siren began to bellow throughout the ship.

* * *

Pierre Antoine was about to drive himself into Nixie when the alarm sounded, its piercing wail interrupting his sexual assault. "Goddamn it!" he shrieked, aborting his pelvic thrust. He planted one hand in the center of Nixie's chest and clamored to his feet. She gasped as the weight of his body pushed the air out of her lungs. As he rose from the bunk, she immediately curled up into a fetal ball. Pierre grabbed his jumpsuit from the floor with an angry swiping motion and hurried toward the hatchway. He opened it, still naked, and stepped into his garment as he rushed into the passageway.

* * *

Molly had been squatting silently in the hold when the sound of the Master Alarm erupted from somewhere above her. It was terribly loud. She sat down hard on the rough metal decking and put her hands over her ears to mute the sonic maelstrom. It didn't work. The sound coursed through her fingers, deafening her.

The hold was bathed in a blood-red glow, and a strobe light was flashing like lightening in a violent electrical storm. Molly looked for signs of fire, but there were none. There was no burning smell, no change in cabin pressure or temperature. She looked at the girls surrounding her. Tormented expressions filled their faces, but she could not hear their screams of terror. The skull-cracking noise of the alarm drowned out all other sounds. Some of them were crying; others were wide-eyed with dread. It was as if she was looking through the gates of hell, into a sea of lost souls, the company of the damned. For the first time in her young life, Molly wondered if she was going to die.

* * *

Nixie lay motionless on her bunk. She was utterly lost. She had closed herself off, mentally retreating into the labyrinth of her mind. She had disconnected herself from her body and her senses. She didn't know what had happened. She wasn't sure if it was safe to venture out of the psychic cocoon she had spun around herself. Had her father left her bed without raping her? Was it safe to open her eyes? It was as if she had climbed into a bunker in the midst of a terrible battle and suddenly all had grown silent.

However, it wasn't silent. There was a loud noise. She not only heard it, but felt it in her chest. There was something familiar about it, it represented something important. Nixie struggled to remember, and then she did. In the back of her battered brain, a voice called out to her. It was a command voice, the voice of a captain. "Alarm!" it said. "You must act! Act now! Suck it up, captain. Regardless of your circumstance, of how you happen to feel at the moment, you must act!"

Nixie unfolded her body and swung her bare feet off the side of the bunk. She got on her feet and padded to the hatch. She could see a sliver of light slipping past the seal. Her father had rushed from the cabin and left the hatch open. She leaned forward and peeked into the passageway. A man with grease on his jumpsuit was rushing past her cabin. Nixie jumped back, but the man did not see her. She thought about the grease. The man was the ship's engineer, and he was running toward the forward compartments.

"You must act quickly!" her inner voice commanded. "You are a captain, and it is your job to act decisively. This is your moment. Do your duty!" Nixie pushed the hatch open and stepped boldly into the corridor.

* * *

Ice and Sprite stared out the forward viewport of the jumpship. They were close enough to *The Cassiopeia* to see the dumbfounded expression on her pilot's face. Sprite glanced at her companion. She could tell that Ice was working out tactical scenarios in her mind. There weren't many options. The element of surprise had been lost, and they had no way of stopping the larger ship. It was likely that *The Cassiopeia* had some sort of weaponry. They might be able to turn tail and run, perhaps survive, but that would mean the end of their mission.

There was a noise in the back of the cabin. Ice and Sprite exchanged mystified glances, then looked aft to determine what had caused it. Addison Traynor was floating by a stack of cases, a sheepish expression on her face.

"Addy!" Sprite scolded. "What are you doing here?"

Ice was miffed. She reached under her seat and pulled out a pulse-pistol. Before either of the other women could react, she had the gun trained on Addison's chest. The laser sight cast a bright red dot directly over her heart. "Who is she?" Ice asked coldly.

"Don't shoot her!" Sprite stammered. "She's my friend." Ice lowered the weapon.

Addison swam through the crowded passenger cabin and planted herself in an empty seat behind Ice. "Strap yourself in," Ice commanded.

The girl fumbled with the safety harness. Sprite leaned over to help her. "What do you think you are doing?" she chided her friend.

"You looked so worried when I saw you in your quarters on Ankrum Platform," Addison explained meekly. "I just had to come and help you." Ice snorted. "Honest!" the girl pleaded. "I have skills. I can be useful."

Suddenly, a brilliant glow filled the compartment. There was a popping sound, and all the jumpship's systems shut down. The cockpit displays went dark, and an ominous silence filled in the cabin.

* * *

Nixie turned to her right and tiptoed softly down the passageway toward the stern of *The Cassiopeia*. The corridor came to an end ahead of her, terminated with an open hatch. Beyond it, she could see the ship's propulsion deck. She stepped through the opening and was greeted by a wave of heat, which enveloped her like a blanket. Only then did she look down at herself, realizing that she was still naked. Although she was alone, she felt a pang of modesty and swung the hatch closed. She pivoted away from the entranceway and glanced around for something to wear. There was nothing, not even a scrap of cloth to wrap around her waist.

The temperature in the engine compartment was oppressive, and Nixie suddenly remembered Ice laboring on *The Raccoon's* propulsion deck. She hadn't approved of her crewmate's nudity, but she now appreciated her friend's point of view. It was very warm, but not uncomfortable if one was in the raw. In her mind's eye, Nixie envisioned Ice, her slender body smeared with grease, climbing through the maze of pipes and conduits surrounding the engine. There had been a problem with *The Raccoon's* power plant, and Ice had coaxed her to help. Nixie stepped back in wonderment. The pipes before her were mingled in the same fashion as those she remembered on *The Raccoon*. There was a gap between two large waveguides. She and Ice had slipped through the same opening on their ship to fix something. The operator's console was different, but the drive hardware was identical.

The wailing alarm stopped, leaving the deck silent. Nixie could hear the dull hum of a circulating pump, but the engine was offline. It was the standard procedure when the Master Alarm tripped. A quick scan of the gauges told her the engine had been idled. There were no signs of a malfunction. What were they doing? Why had they sounded the alarm?

The alarm. Once again, Nixie was swept back to the day she had helped Ice on *The Raccoon's* propulsion deck. There had been a problem that was going to trigger the ship's alarm. What was it? She took a step toward the maze of pipes. Ice had shown her where there was an adjustment in an out-of-the-way spot. She had said something about a design flaw in the engine's cooling sensors. It wasn't dangerous, but would set off the Master Alarm.

Nixie wondered if her father's engineer knew about the problem. The though of him gave her a shiver. "Act!" said the captain's voice in her head. "Don't dwell on your pain; focus on your duty!" Nixie sidled up to the engine piping and stepped into the intricate jungle of metallic limbs. She touched a hot pipe and flinched. This was no place for bare skin. She pushed onward, straining her memory.

Finally, Nixie saw a squat canister with several pipes jutting out of it. This was the spot, she told herself, where Ice had made the adjustment. Nixie reached behind the device, probing with her fingers. There was nothing there. Nixie dropped her hands in frustration. Maybe this engine was modified. Perhaps the design flaw had been corrected.

Nixie pounded the canister with her fist and stared dejectedly at the decking beneath her toes. She shifted her weight to her other foot, and her body moved a few centimeters to the right. She saw a flash of red behind the canister, a few centimeters above the decking. It was a knob. Nixie's memory became clear as crystal. Ice had turned that knob to prevent a false alarm in the engine cooling system. If she could convince her father and his men that the ship was about to explode, maybe she could escape.

Nixie dropped to her knees, then lay flat on the rough decking. She didn't think about what she probably looked like, naked and greasy, sprawled out in an unladylike fashion beneath the labyrinth of pipes. Rather, she stayed focused on her plan, her duty to fight against her captors. She reached behind the canister and gave the knob a sharp twist.

* * *

Pierre Antoine burst onto the flight deck and stared through the forward viewport. He couldn't believe his eyes. "Who are they?" he shouted.

Driver pivoted in his seat. "What?"

Pierre could hardly hear him above the raucous sound of the ship's alarm. "Turn off that damned alarm!" he commanded at the top of his voice. Driver punched a button, and there was silence. "I said, 'Who are they?'"

"We don't know, sir."

"Did you try hailing them?"

"No, sir."

"Why didn't we see them on the network sensors?"

"No idea, sir. They should have been on the scope."

"I don't like this," Pierre muttered.

"Do you want to hail them?" Driver looked worried.

"No." Pierre decided. "They're up to no good. Fire the disruptor, Star."

"Aye, sir," the woman with copper-colored hair replied. She aligned a pair of cross-hairs on the display in front of her and pressed a glowing red icon. A surge of energy thrummed beneath their feet, and a charge of luminous amber plasma erupted from somewhere under the viewports. It engulfed the tiny jumpship.

* * *

Addison Traynor flinched. "What just happened?" she bleated. Ice and Sprite looked back at the larger ship. A crowd of faces filled *The Cassiopeia's* viewport. A small dish, mounted on the ship's nose cone, was glowing with a diminishing amber light.

"What did they do?" Sprite asked worriedly.

"Hit us with a disruptor," Ice shot back. "Fried our electronics."

"Can we fix the ship?" Sprite's voice was thick with fear.

"Not out here."

One of the figures on *The Cassiopeia's* flight deck waved to them through the viewport. Then, the larger ship began to pitch again, her nose dropping out of sight, her metallic belly completely blocking the stars. Sprite pulled her card comp out of her pocket and tried to link with Wiley/Athena. The small device was dormant in her hand. It was burned out, too.

The transfer ship completed its pitch maneuver and once again presented its stern to the jumpship. Her dual ion-emitters pulsed to life, offering a dull blue glow that belied their tremendous power. Sprite and her companions floated helplessly in the darkened jumpship as *The Cassiopeia* accelerated away from them.

* * *

Nixie heard the engine come to life as she freed herself from the tangle of pipes and waveguides. She returned to the hatch and cracked it open, hoping to find the passageway devoid of ship's personnel. Her luck ran out. The man whom she had identified as the ship's engineer was less than three meters in front of her. Two other men followed directly behind him. The engineer grinned when he saw her. He closed the distance between them with a burst of speed. Before Nixie could react, she was thrown face-down on the deck. The man smelled of sweat and grease. He straddled her, bellowing like a bull rider at an old-fashioned rodeo.

Nixie grimaced as his weight jammed her pelvis against the non-skid decking, but she did not surrender to her situation. She tucked her arms under her breasts and pushed against the floor, so she could breathe. Her inner voice was alive, shouting in her mind. "Think!" it commanded. "Don't react."

Nixie heard, rather than saw, the growing number of people filling the passageway. There was an excited chatter of voices, each making some reference to her nakedness. Her father's voice boomed above the rest, demanding silence. "Damn," Pierre Antoine barked as he pushed his way through the crowd. "Get off her, Wrench! Let her up."

Nixie was pulled to her feet. A dozen eyes were upon her, gaping at her exposed flesh. Nixie stood defiantly, her eyes locked on Pierre's face. They blazed at him with hatred's fire.

"My, oh my," Pierre purred. "It looks like our little plaything has recovered some of her spunk." The men laughed, but Nixie stood firm. "Maybe we ought to have ourselves a little party right here, right now." Pierre fingered his crotch.

Nixie pulled against the men who were gripping her arms. "Bass-turd!" she hissed. "I'll tie yer rope-a-dope in a knotty-knot and smasher-een yer ball-bearings!"

Pierre feigned a look of fear, then laughed. His men joined him. "I like aggressive women!"

A voice erupted from the ship's intercom. "Captain? We're coming up on the passenger ship."

Pierre's face fell. He was obviously disappointed. "That's twice that we've been interrupted, child." He reached forward and fondled Nixie's breast. She glared at him with stone-cold eyes. "We'll continue this later." Pierre looked up at the men holding her. "Throw her in the hold with the others," he commanded them. "Everyone?" Pierre rubbed his hands in anticipation. "Get to your stations. We've got some fresh meat to catch!"

CHAPTER FIFTEEN

Nathan Trent grew tired of the observation deck on *The Martian Princess*. The space line had extolled the romance of interplanetary travel. Their netsite had used the ship's observation deck as a selling point, featuring dramatic scenes of Earth and Mars through the viewports. In reality, the breathtaking views only existed in planetary orbit. Even the Moon, with its dimpled-gray desolation, was something to look at, but in the void between planets, there was very little to see. Even at her considerable speed, the stars stood still in the inky void.

Nathan slipped his arm through the handle of his go-bag and swam toward the circular opening that led to the upper cabins. He floated into the opening and began to feel his weight returning. The circular staircase was positioned precisely at the point when the g-force of the upper deck began taking effect. Nathan gripped the railing and planted his foot on the first tread; then he climbed upward into the gravitational field.

Nathan paused at the threshold between the exercise cabin and the lounge. He always scanned a cabin before entering it, measuring the potential risk. A middle-aged man was sitting off to one side, toward the back of the compartment. Nathan had been watching him for the duration of the trip. He was the only passenger who seemed out of place. Nathan entered the lounge. The man didn't look up, but Nathan could tell he was watching him. He had skills, the kind that could get you killed if you didn't take them into account.

Nathan shifted his grip on his go-bag, so he could draw his pulse-pistol. It was a meaningless gesture to the unobservant, but the man flinched slightly, and Nathan knew he was in the presence of another warrior. The seat next to the stranger was empty, so Nathan approached the man and sat down. He was trained to act unpredictably, to keep his foe off balance. Since he and the man had now marked each other, it made sense to approach him rather than retreat.

"That observation deck gets pretty boring after a while," Nathan remarked offhandedly.

"Got that right," the stranger said, not taking his eyes off the digital tablet in his hand. "The whole trip has been pretty boring, if you ask me," he added.

Nathan grunted in agreement. His go-bag now rested on his lap, the pulse-pistol just beneath the fold of cloth covering its contents.

"Mr. Trent," the man said softly. Nathan didn't move, but his brain took a step closer to ordering his hand to pull out the weapon. "I am aware of your special skill set." He tapped the tablet and pressed his thumb against the surface. An instant later, the screen displayed an official-looking identification. "I also know that you have a weapon in that bag and could kill me before I could even think of defending myself." He handed the tablet to Nathan. There was a picture of the stranger on the screen. He was Samuel Hopkins, a security officer employed by the space line company that owned *The Martian Princess*. "We're on the same side, Mr. Trent."

Nathan handed the tablet back to its owner. He studied the man, his steel-gray eyes taking in every nuance in the stranger's facial expression like ground-penetrating radar. Neither man breathed for a few seconds, and then Nathan offered a thin smile. "Now that I know who you are, this trip is really going to be boring." He nodded to the officer, then stood up. He considered going to his stateroom, but thought better of it and headed back toward the observation deck.

* * *

Nixie lay on the floor of the hold. Her father's henchmen had thrown her through the hatch without comment. Her shoulder and hip stung where she had skidded against the rough decking. She was dazed, only faintly aware of the shapeless forms surrounding her. The confidence she had felt on the propulsion deck was draining away, and once again, she felt self-conscious, naked and defenseless. She closed her eyes and tucked herself into a ball, trying to cover her private parts.

"Who are you?" It was a girl's voice.

Nixie opened her eyes. Her ear was pressed flat against the decking. She saw several sets of dirty toes in front of her. No shoes or socks, just toes. They were attached to bare feet. She saw ankles and then the ragged hems of pale green smocks. Nixie picked herself up on one arm, covering her breasts with the other. She looked up.

The voice belonged to a young girl, perhaps ten years old. She towered over Nixie, her hands hanging limply by her sides. She wasn't overweight, but her features were subdued by a layer of baby fat. She had long blonde hair, and her face was smudged with dirt. There were vertical marks under her eyes, the tracks of her tears. "What's your name?" she asked.

Nixie looked at the children who were surrounding her. They were all girls, which made her feel a bit better about her state of undress. They were young, too. Each of them was wearing a pale green smock. They all looked scared. "Name's Nixie Drake," she said slowly. "Howsy-bouts you?" She looked back at the young girl who had spoken.

"I'm Molly Winters. Do you know where we are?"

Nixie rubbed her shoulder where she had struck the floor. She took her hand away, there was blood. She winced, then wiped the crimson liquid on her calf. "We's bustin' our rumpers, pushin' va-cuum to the knotty-Knot."

"You talk funny," said one of the girls. A wavelet of half-hearted, nervous laughter skipped lightly across the hold.

"What's a knotty-Knot?" asked another.

"Rinky-dink Knot!" Nixie said impatiently.

"We don't know what that is," the one called Molly said.

"Rinky-Knot is on the Icy-Line. On Vesta. An ass-troid."

Molly's eyes lit up. "You mean Rinker's Knot!"

Nixie cursed under her breath. "That'sy whats I's been sayin', droopy-head!"

"Where's that?" another girl asked Molly, forgetting for a moment that Nixie was there.

"It's a supply depot run by Meridian Corporation in the Asteroid Belt. It's on Vesta." Molly spoke like a science teacher. She had a keen grasp of the facts.

"The Asteroid Belt!" another girl cried. A murmuring arose in the group as little conversations sprouted here and there.

"I want to go home!" a young girl cried.

Molly didn't take her eyes off Nixie. "Why are they taking us there?"

Nixie didn't speak at first. She knew what lay ahead of them. She looked at their faces. They were all so young and innocent. They were victims of her father.

"I don'ts knows," Nixie lied, unable to tell her companions the awful truth.

"You're lying!" said the girl next to Molly. "Maybe they sent you in here to spy on us!"

A ripple of fear spread throughout the group. Nixie snorted. She stood up and planted her feet on the decking. The children's eyes grew large as she balled her fists and jabbed them into her waist. Nixie glanced down at herself, then arched her back and glared defiantly at the girl who had spoken. "Does I's looky-looks likes a spizee-wisey to you?"

One of the girls snickered, then another. "I guess not," admitted the girl.

Molly stepped forward. "There's one way to know for sure," she said. "Raise your left arm, Nixie."

Nixie was mystified. "Why's you wants me's to dues thats?" she asked.

"Just do it," the young girl asked.

Nixie raised her arm high above her head. A collective gasp filled the hold. Nixie was confused. Then Molly raised her left arm. Nixie could see the tattoo of a barcode in her bare armpit. She shuttered, as one after another of the children raised their hands. Each had the mark. Nixie looked at her left armpit, knowing what was there. She had a barcode, too.

The realization struck Nixie like a runaway comet. The barcode had been there for a long as she could remember, but she had never known why she bore the mark. In fact, she had forgotten about it, dismissing it as meaningless. Now she knew what it was, and it changed everything. She bore the sex-trader's mark. She had been taken from her family. She had not run away from her father years ago. She had run away from her abductor. Pierre Antoine was not her father. She was one of his victims and the girls surrounding her in the hold were her sisters.

There was a commotion in the back of the crowd, and one of the girls worked her way through the throng of captives. She came up behind Molly Winters, pushing past her and stopping in front of Nixie. In her trembling hands was an extra pale-green smock.

* * *

Sprite Logan gave Addison Traynor a withering look. "You shouldn't have come!" she scolded. "As you can see, we are in trouble here. This isn't your fight. You shouldn't be putting your life at risk."

Ice was busy examining all the jumpship's systems. She was frowning, which was out of character for her. The disruptor had shorted out all the semiconductor junctions on board the ship. Comps and sensors were all offline. The life-support system had failed.

"I'm really sorry, Sprite." Addison was close to tears. "I thought I was helping you."

"You're using up oxygen," sniped Ice.

"I promise not to breathe too much," the girl offered. Ice shook her head.

"Just strap in, Addy." Sprite gestured toward an empty seat. Then she glanced out the forward viewport. *The Cassiopeia* was receding into the distance, but not at as rapid a pace as she expected. "It looks like they applied just enough thrust to give them maneuvering room," she remarked.

Ice looked up, her eyes narrowing. "They're on approach," she said, pointing to an object beyond the larger ship. In the distance was a faint glow. Sprite recognized it immediately as the plasma cloud behind another ship. It had to be *The Martian Princess's* ion-emitters. Pierre Antoine's ship was directly behind her, bearing down on the unsuspecting craft. It was lined up behind the ion cloud to avoid detection, just as they had done.

"We're going to lose them!" Sprite proclaimed. The jumpship was still moving forward, thanks to Newton's first law. They were an object in motion, remaining in motion, but they had no unbalanced force to control the ship. Fortunately, their course had been true, and the jumpship was lagging behind the other ships by only a few kilometers.

"You've got a portable thruster," Addison chirped from her seat.

Ice glanced back at the gimbaled device in the back of the cabin. It was a small, self-contained rocket motor used to stabilize tumbling salvage. Its electronics package was as fried as the rest of the ship. "It's burned up," Ice replied.

"Just the controller," Addison shot back, "but it can be ignited with a battery. You can jury-rig a manual throttle. Just open the fuel valves, throttle it back, and energize the igniter."

Sprite looked at her friend with new respect. "Where did you learn about rocket engines?"

"I read a lot," she quipped.

"It's got to be mounted on the hull," Ice challenged. She gestured toward a locker where a lone e-suit hung. "The e-suit is dead, too."

Addison was about to speak again, but Sprite cut her off. "I can go outside with my nanoskin."

Ice nodded. "I saw your mother and father do that at the space-elevator."

"I know you did," Sprite grinned. Her parents had tested the revolutionary skin on themselves, prior to using it to save Sprite's life. They had ventured out into the vacuum and cold of space to locate a cache of killer nanobots.

Ice set her jaw, accepting the plan. She turned to Addison. "Can you rig it up?" Addison's eyes grew wide, then she nodded with a smile.

* * *

Pierre Antoine strapped himself into the captain's chair on *The Cassiopeia's* flight deck. The stern profile of *The Martian Princess* was magnified in a three-dimensional holodisplay in front of the command console. Driver inched the ship closer to its prey. "When do you want me to pull alongside her, sir?"

Pierre wanted to remain behind the passenger ship until the very last moment. He pressed a button with his left hand. Two members of his crew appeared in a small display built into his seat's armrest. He studied their faces. "Are you ready in the grappling pod?"

"Yes, sir," replied the crewman named Mo. "We're all set to snag her and punch into the airlock."

"Very good," Pierre acknowledged. "Star, get ready to disrupt the target."

The copper-haired woman nodded to him and swung back to her console. "The target is locked, sir."

Pierre pressed another button. "Boarding team, what is your status?"

"We are ready, sir."

"Okay, Driver, let's bring *The Cassiopeia* along side her."

* * *

Nixie Drake slipped on the smock and thanked the girl who had brought it to her. She looked into the children's faces and felt an odd role reversal. For much of her life, she had hidden behind her youthful appearance. Now she was the oldest person in the group, and it was obvious that everyone was looking to her for a sign of hope. She could see the desperation in their eyes and feel the weight of their silent pleas.

"Do you know anything about spaceships?" the one called Molly asked.

The absurdity of the question buoyed Nixie's spirits. "I been a shipper-skipper on my owny-boat. Had a crewy-dewy an all 'bout that."

There was a hush in the room, and then a small, thin voice partway back in the crowd whispered loudly, "She's a captain!" The comment was followed by a pregnant silence as the group became charged with hope and expectation. Nixie was overwhelmed. She had chased after respect for years, failing to receive it from her crew. Now she found it here, among this ragtag clutch of kidnap-victims.

"How do we get out of here?" Molly asked.

"I gots a plan," Nixie explained. Everyone started to chatter at once, and she gestured for them to be quiet. "Firsts of all, it's 'portent not to distract any 'tention."

"You mean attract attention, don't you?" It was Molly again.

Nixie smiled. "Yessir doodle I do, girl. I ain't so grand at wordy-ness-likes, buts my nogger thinker's fine."

Back in the ranks of children, the same little voice whispered loudly, "She says she's not good at talking, but her brain works good!"

Nixie grinned at Molly, and the younger girl couldn't help but smile back at her. "I'll try to speaks easier to ya," Nixie started. She cleared her throat, mustering all of her linguistic skills to express herself clearly. "We stays quiet," she began. "They's lots of 'dults on this ship. I mean, there are lots of adults." She put extra emphasis on the "a" in "adults." The hold was silent. Nixie had never had so many people hang on her every word. She told them about her plan to set off the ship's Master Alarm. She warned them that it would be loud like before. She reassured them that even though their kidnappers were going to get scared, nothing bad was going to happen to the ship.

"Theys're gonna high-tailor themselfs off this shipper. Gonna save their own butty-butts for 'nother day. THEN," she paused with a flourish. "Thisser-shipper will blong to us!"

* * *

Nathan Trent was on *The Martian Princess's* observation deck when *The Cassiopeia* came up alongside her. The massive vessel's hull seemed dangerously close to the viewports, as the dull-gray behemoth eclipsed the distant stars. There were gasps in the compartment, followed by shrieks of fear. Nathan shot toward the stairwell like a greased bullet. He had just entered the upper deck when there was a subtle popping sound, and everything went dark. The synthetic gravity system failed, and frightened voices filled the interior of the ship.

Nathan knew immediately that the intruder had triggered an electromagnetic pulse (EMP) weapon, destroying the ship's electronic systems. Every circuit with semiconductor junctions was reduced to fried chunks of silicon. He gripped his go-bag tightly, realizing that they were under attack. His pulse-pistol was shielded against EMPs, and he knew he was going to need it. The marauders would probably breach the airlock. Soon, the civilian ship would be filled with heavily-armed pirates. He paused, letting his eyes adjust to the darkness. He had chemical lights in the go-bag, but they would draw attention to him, and he didn't want that. The darkness was his ally; there was safety there.

* * *

The cabin of the little jumpship was a flurry of activity as she floated in space, several kilometers behind the two larger ships. Addison Traynor labored over the maneuvering rocket, stripping away its useless electronics and preparing it for manual operation. Sprite had pulled her nano-mask from her bag and was adapting one of Ice's air canisters to the breather, in order to extend the duration of her upcoming EVA. Ice sat in the pilot's seat, pressing an antique set of binoculars to her face and watching the distant spacecraft.

"They just fired their disruptor," she reported. "*The Martian Princess* is dead in space." Sprite never imagined her stoic companion as a play-by-play announcer, but Ice was doing a fine job, terse and to the point. "Their grappling pod is extended," she reported. "They're about to breach the outer airlock hatch."

Sprite finished connecting the air canister to her mask and checked the straps of the harness that would hold the air-bottle to her back. She glanced through the viewport. The other ships seemed so far away. A shiver went up her spine as she realized the full gravity of their situation. If she failed to steer the jumpship to the other ships, if she was off-course by even a degree, they would drift out into the ocean of darkness and certainly die.

CHAPTER SIXTEEN

A muffled clanking sound reverberated through *The Martian Princess's* space-frame. Nathan recognized the sound of the grappling collar slamming against the ship's hull, near the main airlock. There were several more thuds, as powerful grippers latched into various anchor points to hold the two ships together. They were about to be boarded.

Samuel Hopkins glided through the exercise cabin toward the main airlock. He had a pulse-pistol in his hand. He flew past Nathan and grabbed a handhold near the hatch that led to the flight deck. He pounded on the metal, but there was no response. He cursed, knowing full well that the captain would not open the hatch for any reason. Then the man took up a defensive position next to the inner airlock hatch.

Nathan remained in the shadows. He knew Hopkins would be the first man to die. The boarders would blast their way into the ship. Any direct response to their aggression was suicide. Nathan floated over to one of the treadmills in the exercise compartment. The conveyor mechanism was almost thirty centimeters tall. He angled his body until it was parallel with the deck and "lowered" himself until his body was completely hidden behind the conveyor. Then he pulled his pulse-pistol from the go-bag.

A powerful blast shook the cabin. There was a series of screams in the lounge. Nathan could tell that most of the passengers had retreated into the corridor outside the staterooms. There was no safe place to go. A lot of innocent people were about to die.

Samuel Hopkins braced himself against the e-suit locker and trained his pistol on the inner airlock door. A red dot appeared on the hatch-panel, and hot metal began to dribble down its surface. The dot began to move, cutting a perfect rectangular path around the perimeter of the door. The severed panel clanked to the floor, and a rush of air swept through the passageway as the atmospheric pressure equalized between the two ships. Hopkins fired his pistol as the slab of metal hit the decking, but there was no one in the airlock. The hole had been cut by a robotic laser, which, even now, was retracting into the recesses of the offending spacecraft.

Nathan reached quickly into his go-bag and pulled out what appeared to be earmuffs. With one hand, he deftly arched the device's springy band over the top of his skull, clamping the two padded cups over his ears. He had just cinched up the protective device when a pulse of energy sent a shockwave through the shattered airlock, lifting and blowing the remains of the inner door in its fury. Nathan lowered his head behind the treadmill.

Samuel Hopkins' body was pummeled by the kinetic wave. His chest cavity was crushed, and his eyes burst from the immense pressure. Thankfully, he was killed instantly. His body went limp and hung in the passageway. Spherical droplets of blood driven by internal pressure erupted from his body, creating a ghoulish mist. Then the boarding party flooded through the airlock like a swarm of angry bees.

* * *

The young girls in *The Cassiopeia's* hold flinched as the ship shuttered. There were sounds of metal on metal, then a muffled explosion. Nixie tried to calm them. Her years of experience had taught her the meaning of every sound. The ship had grappled another vessel, she explained. The explosion was the breaching of the other ship's airlock. The girls understood but were still frightened. They had been under intense stress for weeks, and the slightest thing sent them into emotional tailspins.

"When is the alarm going to sound?" Molly asked quietly. "You said it was going to happen soon."

"No fretty-frets from you, Molly-Polly," Nixie demanded. "Close them pipy-pipes. You's gonna haywire the peeps with talk like that."

"My name's Molly Winters," the girl corrected.

"Don't cares what season you is." Nixie turned her back on Molly, not wanting the girl to see the concern in her face. The engine sensor should have triggered the Master Alarm by now, and Nixie was beginning to wonder if she had made a mistake. She was still tormented by her decision to carry Remson Burke's big blue flight case back from Mars without a proper inspection. She felt guilt rising again in her chest. She had been lucky that her mistake hadn't killed anyone. Now, she looked at several of the young girls who were crouching in a corner of the hold. If she failed this time, she would have their blood on her hands.

* * *

Nathan lay prone on the deck behind the treadmill as the intruders coursed into the ship. They were dressed in dark body-armor and had bright lights attached to their helmets. The leader barked orders to his men. "You two go below to the observation deck. The rest of you head aft to the staterooms." Nathan put his head down as a heavily-armed man paused at the entrance to the exercise room. "Clear!" he shouted. The rest of the boarders swam past without giving the room, or Nathan, another thought. He counted his foe. There were six men, plus the two who had gone to the lower deck. From the sounds of it, the leader was still in the corridor near the airlock.

Nathan heard screams. Then he heard the telltale sound of pulse-weapons. The cries for help were cut off in mid-syllable. The pirates were killing unarmed civilians, but Nathan's training taught him to think tactically, not emotionally. If he ventured out into the corridor, he would have to fight his enemy on two fronts. He would have to strike his foe in the lounge but would risk an attack from the rear by the men who had descended to the lower deck. There had been only a few people on the observation deck when the opposing ship had come alongside them. The armed men would subdue the passengers and come back to the main deck to join their comrades. Only then would he launch his counter attack against these merciless thugs.

Nathan waited patiently. The moments passed slowly, but he did not move. Then there was a voice in the corridor. "We've got four," said a gruff-sounding man.

"Good. You and Barney take them back to the ship." Nathan recognized the leader's voice.

"You got it, boss," was the reply.

Nathan realized the two men who had gone below were taking something back to their ship. He pushed off the decking, his body rising over the treadmill. Then, he floated to the hatchway. He led with his pistol, poking its barrel out of the cabin. Then he hazarded a stealthy look. The man who had given the orders was hovering near the forward hatch. In his hand, he held what looked like a toilet plunger with a pistol grip. He pressed the cup-shaped end against the sealed hatch and pulled the trigger. There was a muffled pop. He pulled the device away from the hatch, revealing a jagged hole in the metal.

Nathan raised his weapon. He unconsciously judged the angle of his hand and squeezed the trigger. A highly-focused pulse of energy struck the man on the back of his head. Streams of blood and brain-matter streamed out from his ears like twin opposing geysers. His body went limp.

Nathan glanced at the hole in the hatch, now covered with the man's blood. He recognized the tactics. The boarders weren't interested in the flight deck or its crew. If they were, a whole group of them would have been standing by, ready to storm the forward spaces. They were assaulting the integrity of the internal hatchways, so they could decompress the ship. But why hadn't they simply punctured the hull, killing everyone? With the crew and passengers out of the way, they could have plundered the ship at will. He thought about the men who were taking something back into their ship. These guys wanted something else. They wanted to keep someone alive.

Nathan shut his first victim out of his consciousness and turned aft. He flattened his body against the side wall of the passageway, then inched his way to the lounge, head-first along the bulkhead. There, the carnage was almost complete. Men and women were screaming as the pirates discharged their weapons indiscriminately. Everything that wasn't bolted down was now hovering, creating a swirling sea of debris.

Bodies were floating everywhere on meaningless trajectories, bouncing off bulkheads and tumbling head-over-feet like discarded rag dolls. Nathan positioned himself behind one of the dead, his pistol at the ready. He saw several of the young passengers stacked like cordwood near one of the viewports. They were unconscious, their hands and feet bound with plastic restraints. Nathan realized immediately that the boarding party was after the children. They had taken four of them from the observation deck. These bastards were human-traffickers.

A woman screamed. Nathan moved from behind the body and repositioned himself for a better look. A mother was shielding her daughter, pleading for mercy. One of the marauders raised his weapon. The woman put up her hands helplessly. Nathan shot from the hip, hitting the man in the torso. The shockwave deformed his chest cavity, his ribs cresting and falling under his abdominal muscles as the pulse liquefied his internal organs.

A second intruder watched, dumfounded as his comrade's lifeless body flinched and went limp. Only then did he lift his pulse-rifle. Nathan could tell from the man's response that he wasn't a trained soldier. He was much too slow. Nathan squeezed off a second shot and killed the man.

Another pirate was entering the lounge from the aft corridor as Nathan fired his second shot. He ducked out of sight before Nathan could react. There was a chatter of men's voices from the passageway. Nathan pulled himself down behind one of the couches, his pulse-pistol leveled at the spot where the man had disappeared. Then he heard a sound from the forward end of the lounge.

Nathan remained calm, his pulse barely above sixty beats per minute. The enemy was on both sides of him, now. The two men who had taken four of the children to the pirate ship had returned. He craned his neck in the direction of the sound. He was right. Two men appeared in the forward hatchway. They paused, momentarily disoriented by the hellish stew swirling around the cabin. Nathan struck like a python, two bolts of energy flashing in quick succession from the muzzle of his pistol. Both men twitched, then hung silently in the zero-g.

Nathan pivoted back toward the aft passageway and saw the top of a man's head appearing around the hatch seal. In a single fluid motion, born from years of training, Nathan brought his weapon to bear and fired again. The head jerked violently, issuing a red and gray plume of cranial debris.

* * *

"We're taking casualties here!" The voice was laced with urgency as it filled *The Cassiopeia's* flight deck. "There are soldiers on this ship!"

Pierre Antoine cursed. "How many?"

"Buster and Pete are gone. So are Chuck and Emmett. Lorenzo isn't answering his comm."

"I meant how many soldiers?" Pierre was shrieking.

"We can't see them." The sounds of a commotion interrupted the man's report. "Somebody just shot Smitty. Blew his head right off!"

"Get back here!" Pierre raged. "We're gonna cut her loose!"

* * *

Sprite and Ice maneuvered the portable thruster into the jumpship's airlock. Sprite donned her facemask and dialed up the temperature of her nanoskin. The harsh cold of space would kill her instantly without the molecular-engineered membrane that covered her body. She slid into the lock and then gave Ice a thumbs-up.

As soon as the lock decompressed, Sprite used the manual control to open the outer hatch. She secured her tether to a handhold next to the opening and fastened a second line to the thruster. She felt a chill and increased the temperature of her nanoskin again. Keeping one hand on the handhold, she pulled the rocket engine out of the lock and carefully inched her way to the utility tray, which was attached to the exterior of the fuselage directly over the cabin.

Sprite attached the thruster and unlocked the gimbals, swinging the bell of the motor so it pointed aft. She looked over her shoulder at the distant ships, judging the thrust angle necessary to steer the jumpship toward its target. She decided to ignite the motor at zero degrees, pushing the little craft forward. Then she would experiment with slight changes in the thrust vector and see how the ship responded.

The motor ignited immediately, and Sprite was startled by the vibration that radiated through the metal plating under her feet. A reddish glow appeared behind the rocket nozzle, the plume of hot gasses coursing aft and pushing the little ship forward. She felt the acceleration, her body leaning toward the gimbals. She gripped the makeshift handles on the device and pivoted the engine slightly to her left. The nose of the jumpship swung to the right.

The two spacecraft drifted across the little ship's centerline as the rocket motor drove the jumpship into an overcorrecting yaw. Sprite panicked and swiveled the rocket to the right and then looked behind her. The nose was coming back to the left. Immediately, she pivoted the motor to zero degrees and locked it in place. She looked behind her again. The jumpship was aimed directly at the other two ships. Sprite turned to the motor and closed the fuel valves. The plume of hot gas winked out as the rocket shut down.

* * *

Nathan wove his way past the dead bodies in the ship's lounge. He would press his assault and defeat his enemy. No other thought distracted him. He was a killing machine with a singular purpose. He reached the aft bulkhead. The body of an elderly woman floated near him, her face contorted in a death-mask of pain. Nathan recognized her. She had been obsessed with her appearance, always looking at herself with a small pocket mirror she kept in her handbag. Nathan looked at her hands. Sure enough, her corpse was clutching the bag. He pried it out of her dead fingers.

He pulled the mirror from the handbag and then moved closer to the hatchway that led to the staterooms. He hovered next to it, his pulse-pistol in one hand, the mirror in the other. He could hear voices from the passageway. He heard a man pleading for his life, then the distinctive sound of a pulse-rifle discharging. There was the subtle "plunk" of the shockwave distorting its human target. The unseen man was dead.

Nathan heard other voices. They belonged to his enemy. There was urgency in them. Nathan took a deep breath. Six men had passed by the exercise cabin while he was hiding behind the treadmill. There had been a seventh man at the forward hatch and then the two who had transferred four children to the pirate ship and returned while he was in the lounge. There were nine in all. Nathan had killed six of them, leaving three men in the aft compartments.

Nathan slid his shoulder until it was up against the hatchway; then he reached out and positioned the small mirror at a forty-five degree angle. He let go of it gently, and it hung almost motionlessly in the zero-g. He gave it a nudge, and the little mirror drifted toward the open hatch.

Nathan gazed intently at the reflection. He saw two men cowering at the other end of the dim passageway, their lights making them perfect targets. Amateurs, he thought. They hadn't a clue how to use the darkness to their advantage. Nathan moved his gun-hand forward until it was clear of the hatchway seal. He positioned his pistol without taking his eyes off the little mirror. His eyes narrowed, judging angles and distances to his targets from the tiny reflected image.

Nathan squeezed the trigger. The pulse-pistol discharged, and one of the men was dead, pulverized by the shockwave. His companion began to react. Nathan saw the remaining pirate look toward him, but he was confused. He could not see his enemy. The lone pistol at the edge of the hatchway was invisible in the darkened corridor. Nathan fired once more, and the remaining man joined his comrade in death.

Nathan pitched his body through the hatchway and swam quietly toward the back of the ship. The screams and pleadings of the passengers had been replaced by a sepulchral silence. Death surrounded him, but he paid no attention to it. By his count, there was only one man left. Until he was dead, Nathan could think of nothing else.

A muffled voice wafted up the passageway. It belonged to the last intruder. Nathan followed it to a partially-open stateroom. "Get me out of here, boss!" the man was whining. "The soldiers have me trapped!"

A tinny voice answered back. "We can't risk the ship, Waldo! You gotta understand that."

"No!" The man was almost hysterical.

Nathan glanced through the open door and fired his pistol one last time. The man's face erupted, spraying brain and blood throughout the stateroom. Nathan immediately returned to the lounge. He knew what was going to happen next. The enemy captain had not expected any resistance. He had lost his entire boarding party. He had told his man that he could not risk his ship. That meant the captain was going to leave. He was going to disconnect from the shattered airlock, and the resulting explosive decompression was going to kill any survivors who were left.

The woman he had saved was still clutching her daughter. "Come with me!" he commanded, grabbing her by the arm. "We've got to go to the e-suit locker!"

Nathan pulled both of them along as he swam forward through the lounge. The child had her face buried in her mother's bosom. The woman was trembling but remarkably unaffected by the sea of bloody corpses.

When they arrived at the e-suit locker, Nathan looked at the shattered airlock, which was located directly across from the locker's hatchway. The enemy ship's outer airlock door was already closed. They were running out of time.

Nathan grabbed an e-suit. He realized immediately that the life-support system was useless. It had been destroyed by the EMP that had disabled the ship. He pulled a couple of chemical warmers out of his go-back and dropped them down the pant legs of the suit. He hoped they would be enough to keep him from freezing to death before he boarded the enemy ship. He donned the suit with cool efficiency, slinging the air-supply onto his back and seating the helmet into its neck-seal.

A loud metallic sound resonated through *The Martian Princess*. The enemy ship was disengaging the grappling hooks, which held the ships together. There wasn't much time. He energized two more sets of warmers and deposited them in two of the other e-suits. The mother insisted on suiting her daughter first. The child's body was too small for the suit, but they labored to put it on her anyway.

Nathan was holding the girl's helmet when the enemy ship broke the seal on the docking collar. The sudden hurricane of air snatched the helmet from his hands. Nathan looked out the locker hatchway and into the disabled airlock. He could see the emptiness of space through the jagged opening. In the blink of an eye, both the mother and her daughter were sucked out of the e-suit locker and blown into space. Nathan grabbed a handhold with both hands and held on.

CHAPTER SEVENTEEN

S prite rode the jumpship like a stallion, kneeling on the ship's back as it flew toward the mated ships. They were much closer now. She could easily see the grappling pod and the metallic fingers that bridged the gap between the two vessels, holding them together. It was time to swing the portable thruster around and slow their approach.

Sprite unlocked the pivot and swung the rocket nozzle until it was facing the nose of the jumpship. She pressed the igniter, and the little motor flared into life. She watched the distance between the ships stabilize. She shut down the rocket when she was less than a hundred meters away.

Without warning, Sprite saw the grappling-hooks disengage from *The Martian Princess*. Her hopes faded as she realized the sex-traders were about to separate from the stricken vessel. They would fire their main engine and continue on to Rinker's Knot, leaving them behind to perish in the merciless cold of space.

Sprite's thoughts were interrupted when the slave-traders fired their vernier thrusters. The little rockets pushed *The Cassiopeia* away from the other ship, and the docking collar pulled free of the disabled ship's hull. Instantly, a cloud of debris erupted from the opening, carried into space on violent currents of escaping air. There was no sound. It was like watching an ancient silent movie.

Sprite saw the first body emerge from the open airlock. It was a young girl. She flailed about, trying to grasp the wind as she rode the column of air into the vacuum of space. Then her tiny body grew still as her life was stolen away. Sprite tasted acid rising in her throat. She gripped the handles of the rocket motor and looked away in horror. She had not fully appreciated the evil that gripped the hearts of Nixie's captors. Sprite looked back. More bodies cascaded out of the ship, tumbling like broken dolls into the void. Gradually, the maelstrom lost its breath, and the cloud of bodies and debris disbursed in an ever-widening reminder of the acts of violence committed within *The Martian Princess's* hull.

* * *

An unbearable despair had settled over Stephen and Rene Winters. The authorities had told them there was little hope for their daughter. They had exhausted every idea and contact they could muster. There was nothing else they could do. Their hope was flagging and with it, their belief in goodness. Waiting and not knowing were the greatest curses of their lives. They were helpless and cut off.

Stephen stood in the shower, the hot water coursing down his skin. He didn't feel it. In fact, he didn't feel anything anymore. He had always been an enthusiastic man. He was once full of good humor, a trickster by nature. Now he was morose, a lifeless automaton who shuffled through his day on autopilot. He was numb.

He looked at the bar of soap in his hand. His daily showers had eaten away at it, dissolving the waxy brick. Now it was paper-thin. He palmed it, and the bar broke into several useless pieces. He stared at the sticky fragments in his hand. Molly was dead, he thought. Then he hung his head, his tears mingling with the scalding water.

* * *

Nixie stood vigil with the children in *The Cassiopeia's* hold, listening for the sound of the Master Alarm, which would announce the beginning of their revolt. She counted backwards from ten in her head, hoping for the piercing siren to ring out when she reached zero. The alarm did not sound.

The hatch opened without warning, and two members of the crew pushed the inert bodies of four children into the hold. They tumbled to the deck, their hands and feet tied with plastic restraints. Nixie watched the men's faces. They looked worried. Something was wrong.

The ship's intercom blared to life. It was Pierre Antoine's voice. "All hands! Get to your stations. The boarding team is under heavy fire! We're decoupling from *The Martian Princess*."

Nixie smiled innocently at the two men. "Aw. Ain't that toosy bad," she said sarcastically. "Soundy likes your jobby-job went to poopy-dupe." The men stepped back into the passageway and started to close the hatch. "Hope you die, you bass-turds!" Nixie shrieked. The hatch clicked shut.

Nixie turned back toward the other girls. Her bravado was only skin-deep, and although she could not show it, she was worried. Molly Winters started to clap. Several of the other girls shouted with glee. Then cheers spread throughout the hold like a wildfire.

Nixie wanted to feel the same exuberance as her companions, but she could not. She knew her plan had fallen apart. The Master Alarm should have sounded long ago. Without it, their captors would have no reason to abandon their ship. All the cheering waifs surrounding her were going to be sold into slavery and would spend their remaining days at the mercy of lustful men. Nixie raised her hands as an expression of triumph she did not feel. She knew the hope she was giving these girls was false hope, as much of an illusion as Captain Grit had been.

* * *

Nathan Trent was pummeled by the swirling vortexes that accompanied the avalanche of air that stormed the gaping airlock. He held on with all of his strength as the contents of the e-suit locker were sucked out of the hatchway, across the corridor, and through the airlock into the vacuum of space. His go-bag was gone, but he had had the forethought to tuck his pulse-pistol into the utility pouch on the front of the e-suit.

Gradually the wind lessened, dwindling to a coarse whisper, then muttering into silence. Nathan let go of the handhold and swam out into the corridor. The interior of the ship was swept clean by the maelstrom. He propelled himself into the airlock and floated in the gaping orifice where the outer hatch had been. The space beyond was littered with bodies and debris, some of it bouncing off the hull of the intruder's ship. The gap between the two vessels was widening. The enemy ship had fired her vernier thrusters, pushing her away from the stricken ship. The air-geyser from *The Martian Princess's* airlock had given her lateral thrust of her own, but the force was causing her to spin slowly about her center of mass.

Nathan felt the cold of space cutting through his disabled e-suit. He knew that even the best training couldn't save him now. He was a warrior, and he had fought valiantly against his enemy, but they had won. The commander who had ordered the deaths of so many innocent people was warm and safe aboard his ship. He had lost his boarding party, but he would live. He would continue to terrorize his victims, stripping children away from their parents.

An icy calm settled over him. His eyes fell on the emitter pod that skirted the aft section of the enemy ship. The two ion-emitters were hidden behind the cowling, but if he could climb to *The Martian Princess's* stern, he might be able to get a clear shot. Nathan reached for a handhold on the exterior of the hull, taking care not to puncture his e-suit on the jagged edges where the airlock hatch had been. He climbed from gripping point to gripping point, until he was on the midline of the ship. Then, he began to work his way aft, toward the tail section.

He was halfway to his destination when a brilliant bluish glow erupted from the enemy ship's ion-emitters. She was getting underway. He was too late! Nathan had to act. Without any further thought, he leapt off the hull toward the tail section of *The Cassiopeia*. He began to tumble as he flew through the intervening space between the two vessels. He reached into the utility pouch and withdrew his pulse-pistol. He extended his arm and sighted down the barrel, judging the ever-changing angles caused by his tumbling body. He did not want the last shot of his life to miss its target.

The nearest ion-emitter moved across his sight, and Nathan squeezed off the shot. The shockwave from the pistol hit the central element of the emitter, destroying the complex mechanism. The blue fire flickered out as the massive device failed. The other emitter grew brighter as Nathan tumbled toward its ion cloud. He lined up his weapon for a second shot, but when he pressed the trigger, the pulse-pistol didn't fire.

Nathan stared into the blue plasma, facing his death with eyes wide open. The plasma envelope shuttered and winked out as the functioning ion-emitter shut down. Nathan crossed in front of it safely, but he was out of control. In the void of space, there were no handholds, no tethering points, and no solid ground. His body continued to tumble as he drifted off into the cold darkness of space.

* * *

Nixie heard *The Cassiopeia's* propulsion system engage. It was a haunting reminder of *The Raccoon*. The power surge was smooth, the signature of a fully functional engine. Her hope was slipping away with each passing moment.

Suddenly, the pitch of the engine changed. A loud hum coursed through the ship's space frame, and there was an explosive sound from somewhere in the aft section of the ship. The lights in the hold flickered, and many of the children screamed. Then the Master Alarm began to wail. Within seconds, the main engine shut down, and there was a flurry of activity in the passageway outside the hold.

Nixie breathed a sigh of relief. Her plan was working, but she knew something more serious had happened. Her sabotage would not have caused an explosion. Her years of experience had taught her that spacecraft could fall victim to many technical problems. The unfolding events might have the desired effect, forcing their captors to abandon ship, but she and her young companions were still immersed in a sea of peril. All of her knowledge and cunning might prove to be inadequate. Nevertheless, Nixie set her jaw, refusing to bow again to her insecurity.

Molly Winters nudged Nixie's elbow, her eyes wide with fear and anticipation. "When do we get out of here?" she shouted into her ear.

"We gots ta wait 'till the bass-turds leave the shipper," Nixie yelled back. Then with an even louder voice, she addressed everyone in the hold. "'Larm'sa falsie. Wheeze gonna beezee okee-dokey!"

* * *

Pierre Antoine cursed as the flight deck shuttered under his feet. The Master Alarm sounded, and pulsating red icons filled the ship's status screens. At the same time, his engineer's voice erupted through the ship's comm system, filling the bridge with his trembling words. "Propulsion is offline, sir!" he squealed. "I've got over-temperature indicators on the main reaction chamber. The starboard emitter shut down. It unbalanced the system, and the mismatch overloaded the power circuits!"

"Mute that damned alarm!" Pierre shrieked at Star. She pressed an icon on her display, and the ear-shattering alarm went silent. Red flashing lights still blinked angrily throughout the ship. Pierre turned back to the comm system. "Can you fix it?" Pierre shouted at his engineer.

"I could if we didn't have the thermal overload. It's gonna go critical on us, sir. We're all dead if we don't get off this ship!"

"Shit!" Pierre screamed. "How did everything go to hell so fast?" He was stunned by the loss of his boarding party and now a major malfunction on his own ship. "Abandon ship, everyone! Get to the hanger bay and prepare the jumpship for immediate departure!"

* * *

Ice watched from the jumpship as *The Cassiopeia* detached from *The Martian Princess*. She had watched the weapon flashes through the passenger ship's viewports and knew there had been a slaughter. Her suspicion was confirmed when the dead bodies flooded out through the shattered airlock. The men who had Nixie were ruthless killers.

Ice grabbed her binoculars when the e-suited figure appeared in the airlock hatchway. The boarders would not have worn suits, so this man must have been a passenger on the disabled ship. She studied him as he climbed up the side of the ship's fuselage. He was on a suicide mission. His suit couldn't be functioning. He would have air to breathe for a while, but without a heater, he would freeze to death long before he suffocated.

When *The Cassiopeia's* engines came to life, Ice knew they were in trouble, but her concern was temporarily over-ridden by the actions of the e-suited figure. She watched as he leapt from the disabled ship. She saw him draw his weapon as his body tumbled toward the enemy ship's stern. Then she witnessed his impossible shot, sending a crippling pulse directly into the starboard ion-emitter.

This man was a member of special forces. She was certain of it. They were the only ones who could make a shot like that. She knew because she had been one of them. This stranger was a brother-in-arms. She pulled the binoculars from her face as the man continued to tumble across the stern of *The Cassiopeia*. His body gyrated about his center of gravity as the dark void swallowed him up in its infinite maw. She knew she was powerless to save him, but if she could, she would gladly give her life to pluck her fellow warrior from the jaws of danger.

* * *

Nixie looked up as the hatch opened once again. Two of Pierre Antoine's men appeared in the opening. They were holding pulse-rifles. The girls screamed at the sight of the weapons. Pierre appeared from behind his men. They stepped aside dutifully, and he entered the hold. He nodded at Nixie. "I see you got some clothing," he taunted. "That rag looks good on you." Nixie spit at him. "Defiant to the end, aren't we, Miss Drake?" Nixie glared at him, the fire in her eyes rekindled. Pierre smirked. "Something's different about you," he remarked. "You should never have run away from me years ago. I don't like losing things."

"I ain't no thingy," Nixie growled.

"That's where you are mistaken. You've been my property ever since I took you from your parents." Nixie's hands were balled into fists. Pierre looked down at them. "You've got spunk. I'll hand you that." He sighed. "I can't stay long. The propulsion system is overheating, and we are abandoning ship. Alas, we don't have room for you in our jumpship, so you're going to have to stay here and die. Sorry about that." Pierre turned back toward his men dismissively and disappeared through the hatch.

* * *

Sprite was repositioning the small rocket motor to keep up with *The Cassiopeia* when Nathan Trent had leapt from his perch on the back of *The Martian Princess*. She had swung the motor around, and her back was turned when he had fired his pulse-pistol. She ignited the rocket and looked over her shoulder to check her heading in time to see the enemy ship's engines fail. Realizing she now needed to break the ship's momentum, she shut down the thruster and once again pivoted it around until the nozzle was facing forward. When she threw the switch, the rocket didn't fire. Sprite tried again, but to no avail. The jumpship was now traveling faster than *The Cassiopeia* and would soon pass her.

A lump formed in Sprite's throat as pure anxiety kneaded her stomach like a lump of bread dough. She slid toward the jumpship's nose and climbed down outside the forward viewport. Ice was staring at her through the aluminum-silicate glass. Sprite touched the faceplate of her mask to the glass and shouted, "We've got to slow down, but the thruster won't fire!" The sound waves from her voice were transferred through the viewport. Ice nodded in understanding.

Ice climbed over the control console and put her face to the viewport, directly in front of Sprite. "Use the winch!" she shouted.

"The winch?"

"Yes! Play out enough cable and jump!" She motioned toward the enemy ship.

"You want me to jump?"

Ice nodded.

"With the winch cable?"

Ice nodded again. At that moment, Ice saw movement under *The Cassiopeia*. A sleek silver jumpship shot out from beneath her hull and streaked away.

* * *

Pierre Antoine had lost over half his crew in the firefight on *The Martian Princess*. Now he sat beside Driver, who had just opened the hanger-bay doors in the belly of his doomed ship. The pilot undocked the jumpship from her moorings and used the vernier thrusters to push the little craft away from *The Cassiopeia*. Pierre watched the curved hull of the larger ship rise above them as the sleek jumpship dropped through the open belly of its mother. Then Driver punched the main thruster, and the jumpship shot forward.

"Get us back to Copernicus Base!" Pierre commanded. Driver responded with a nod, laying in the course with the ship's nav-AI.

"Sir!" It was Star. The copper-haired woman was gazing out the tiny viewport in the rear of the cabin. "The jumpship that was following us is much closer now."

"It doesn't matter," Pierre said dismissively. "When *The Cassiopeia* blows, it will take everything within thirty klicks with it." A grim fatalism descended over him. At least he had taken care of the Drake girl. Losing the shipment of girls was a different matter. He had been trying to improve his customer service. Remson Burke and his superiors weren't going to be pleased. Pierre would have to make good, of course. He would have to get another ship and round up more skin-goods. He cursed silently. It was going to take years to recover from this fiasco.

* * *

Nixie did her best to calm the girls, but their days and weeks of captivity had worn heavily on them. She called for silence, telling them that the sounds of the ship were her window to what was happening outside the hold. She lay down on the deck, placing her ear against the cold metal. She had to be certain that their captors had left the ship. If they ventured out of their prison too soon, Pierre Antoine's men might kill them all.

Nixie felt a distinctive clunking sound vibrate through the ship's framing. She was sure it came from thrust-bolts retracting in a docking mechanism. The ship's crew had boarded a jumpship on *The Cassiopeia's* hanger bay, and the little ship had just been released from its cradle.

Nixie got up and approached the hatch. It was virtually the same as the ones which had been on *The Raccoon*. Many times, she had helped Ice repair them, and she knew how to disengage the locking mechanism. She reached up behind one of the panels and found the cable she was looking for. She disconnected the electrical coupling with a quick twist of her wrist.

Nixie looked over her shoulder. The other girls had gathered around her in a semicircle, scarcely daring to breathe as they watched her. She gave them a confident smile, then gripped the latch-handle. Nixie pushed down on the lever, and the hatch popped open.

* * *

Sprite climbed back to the jumpship's airlock. A small winch was built into the hull, next to the outer hatch. She disengaged the locking mechanism and painstakingly withdrew the slender winch cable, playing it out as far as it would go. She kept an eye on *The Cassiopeia*. If she didn't hurry, they would pass the larger ship and drift off into the void.

Sprite secured the end of the winch line to her tether harness, then released the shorter safety cable and stowed it on her hip. She planted both feet against the hull, her eyes on the larger ship. The distance between them was narrowing at a slow but inexorable rate. She judged the angle necessary to intercept *The Cassiopeia's* hull, wishing she had a personal mobility unit to ride across the gulf that separated the two vessels.

A ripple of anxiety tied a knot in her stomach. She hesitated, her fear overwhelming her inner fighter. She couldn't do this. She looked away, trying to calm herself with the beauty of the interstellar ocean, and saw a tiny human-form tumbling in the inky blackness. It was the brave stranger from *The Martian Princess*, who had disabled the sex-traders' ship. He hadn't been afforded the luxury of a tether or a winch line. Nevertheless, he had done what was necessary.

Sprite pushed away her fear, steeling herself for what she had to do. She gripped the winch line tightly, inspired by the unknown man's bravery. Then, she hooked her toe under a handhold and bent her knees, crouching like a frog against the side of the jumpship. She disengaged her toe and took one more careful glance at her target.

As Sprite pushed away from the jumpship, her foot brushed against the handhold she had just used. She hadn't pulled her toe out enough before leaping, and she began to spin, careening uncontrollably in the wrong direction. She swore, angry with herself for being so clumsy at such a critical moment. She would miss *The Cassiopeia*. The jumpship would pass the larger ship, and they would die. Her companions had put their lives in her hands, and she had failed them.

CHAPTER EIGHTEEN

Nixie was the first one out of the hold, glancing fore and aft to make sure there were no crew members still on board. A river of children coursed out of the hatchway behind her. Nixie moved forward, pausing briefly in front of the ship's multi-cabin. She pivoted on her heel and glanced through the crowd for Molly Winters.

"Hey! Molly snowflake! Move yer cedar-rumpus up here!" Nixie wore a playful smile.

"It's Winters," the girl complained.

Nixie ignored her. "I'm makin' you my firsty-first off-sir."

Molly's eyes grew large. "You mean it?"

"Absotively, posolutely." Nixie nodded. "Now I gots to go to the 'pulsion deck. You set the girls down on their fanny-wackers and get them somethin' to stuffy two-shoes into their tummy-tums." She gestured toward the food dispensers.

Molly gave her a mock salute and began herding the children into the multi-cabin. Nixie threaded her way aft through the melee.

* * *

Sprite gripped the winch cable in both hands and began taking up the slack. She knew she would have to try again, but she didn't have time to "climb" the full length of the line. She pumped her arms rapidly, pushing the loose cable past her fingers. She watched the line straighten as her body pitched away from the jumpship. Everything was spinning, and she struggled to keep a firm grip on the cable.

Sprite wrapped the winch-line around her wrist. It was only seconds before her full mass snapped the cable taut. She looked down at her left forearm and punched one of the control buttons for her nanoskin. Instantly, the envelope which covered her body grew as hard as diamond. The cable stretched tightly between her and the jumpship, cinching harmlessly against her impermeable outer shell. Sprite readjusted the skin's toughness and started pulling herself back to the jumpship, climbing hand over hand. All the while, she prayed that there would be enough time to hurl herself toward the other ship again and fasten the two vessels together.

* * *

Nixie kept watch for any of Pierre Antoine's men as she rushed toward the propulsion deck. She glanced in every cabin as she worked her way aft, finally checking the room where she had been held. The crew was gone. They were alone on the ship.

Nixie went straight to the engineer's console. She scanned the instruments, noting the abnormally high thermal readings. She hoped they were caused by her sabotage of the sensors and not because of a real malfunction in the engine's cooling system.

Nixie almost overlooked the other fault indicator that was blinking on the engineering display. The Cassiopeia's engine was a powerful ion-drive. Two large emitters protruded from her stern and squirted highly-charged particles like a garden hose, giving the ship her forward thrust. Nixie didn't understand the details, but she knew that the emitters had to be tuned precisely to the rest of the engine. Any mismatch would cause some of the immense energy to be reflected back into the engine. The result would be catastrophic.

The display in front of her indicated that one of the emitters was malfunctioning. Fortunately, the drive AI had sensed the problem and shut down the engine, but Nixie had no idea how to solve the problem. They had gained their freedom from the sex-traders, only to be marooned on a disabled spacecraft.

* * *

Sprite was breathing heavily when she finally returned to the jumpship. She grabbed the handhold that had previously caught her toe and repositioned herself for another leap toward *The Cassiopeia*. The two crafts were side by side, ships passing in the night. Sprite panicked when she gauged her trajectory to the nearest anchor point on the larger ship's hull. She had run out of time. She had to jump immediately. Sprite poked her toe under the handhold again and squatted down. She removed her foot and gently floated a half meter away from the rung. She looked up at her target one more time and leapt from the jumpship's hull with every ounce of her strength.

Sprite flew straight and true, a space angel gliding effortlessly through the darkness. The winch cable snaked behind her in slow motion, its meandering curves untwisting and straightening as the slackened line stretched out. Her flight was silent, except for the breath sounds in her mask and the sound of her heart beating in her chest. Sprite stretched her arms forward, like a high diver reaching for the water's surface. She willed her body to land near an anchor point on the transfer ship's hull.

The massive ship's beam loomed in front of Sprite. It was going to be close. A row of anchor points dotted the vessel's fuselage, running from near the stern to her nose. Sprite fixed her eyes on the one nearest to the nose of the ship, her hand gripping the clip on the end of the winch cable. She was twenty meters away.

Everything seemed to be in slow motion as time dilated. Sprite saw that she was going to strike the hull, but miss the last anchor point. Her heart fell as the cruel course of events unfolded before her. She could not swim toward the anchor point. Her flight had been determined the second her feet left the jumpship's hull. She was ten meters from failure.

The last anchor point slipped silently out of reach. Cold gray metal plating filled Sprite's field of view. She was almost past the larger ship. She could feel the line begin to pull against her, decreasing her velocity. She glanced back at the jumpship. The winch cable was almost straight. She was going to run out of line before reaching *The Cassiopeia*!

Sprite looked down at the harness that held her air canister. She saw her tether coiled in a hook and loop strap. She ripped it from her waist and fastened one end of the tether to the winch cable. The other end was still secured to her harness. Then, Sprite let go of the longer cable and let it float free on the end of the tether. She was five meters from her target.

Sprite's tether was uncoiling. She wondered if it would be strong enough to withstand the pull of the jumpship. She imagined the slender braid unraveling under the strain. Perhaps one of the clips would shatter. She was only three meters from the larger ship.

Sprite scoured the massive hull for a place to secure her line. The fuselage was narrowing toward the flight deck. She was approaching the ship's bow at a terrifying rate. Sprite would slide past *The Cassiopeia's* forward viewports and career over her nose. After that, the ship would be out of reach, and she would be dragged behind the jumpship like a tin can fastened to the bumper of a honeymooner's car. She was only one meter away.

Sprite struck *The Cassiopeia's* hull just aft of the forward viewports. The winch cable and tether pulled her laterally along the surface of the hull. Her body began to tumble against the metal. She spread out her arms, hugging the skin of the ship in an attempt to steady herself. She slid spread-eagled over the smooth glass of the viewport, one hand gripping her tether. The flight deck flashed by beneath her, then all she could see was the blunt nose of the ship. She was going to die.

At the last possible moment, Sprite saw a ring protruding from the very tip of *The Cassiopeia's* nose. It was an anchor point! She reached down and unsnapped the tether from her harness. She gripped it with all her strength. She could not fail! She must not fail! If it slipped from her fingers, her friends would die, and she would be lost forever. Sprite reached out her arm. As her body slipped past the nose of the ship, she hooked the tether's clip into the anchor-ring and snapped it closed. The line drew tight, and she grabbed it. The cable sang like a bass string on a grand piano, its vibrations coursing through her hands and into her bones. It was the most beautiful sound that Sprite had ever heard.

* * *

Nixie Drake left the propulsion deck and descended to the hanger bay. As she suspected, there was an empty cradle where a jumpship had once been secured. The immense doors were open, revealing the ink-black sea of space. She closed the bay and locked it, making sure Pierre and his men could not return to the ship. Then she returned to the main deck. *The Cassiopeia's* bridge was her next stop.

Nixie strode forward through the main passageway with a captain's purpose. This was her ship now, and damaged or not, she would not lose her. She peeked into the multi-cabin as she passed by. The children were sitting quietly at the tables, filling their bellies with food. Molly was supervising several of the girls who were distributing beverages. She didn't linger, but proceeded forward through the passageway, toward the bridge.

Nixie felt a wave of pride as she entered the flight deck. She scanned the displays, noting the flashing red icons on the engineering screens. The life-support system was nominal, as was the ship's electrical system. She stood quietly next to the pilot's seat, examining the controls. The ship was dead in space, but every system was normalized. Pierre's pilot was a pro. At least there was that.

"There a brain-bucket on this shipper?" she asked with a gravelly tone.

There was no response.

Remembering how long it took to teach *The Raccoon's* AI to understand her dialect, Nixie paused and chose her words more carefully. "Ship's AI," she enunciated clearly. "Report in."

Still no answer.

Nixie turned and glanced at the racks of electronic gear on the aft bulkhead of the flight deck. To her surprise, she saw a gaping hole where the ship's artificial intelligence system would have been located. Bundles of cables were cut away, leaving nothing but blunt-ended wires. Pierre Antoine had taken the ship's AI with him. Her heart sank. *The Cassiopeia* couldn't be flown without it.

Nixie turned her attention to the communications system. As she suspected, the ship's comm gear was smashed beyond repair. There was no way to fly and no way to call for help. She and the children were still prisoners, now sentenced to lives in the solitary confinement of a disabled ship.

Nixie heard something bang against the hull over her head. She looked up instinctively. There was a scraping sound as if something was being dragged over the skin of the ship. She turned around, just in time to see a human body slide past the viewport. It was a woman. She wasn't wearing an e-suit, and she was hanging on to a tether of some kind. The woman disappeared from view, and Nixie's attention was drawn to the small spacecraft that was fastened to the other end of the long cable. Her eyes narrowed. It was her jumpship.

Nixie stared in disbelief. What was her ship doing out here? Then she heard metal clicking against metal from beneath the viewport, followed by a sound resembling a vibrating string, its deep bass note resonating through the ship's framing. There was a tugging sensation, and Nixie realized immediately that the two ships were now tied together.

Nixie's mind went into overdrive, trying to make sense of what she had just seen. Had Pierre Antoine stolen her jumpship? Had he returned, only to find the hanger bay closed and locked? Was he going to force his way back on board? Nixie pushed away her emotions. It didn't make sense. As far as Pierre knew, the ship was still a ticking time bomb. He would not risk his life returning to *The Cassiopeia*. And then there was the crazy woman who had just flown past the viewport without the benefit of an e-suit. How was that possible? Nixie's mental question triggered a memory. There were a couple of people in the system who could do that sort of thing, and she knew them both. She caught her breath as a new possibility took shape in her mind. For the first time in many days, Nixie smiled.

* * *

The winch cable and tether withstood the tug of the jumpship. The anchor ring on *The Cassiopeia* became a pivot point, and the little ship began to arc toward the larger ship. Fortunately, the vessels were no longer side by side, and the two hulls did not smash together. Sprite gripped the cable with both hands, painfully aware that her tether was now part of the line which kept the ships from separating. She dared not move, lest she drift off into space. She considered pulling herself along the cable and going back to the jumpship, but the risk was the same no matter where she was. She resolved to save her energy and work the problem. There had to be a way to get to safety.

Sprite considered trying to pull the jumpship closer to *The Cassiopeia*, but she doubted she could do it. She would have to grip the cable with her arms outstretched and pull her hands together, creating a loop in the winch-line. It would take more strength than she could muster, and if one hand slipped, she'd probably set herself in motion and float beyond reach of the cable.

Sprite felt a deep chill in her fingers. The nanoskin was having trouble protecting her from the cold. She let go of the cable with her right hand and pressed the temperature control on her left forearm. She felt a surge of warmth. Sprite wondered about the limits of her nanoskin. She had become accustomed to it over the last three years. The burns she had endured at the Meridian research settlement on Ceres had nearly killed her. The nanoskin that covered her body had saved her life, and she had come to rely on it. She took a deep breath of air, then realized she had no way of knowing how much oxygen remained in the tank on her back. What was going to kill her first? She decided she would rather freeze. Freezing to death was relatively painless. She would become groggy, then fall asleep. It was far better than suffocation.

Sprite thought of Kell. She felt a cold tear on her cheek as she remembered how they had embraced on the Ankrum dock. She could hear his voice in her mind, whispering "I love you." She felt like she had been stabbed with a dagger when she remembered him telling her how he never wanted to lose her again. She was going to break his heart. He was going to die wondering what had happened to her.

Sprite shut the thoughts from her mind. As long as she was alive, there was hope. She thought of the e-suited figure who had fired his weapon on *The Cassiopeia*. His suit electronics had been destroyed, but he still managed to use it to venture outside his ship. There was an e-suit on the jumpship. Maybe Ice would put it on and bring a tether to her. Sprite glanced over at the little craft. Her spirits fell when she saw the outer airlock hatch. She had left it open. There was no way for Ice to exit the ship. She would have to decompress the cabin, and Addison would die.

Sprite saw a light glinting off the winch cable. Its source was over her shoulder. Her pulse quickened. The light grew more intense; then it disappeared. Sprite craned her neck and saw an e-suited figure orbiting around her left side. Whoever it was had a personal mobility unit. Its lights were blinding. Sprite squinted, unable to discern the face of her rescuer. She wondered for a moment if the sex-traders were still on board the ship.

The space-walker came to a stop directly in front of her. The jets on the PMU spit silently, and the stranger approached within a half-meter of Sprite's face. The brilliant lights winked out, and everything was ink-black. As her irises dilated, Sprite saw a youthful face grinning from beneath the e-suit's faceplate. It was Nixie Drake.

Nixie tipped her head forward and gently touched her helmet to Sprite's facemask. Sprite could hear the life-support system humming through the clear material. Then she saw Nixie's lips move, and a gravelly voice whispered to her. "You one of them Logan peeps?"

* * *

Ice watched the e-suited figure approach Sprite. In her own subdued fashion, she was grateful. Ice had known some people who deserved to die in space. Sprite wasn't one of them. She was a brave woman. She had volunteered for the rescue mission because of the kindness that Nixie had shown to her family. She wasn't trained for combat or deep-space EVAs, but she had put herself on the line for her friends. Sprite had earned her respect.

Ice's thoughts turned to the marksman who had made the impossible shot while tumbling past *The Cassiopeia's* ion-emitters. Ice closed her eyes, imagining him spinning out of control, beyond the ships and into the lonely dark. The life-support system in his suit was fried. He must have put some chemical warmers in the suit, or he would have been frozen as soon as he exited *The Martian Princess's* airlock. He was getting cold, and his air-supply was running out. Like Sprite, he didn't deserve to die either.

Ice had been out of the special forces for over six years, but the training had never left her. She didn't know the stranger's name, but his peril was like a mythic siren, summoning her to his side. He was a fellow soldier, and letting him tumble off into the endless void of space was unacceptable. Unfortunately, there was nothing she could do.

* * *

Nixie pressed the end-clip of a tether into Sprite's hand. She accepted it with a broad smile and immediately snapped it onto her harness. She let go of the winch-cable, flexing her stiff fingers to restore circulation. Nixie rotated away, taking her in tow back to the airlock. When the chamber was repressurized, Nixie pulled off her helmet.

"You offer yer eggy-noggin, girly?" she growled. "Where's yer 'dults?"

"Home," Sprite offered simply. "Ice and I followed you out here."

Nixie frowned. "Icy's here?"

"In the jumpship with another friend of mine."

"Gots 'pulsion troubles? Don't see it movin' much."

"Pierre Antoine fired their disruptor at us. The EMP fried all of our electronics."

Nixie understood. "We besty goes 'n gets 'em," she said softly." She gestured toward a row of e-suits. "Putsy a reg'lar suity-suit on yer butt." She pointed at the outer airlock door with her thumb. "You beezee lots more warmy-warm out there."

Nixie waddled out of the airlock as Sprite grabbed the nearest e-suit. The young captain returned a couple of minutes later with a portable thruster. It looked like a miniature version of the one Sprite had used to steer the jumpship. She explained that she had opened the hanger bay, so they could bring the stricken craft on board.

The women checked each other's suits, then Nixie cycled the airlock. Each had a personal mobility unit, so they shot away from the ship on jets of compressed air, their lights piercing the darkness of space. It took only a few seconds for them to reach the jumpship. Sprite maneuvered to the viewport and told Ice what they were going to do.

Nixie attached the portable thruster to the utility tray and activated the unit. Then she took a pair of cable cutters from her tool pouch and cut the winch line. Using a remote control built into her PMU, Nixie fired the thruster, steering the jumpship like a child's toy, back toward *The Cassiopeia*. Nixie flew the jumpship under The Cassiopeia's belly, then carefully maneuvered the disabled craft toward the open hanger bay. Once inside, the little craft was securely clamped into its cradle.

Moments later, Nixie and Sprite stood, helmets in hand, before the jumpship's hatch. There was an audible hiss as Ice cranked open the panel. The older woman stepped out of the hatch. She stood squarely in front of Nixie, her eyes fixed upon the younger woman. Nixie held her breath, unsure of what to say. Ice had not defended her when their crew broke up. She wasn't sure if she was friend or foe.

"Permission to come aboard, Captain," Ice intoned.

Nixie's jaw dropped. The stoic woman was deathly serious, her request an acknowledgement of her respect. Nixie gave her a mock salute. "Getcher butty-butt over here, Icy!" Ice stepped forward and offered to shake Nixie's hand. The young captain took it enthusiastically. "Welkey-Delky to my newsy shipper! She's a bitsy-broken, but wheeze gots air and heaty-heat!"

Ice nodded. "Can I borrow that PMU and an e-suit?"

Nixie paused, somewhat befuddled. "You's goin' EVA? You just gots here!"

"Have to run a quick errand," Ice offered mysteriously. "I'll need a spare life-support system, too."

* * *

Nathan Trent knew he was going to die. He had known his life was over the very second he had leapt into space without a tether. He had watched with cold detachment as the spaceships grew smaller in the distance, his body transformed into a tiny interplanetary vessel, pitching this way and that. He took a measure of satisfaction from the knowledge that his final act was to strike back at the enemy. He had fought against the agents of inhumanity. He had brought the battle to them, and although he was going to die, he had not left them unscathed.

Nathan closed the sunshield on his helmet to block out the stars. He was tumbling uncontrollably, and the spinning points of light made it hard for him to concentrate. He withdrew into a Zen-state, slowing his heart rate and clearing his mind for the end. He was cold, and although he had slowed his breathing, the air in his e-suit was growing stale.

He thought of his brother on Mars. Some nameless bureaucrat was going to pay him a visit and break the news that *The Martian Princess* had failed to arrive. He would be shattered by the news, perhaps relapse into his alcoholism. Nathan was sorrowful, wishing he could have seen his brother again, but then he remembered his training. "Duty above all," he had chanted with his comrades. Duty above all. Duty had trumped a visit with his family. Duty had trumped his hopes and dreams. Duty trumped everything.

Something touched Nathan's arm. It was a human touch, a hand. He felt a change in acceleration as his body ceased tumbling. He thought it was a dream. Perhaps it was the arms of death embracing him, welcoming him home from life's battlefield. Something retracted his sunshield, and Nathan opened his eyes. Before him floated a woman. He looked into her eyes and saw an ancient soul. She leaned forward and touched their faceplates together. "Stay with me, soldier," she called to him. Nathan nodded, and the woman disappeared.

Once again, he thought he was dreaming and the woman was a figment of his imagination. Perhaps she was an angel, although Nathan was skeptical about such things. He felt something on his back and then heard the familiar sound of a life-support system churning the air in his suit. Warmth wrapped itself around his body, and Nathan felt death release its grip on him.

The woman reappeared in his field of view. He could feel her strength as she gripped his forearm. He could see her strength when he gazed into her eyes. He recognized a kindred spirit. She was a warrior, a sister, a comrade-in-arms. Nathan offered the angel a weak thumbs-up as she carried him out of the darkness of oblivion.

CHAPTER NINETEEN

olly Winters watched Ice carry Nathan Trent to *The Cassiopeia's* infirmary. She was amazed by the woman's strength and secretly vowed to emulate her in later life. She stood in the hatchway as Ice laid the man gently on the examination table. Molly recognized the small cabin. This was the place where she had been forced to remove her clothing and endure the taunts and insults of the man called Mo. She stepped back into the passageway but did not leave.

Molly studied Ice's movements. The woman straightened her fingers as she withdrew her hands from under the man's shoulders and knees. She had pianist's hands, but Molly suspected the muscular woman was not a musician. The woman moved like a dancer, but she was certain that Ice had never been on a stage. Molly concluded that she was a soldier, full of power and grace, secure in her skin, agile minded and fearsome in the face of danger.

Molly watched as Ice gave the man a sedative and gently spread a blanket over his inert form. She marveled at the woman's abilities as she threaded an intravenous line into one of his veins and started a saline drip. The young girl felt safe near Ice. The warrior-woman's strength transformed the infirmary from a place filled with terrible memories into a chamber of healing.

Molly stepped into the cabin. "Is he going to be okay?" she asked tentatively.

"Who are you?" Ice's voice was quiet, but it had an edge of steel.

"Molly Winters. I was one of the..."

"Hostages." Ice finished for her. "He's a strong man. He's going to sleep for a while. He'll live."

"I'm glad," Molly murmured. "What's your name?"

Ice turned away from Nathan, giving the young girl her full attention. Molly tensed. "I'm a friend of Nixie Drake's," Ice replied. "My name's Ellie Karlsen. You can call me Ice."

Molly stuck out her hand. "Thanks for saving us," she stammered.

"You're not home yet, girl." Ice took another look at Nathan Trent, then turned back to her. "Have one of the kids keep an eye on him. Let me know when he wakes up."

"Yes, Ma'am," Molly promised.

* * *

Nixie sat in the captain's chair on the bridge of *The Cassiopeia*. Most of the systems were on standby. The ship's engine was disabled; her AI was missing. The ship was a wreck, an impotent hunk of metal floating in the endless expanse of outer space. Sprite Logan sat in the pilot's seat, the chair twisted around so she could face her friend. Addison Traynor was bent over one of the other stations, studying the various screens and knobs that occupied that section of the flight deck.

"Taint su-prised muchy-much, Spritey, buts I's never 'spected ta see ya skinny-dippy outside my viewport!" Nixie laughed with a gravelly cackle.

"I was dressed!" Sprite said defensively.

"Butcha were missy-missin' your e-suit. Taint natchal swimmin' in the void like that."

"The jumpship's e-suit was destroyed by the disruptor," Sprite explained.

"A focused electromagnetic pulse-weapon." Addison pointed at the screen in front of her. "This is the targeting console for it."

Nixie shook her head. She wasn't sure what to make of the girl. "Tells me, Spritey, whats missy trainer-wheels doin' here?"

Addison pivoted around and gave Nixie an intense look. "Traynor wheels?" she echoed quizzically.

Sprite giggled. "Her name is Addison Traynor, Nixie."

"Nosey matter," Nixie shrugged.

"She's a friend of mine from Ankrum Platform. We're classmates."

"I stowed away on the jumpship. I helped Sprite find you," Addison said proudly.

Sprite gave her friend an oblique glance. "She helped us rig a portable thruster."

There was a sound at the hatchway, and Ice entered the flight deck. She nodded at Sprite and Addison, then turned to face Nixie. "He's resting in the infirmary," she said simply.

Nixie studied her old crewmate. "Whoozy?" she asked.

"Don't know, but he's special forces. I'm certain of that," Ice said confidently. "He's the one who disabled this vessel. Very few people could have made that shot."

A shadow crossed Nixie's face, but she said nothing.

"It's good to see you, Nix." Ice looked at her hands. "I'm glad you're okay." Nixie shifted in her seat. Clearly, there was unfinished business between them. Ice looked up at her. "There's something you need to know." Nixie gave Ice an expectant stare. The older woman paused, a fleeting shadow crossing her otherwise dispassionate face. "It wasn't by chance that I was your first recruit. I joined your crew because of Momma Kate."

Nixie's jaw dropped. "Momma Kate?"

"Like you, I lived with her for a while. My parents were afraid I would die in the Thorium fields of Mare Insularum. When I left the special forces, she asked me to sign on with you. She wanted me to watch your back."

"You node all longwise 'bouts Gritty?" Nixie was crestfallen.

Ice nodded. "I did. And I was damned mad at Spif and Slake for treating you the way they did, too."

A single tear formed in Nixie's eye. "You 'bleeved in me?"

"Always, Nix. You've been a damned good captain." Ice looked at her squarely and nodded with respect.

"Wow-wy Dow-wy," the younger woman muttered, letting out a long breath.

"Is there anything you would like me to do, captain?" Ice had said her piece. Now, she was all business.

Nixie gave her a precocious grin. "I's needs ya on the 'pulsion deck, Icy. I fidaddled with that thermo-sensor thingy you showed me on *The 'Coon*. Master 'Larm's mutated and such."

"I can fix that," Ice replied curtly.

"Your shooter-guy tore up somethin', too."

"I saw him do it. He destroyed one of the ion-emitters."

"Canya fixed it?"

"No," replied Ice. "But I can work around it."

Nixie's face burst into a huge smile. "Now alls I needs is a brain for this bucket." She stuck her thumb out at the mass of twisted wires behind her. "Pierry Ant-won-ette snooky-tooky the AI whiz him when he popped this blow stand."

"That's going to be a problem, " Ice said seriously. "You can't fly one of these ships without an AI."

"Howsy bouts the 'pulsion brain-bucket?"

Ice shook her head. "Two different animals. That AI is specialized, and after I'm done retuning the power plant, we'll need every ounce of her computing power to stabilize the engine."

"Pooper." Nixie's face fell.

"I can help with that!"

Everyone looked at Addison Traynor. She was wagging her butt back and forth in her swivel-seat, a huge smile on her face.

"And how do you think you can do that?" asked Sprite. "People don't build AIs out of spare parts."

"I can fly the ship," Addison announced confidently.

Ice snickered. "I doubt that."

"I'm an AI."

Silence settled over the flight deck. Sprite was stunned. Then she sat forward in her seat. "You're my classmate."

"I was assigned to be your AI-companion. My identity was kept from you so you could fully appreciate how human we can be."

"If you are a machine, you should have been fried with the rest of the jumpship's electronics." Sprite was still in denial.

"My processors aren't based on silicon junctions. I am an advanced system. I can handle this ship with my eyes closed." Sprite leaned back in her seat, flabbergasted. Addison gave her a big smile. "I told you I had skills."

"Nice and tight, Addy-machine! Nice and tight!" Nixie rubbed her hands together gleefully. "Let's gets to worky-derky on this space-bucket! I wants to go home!"

CHAPTER TWENTY

S tephen Winters was sitting at the breakfast table when the message came. He fell to his knees when Molly's face appeared in the holo-display.

"Oh, daddy!" she cried. "I'm safe! I'm on the Moon."

Rene, who was occupied in the next room, rushed into the kitchen at the sound of her daughter's voice. "Is that Molly?" she asked with a trembling voice. She stood next to Stephen and gazed into Molly's face. She reached down and unconsciously ran her fingers through Stephen's hair. "We're coming for you, Molly!" she cried.

Stephen nodded his head. "You bet we are! We'll be there as soon as we can!" The Winters looked at their daughter. Soon they would be together again, and their long vigil would be over. Molly had changed. She appeared older. There was a hardness in her eyes, but she wore a grin as wide as the Milky Way, and she was alive.

* * *

In the weeks that followed their return to lunar orbit, all the children were reunited with their families. Word spread throughout the inner system of Pierre Antoine's human trafficking activities, and he was brought up on charges. Unfortunately, his case never went to trial. Antoine died unexpectedly of a brain hemorrhage before he could be interrogated. His body was cremated before an autopsy could be performed.

Nixie and Ice took possession of *The Cassiopeia*, rechristening her *The Raccoon II*. Nathan Trent recovered from his hypothermia, but suffered some residual nerve damage, which forced him into early retirement from the Terran Special Forces. Ice encouraged Nixie to sign him on as a member of her crew. To Nixie's surprise, he jumped at the chance.

The task of repairing the jumpship's electronics and *The Raccoon II's* damaged ion-emitter was a daunting one. Nixie contacted the crew of *The Celestial Ghost* and secured their help. Raven and her crewmates rendezvoused with the damaged ship and worked side by side with Nixie, Ice, and Nathan to return *The Raccoon II* to service. To Nixie's surprise, they brought Norman, the AI from the first *Raccoon*, and installed him on the flight deck.

* * *

Nixie had just finished tightening a bundle of cables behind Norman's rack when the AI's voice filled the flight deck. "Nixie? You have an incoming message from Stephen Winters."

Nixie floated out from behind the bank of equipment and glanced at the holodisplay in front of the pilot's seat. "Lemmee seeze it on the mainy-display, Normo."

A man's torso appeared in the display chamber. He had gray hair and a chiseled, but friendly, face. He wore a sport coat, with an open-collared dress shirt. Nixie was immediately suspicious.

"Miss Drake?" the man asked politely.

"Yessir, that's meezy wheezy," she replied. Her gravelly voice was pitched a little higher than usual. "We's not buyin' nothin' from nose sales-peeps."

The man chuckled. "I'm not a salesman, Miss Drake. I'm Stephen Winters, Molly's father."

Nixie relaxed. "Molly Snows-flake! Howdy-does her?"

Winters was mystified, then amused. "She's doing famously, thanks to you."

"Whatcha needin', Steve-oh?"

The man almost laughed. "Actually, that's why I contacted you. Molly's mother and I want to thank you for saving our daughter."

"Yer welkee-delcome."

"I want to invite you to a little celebration. Do you know about the Ankrum Platform? It's Cornell University's orbital facility at the Earth-Moon L1 point." Nixie nodded her head. "Could you come here the day after tomorrow? I want to thank you properly."

Nixie had heard Sprite and Addison talk about Ankrum on their way back to the Moon. She knew it was a place for highly-educated people, and it frightened her. "Knotty too surely 'bouts that, Steve-oh."

The man's face fell. "It would mean a lot to me and Rene. Molly, too. Please come, Nixie. I have something important to tell you, and I want to do it in person."

"I dunno."

"It might change your life, Nixie."

"I's hads 'nuff change-ola."

"Just come, okay?" The man was pleading.

"Maybe," Nixie conceded.

"Good! Miss LeRoc will meet you at the Ankrum Dock at fourteen hundred hours the day after tomorrow."

"LeRoc?" Nixie pronounced the last name carefully.

"You know Sprite by another name."

"Yessir," Nixie nodded in understanding. "I dooze."

"Please come, Nixie. I really mean it, and I think you will be glad you did."

"I'll cog-noggen 'bout it," she replied.

"You'll think about it?"

"Yessir."

"That's all I can ask, Nixie. Please let me know what you decide." The man's image dissolved into a sea of noise, then the holodisplay winked into darkness. Nixie sniffed and shook her head. What kind of idiot was she? She had no business going to such a highfaluting place.

* * *

Late the next day, Nixie was alone on the bridge. The repairs were complete, and everyone was gathering in the multi-cabin for a celebration. She lingered there, lost in thought. So much had happened over the last months, and she was glad to put it behind her. She knew a lot more about her beginnings but was confronted with a new mystery: the identity of her parents.

She looked at her captain's chair. It was positioned behind the pilot's seat on a raised platform. It was her place. She was the legitimate mistress of *The Raccoon II*. There were no more deceptions, no more secrets.

"Well captain, I think your ship is rigged and ready." Nixie pirouetted in the zero-g. The voice belonged to Raven. She floated in the hatchway, a broad smile on her face.

Nixie nodded with satisfaction. "I owes ya, Ravee."

"You don't owe me a thing, girl. It was our pleasure to help you put things back together." She was talking about more than just the ship repairs. "Do you remember when we talked in the grappling pod on *The Celestial Ghost*?" Nixie nodded slowly. "I asked you if you had ever considered doing something else."

"And I saidy-said you thats this," Nixie gripped the back of the captain's seat with her hand, "itsy alls I knows."

"Yes, that's what you said." Raven hovered in silence for a moment. "And I told you that you always had alternatives."

Nixie looked out the forward viewport, her eyes fixed beyond the stars. "Yes'm, you diddly-did," she whispered.

Raven moved closer to her and put her hand on her shoulder. "You are an amazing woman, Nixie. Don't ever say "no," when life offers you a "yes.""

Nixie looked deeply into her friend's eyes. Raven was a living example of what she was saying. In that moment, Nixie knew she would accept Stephen Winters' invitation.

* * *

Sprite Logan and Kell Edwards were waiting for Nixie when she arrived at the Ankrum dock. Ice and Nathan accompanied her in the newly-refurbished jumpship. Nixie's pulse was pounding. She felt threatened around highly-educated people.

"Everybody's waiting for you in the boardroom." Sprite could hardly contain her excitement.

Nixie nodded nervously as Kell led the way through the web of corridors and nodes. They passed through the outer ring of residences and into the section of the platform dedicated to research and instruction. Nixie glanced this way and that, taking in the studious men and women who were gazing intently at their work. She felt terribly out of place.

The boardroom lay at the very center of the Ankrum complex. Circular viewports offered breathtaking views of the Moon and the Earth. A large holographic chamber was suspended in the middle of the room. It was perfectly transparent until energized. At the moment, an azure pool covered the base of the chamber, like a round, liquid table. It shimmered, filling the room with a cool, pleasant light.

A small group of people was waiting for Nixie. When she floated through the connecting passage and crossed the threshold into the magnificent room, everyone broke into cheers and applause. Nixie blushed. No one had ever greeted her like this before. She turned, ready to flee, but Ice and Nathan blocked her path.

Nixie turned back and floated into the room. Addison Traynor and Tyson Edwards slid over next to Sprite and Kell, warm smiles on their faces. Molly Winters hovered by the holodisplay with her parents. Nixie recognized Stephen from their previous conversation. Molly introduced the woman as her mother, Rene. Mrs. Winters glided toward Nixie and gave her a bear hug. Nixie didn't like being touched, but the woman's embrace was genuine. She felt a strange warmth, as if being enfolded in the woman's arms was an echo of a long-forgotten memory. When Rene dropped her arms, Nixie saw a familiar face. Kate Sloan was hovering directly behind Stephen Winters. She was bursting with pride. Their eyes met for a brief moment, and Kate gave her a nod and a smile.

Stephen Winters was obviously the leader. He glanced around the room, and everyone settled down. He squeezed Molly's shoulder, then floated over to Nixie. He stuck out his hand, his face blossoming into a huge smile. "Nixie! Thank you for coming!" He pumped her hand enthusiastically. "Rene and I can't thank you enough for saving Molly."

A tear formed in his eye. He kept shaking her hand, apparently unable to stop.

"Jeeze, Louie-zeeze," Nixie offered awkwardly, pulling her hand away. Everyone chuckled, and Nixie blushed.

Stephen Winters dropped his hand, shaking his head in embarrassment. "I get carried away, sometimes," he explained. "Just ask Rene."

Laughter filled the room. Molly's mother nodded. "Just ask everyone associated with Cornell," she offered. There was even more laughter.

Stephen grew serious, raising his hand again for silence. "I want to show you something, Nixie." He nodded to a smart-looking young man across the room, and the massive holodisplay burst into life. The circular blue waters were transformed into a sea of fire, churning with flames of red and orange, which rose up into the air. The surface of the liquid fire parted, and a beautiful multicolored bird rose on magnificent wings. Her beak was turned upward, away from the inferno. The creature was not burned, rather it rose triumphantly above the inferno and hovered there. Her body was sleek and curved, as if it had been modeled after the tongues of fire from which it had come.

Nixie had never seen anything so beautiful. Her eyes were locked on the bird. The holographic tableau touched something deep within her, and she felt a knot form in her chest. She opened her mouth to say something, but words failed her, and she remained silent.

"Do you recognize this, Nixie?" Stephen asked gently. Nixie shook her head. "This is a depiction of an ancient myth. It tells the story of a magical bird who was consumed by fire. She was burned until only ashes remained. Then, according to her legend, she rose out of the ashes as a new bird."

"Wowee," Nixie breathed. "Sheezy's be-you-tea-full."

"Yes, she is," Stephen nodded. "Do you know the name of the bird?" Nixie scratched her scalp. There was a hush in the room. She felt a pang of embarrassment, and she blushed. Stephen noticed her discomfort. "There's no pressure here, Nixie. We don't judge people on "pop quizzes." There was another round of chuckles.

Nixie had no idea what Stephen Winters meant, but she felt safe with him. He was obviously a very educated man, but there wasn't a single thread of superiority in him. "Nossir," she said finally. "I's don'ts nosey her name."

"The bird is called the Phoenix."

"Phoenix?" Nixie echoed.

"That's it. She's your namesake, Nixie. Your name is a shortened form of Phoenix, and like her, you have been on a difficult and painful journey."

A knot rose up into Nixie's throat. She could hardly breathe.

"Nevertheless," Stephen spread his hands, "you are a survivor. You rose from a fiery pit, so to speak, and brought my daughter and many others with you. You rose from your own ashes to fly again."

Tears were streaming down Nixie's face. She felt someone touch her shoulder. It was Ice, standing by her side.

"Now, I had a conversation recently with one of your closest friends." Stephen turned to Kate, and she moved to his side. "For those of you who don't know her, this is Kate Sloan. She is a businesswoman at Copernicus Base." Stephen redirected his gaze toward Nixie. "Kate told me that your life got off to a rough start, and you have always wanted to get an education." Nixie was trembling. She nodded again. "I happen to be the president of Cornell University, and educating people is what we do."

Nixie stopped breathing.

"It would be my great honor if you would come and spend a few years with us at Cornell. We would love to give you the education you always wanted."

Nixie turned to Ice. Her friend offered her a rare smile and a nod of encouragement. Then Nixie turned back to Stephen Winters. "I got's a friend," she began, "who sud-gests ta me that I's shouldy never-never say nosey-no when lifey says 'yessir.'"

Stephen nodded. "Well then, Nixie, what do you say?"

Nixie glanced up at the mighty bird that was flying above the flames. She scratched her left armpit. Then she said, "Yes."

ABOUT THE AUTHOR

Dan Moore lives with his wife Diana near Syracuse, New York. He is a freelance video producer and the proud father of two sons, two daughters-in-law and three grandsons. He holds degrees from Cornell, Boston and Syracuse Universities. Dan has written two previous novels, The Rings of Alathea, and Meridian's Shadow, which is the first novel in the Meridian's Shadow series. He is currently writing his fourth novel, Broken Bridge.

Made in the USA
Charleston, SC
29 March 2012